Praise for the novels of Robyn Carr

"This book is an utter delight."

—*RT Book Reviews* on *Moonlight Road*

"Strong conflict, humor and well-written characters are Carr's calling cards, and they're all present here.... You won't want to put this one down."

—*RT Book Reviews* on *Angel's Peak*

"An intensely satisfying read. By turns humorous and gut-wrenchingly emotional, it won't soon be forgotten."

—*RT Book Reviews* on *Paradise Valley*

"A heart-grabber that won't let readers go until the very end."

—*Library Journal*, starred review, on *What We Find*

"A strong, uplifting tale."

—*Library Journal*, starred review, on *The View from Alameda Island*

"A blissful beach read."

—*Kirkus Reviews* on *The Summer That Made Us*

"A satisfying reinvention story that handles painful issues with a light and uplifting touch."

—*Kirkus Reviews* on *The Life She Wants*

"Classic women's fiction, illuminating the power of women's friendships, is still alive and well."

—*Booklist* on *Four Friends*

HOLIDAYS
IN
VIRGIN
RIVER

ROBYN CARR

Under the Christmas Tree and *Midnight Confessions*

mira

mira™

Recycling programs
for this product may
not exist in your area.

ISBN-13: 978-0-7783-8717-6

Holidays in Virgin River

Copyright © 2022 by Harlequin Enterprises ULC

Under the Christmas Tree
Copyright © 2009 by Robyn Carr

Midnight Confessions
Copyright © 2010 by Robyn Carr

For questions and comments about the quality of this book, please contact us
at CustomerService@Harlequin.com.

Mira
22 Adelaide St. West, 41st Floor
Toronto, Ontario M5H 4E3, Canada
BookClubbish.com

Printed in U.S.A.

Contents

A Note from Robyn Carr

After twenty books, I feel we've become friends. But did I ever tell you how it all began?

When the idea for *Virgin River* started to bubble, the first thing I could see was the glorious snow-peaked mountains of Northern California. I could smell the scent of the pine trees and redwoods. The cold clear air made me tingle. I'd need a soft wool jacket to keep me warm here. Suddenly I felt very awake. This was beginning to feel like a real place. And it was glorious—it held so much promise.

And then Jack's Bar appeared. Rough wood planks covered the walls. A fire was blazing in the stone fireplace. Six or seven laughing people sat at the bar, drinking and nibbling, telling stories to each other. I'm a chardonnay girl myself and am always up for a friendly conversation. This felt like exactly my kind of hangout.

Who was that behind the bar? He looked very appealing. (Not surprisingly! Now you know the kind of man I find attractive.) Competent and strong. Also watchful. Maybe a touch sad? Former military perhaps? He was just the right age to have served in Iraq. And while he looked like he'd be happy to share a joke, he'd seen things he'd prefer not to discuss. He must be the owner. I wondered how he'd ended up in this small shabby town. How could it even support a restaurant?

Walking in now was an attractive young brown-haired woman. Well, she kind of sprawled in. Her hair was disheveled. She made quite an entrance. Everyone turned around to look at her. She needed help. What was she doing here? Her high-heeled soft leather boots were too impractical for a place like this. I couldn't wait to figure out what was going on.

Was that the cook walking out of the kitchen? He was a big guy. Tall and friendly, a welcoming smile. Bald. Now I noticed how good the place smelled. Was that meat loaf? Yes! And evergreens mixed with crackling wood with an undertone of coffee and cookies. I was starting to get hungry. Preacher, I decided immediately—that was the chef's name.

Suddenly I looked out the window of the bar. It was late afternoon and it was starting to snow. Damn, I was going to have to spend the night in this place. Where could I stay? There must be cabins to rent. Maybe a guesthouse? My phone had no cell service. I'd have to ask that Jack guy.

Only now he was talking to that woman. "My name is Mel" I heard her say. Well, I'd just sit down a bit and get my bearings. This was such a cozy, cozy place. It was only October, but it felt like Christmas. I felt like I was home.

At first, *Virgin River* was supposed to be a stand-alone. But the stories kept coming. I wrote the first four books in less than a year. No sooner had I gotten Jack and Mel settled down than in came a terrified wife who'd been abused and was on the run with her young child! Well, Preacher could take care of her. And a handsome ex-marine like Jack must have a lot of army buddies—and of course I just had to help them all find love.

I was spending far more time in the mountains of California than my home in the desert of Nevada. But not only did Virgin River feel like an especially charmed place, it also felt like a respite during this vulnerable time for all of us in the country.

In 2005, when I was writing the first Virgin River novel, war was raging in Afghanistan and Iraq, we were in the depths of recession, my son was an army doctor, the housing market was crashing and I longed for a place like Virgin River, a sweet and simple place where people helped each other. And the letters from readers were flooding in. Some of them told me how much they cried. Some of them told me who ought to get the next love story. A lot of them asked me for directions to Virgin River! I guess I wasn't the only one craving good neighbors, people who really stick up for each other. One reader volunteered to keep all the characters straight for me. Whew, I needed that. I didn't have time to stop writing to create a list.

Writing about Virgin River was a haven from the news. The town wasn't perfect, nor was it perfectly safe. Dangerous things happened—there were bear attacks, floods and medical emergencies, not to mention the violent exes! But everyone in the town was trying to do the right thing. They wanted to work together, even if their efforts were misguided. (Franci and Sean certainly made their fair share of mistakes on the way to their happy ending.) They only needed a little nudge to understand that they were surrounded by neighbors who could help them carry the burden. And of course there was the promise of love, of a strong, loyal mate who makes your heart and head spin.

Okay. I am a romantic.

A romantic who loves the holidays.

I hadn't realized just how many of my stories were set during Christmas. Just think about guilt-ridden Ian Buchanan holed up in his mountaintop cabin, until stubborn Marcie coaxes him out of his shell. Or how about Patrick and Angie, both recovering from a brush with death, and their holiday fling that turns into forever?

Two of my favorite love stories are included here. *Under the Christmas Tree* kicks off with a box of abandoned puppies under the big town Christmas tree. Dogs have a magical ability to bring people together, and Nate and Annie are no exception. (If you know me, you know I just love dogs! Bella and Beau are golden retrievers, brother and sister, often getting each other in trouble, often giving me comfort and unconditional love.)

Midnight Confessions is set at the New Year's Eve party at Jack's Bar. Drew and Sunny are carrying so much pain from the old year, and they both need a lot of help to leave it behind.

But before we get there, let me tell you a bit about how the town celebrates.

First of all, it's very improvised. You'll notice that there is no mayor, no town council. Yes, the same things happen year after year, but each year it's a bit different.

I'd say the kickoff comes the day after Halloween. The kids have had their Halloween day parade. (You can't trick-or-treat in a town where houses are so spread out.) Hunting season is its own holiday in Virgin River, but even the most devoted hunters make sure to be home in time to see all the kids in their costumes.

There are so many small enterprises in town now. Paul Haggerty's construction company is working overtime to get all the homes winter ready. At Cavanaugh Orchard, all the apples have been harvested, and cider is being pressed. It's harvest season for Jilly too, and she's busy making big batches of her curried pumpkin soup.

Thanksgiving is huge. Boxes are collected so that the locals can pack up meals for those in need, which spans a pretty wide swath. The night before Thanksgiving is when old friends gather at Jack's. And on Thanksgiving Day, everybody has a place to go. Virgin River people truly know what it means to give thanks.

At the church, Reverend Noah Kincaid is gathering the kids for the Christmas pageant. And Ellie keeps her eye out for any kid who might need a new coat or some extra presents under the tree. After her difficult past, she knows how hard the holiday season can be. Those at the local school do their best to contain the holiday excitement, but by the time December rolls around, even the bookish kids are in full-time Christmas mode!

Of course, not everyone is able to take a break. Road workers, nurses and doctors work around the clock, and every winter brings its own emergencies. But as always, Virgin River pulls together as a community.

After school gets out, Mel organizes the cookie exchange. Every year there are Santas and trees and ornaments, lemon bars, chocolate crispies, brownies, shortbread, chocolate chip cookies, gingerbread and more. Paige and Brie make their cookies in the bar kitchen. Mel never bakes anything—she can't even boil water.

The big thing is the town Christmas tree. Jack always keeps his eye out for the perfect one. Years ago, Jack had the idea to decorate it with military patches, and since Virgin River has so many military men, the idea really took over. Originally every available man was needed to chop it, haul it into town and stand it up. Jack, Mike and Paul are in charge of this tradition. They use Paul's cherry picker and truck to haul and set up the tree, string the lights and decorate the highest parts. The women help decorate—Mel even went up in the cherry picker while she was pregnant, against Jack's wishes. One thing you can say about Mel—she knows her own mind.

While everyone decorates the tree, they enjoy warm mulled wine, homemade pumpkin-spice lattes and hot chocolate for the kids, plus roasted chestnuts for snacking. And the caroling! Ian and Marcie sing "O Holy Night" every year, and every family has their favorite carol. Then everyone warms up at Jack's Bar with Preacher's famous steak and ale pie, venison chili, or meat loaf and garlic mash.

Every family has a different tradition. (Though some people are like bears. They just hibernate through the cold months.) The big Riordan family opens presents after mass on Christmas Eve. The boys all buy lavish gifts for their mother, Maureen: Chanel, Lladró sculptures and electronics. But their sense of humor shows in their gifts for each other—one year, Sean gave Aiden, the ob-gyn, a subscription to *Penthouse* magazine, so he can know what women look like when they don't have their feet in stirrups.

Of course, not every family can afford to spend a lot of money. There are a lot of hand-knit scarves and hats and homemade candy. But the town makes sure that every kid has a brightly wrapped present waiting for them under the tree. This is also the time when engagements and new babies are announced.

In the magical week between Christmas and the New Year, the families of Virgin River gather together under their thick blanket of snow and take joy in the love they share—no matter how bumpy the road to happiness was. I can't wait for you to meet Nate and Annie and their bundles of puppy joy, and Sunny and Drew as they turn to face a new future together.

After this, Virgin River settles down to hibernate, maybe forever. If you need me, I'll be busily writing away in Sullivan's Crossing, another small town full of complex women and strong, loyal men. Or I'll be in front of my own Christmas tree with my wonderful, loving family—and yes, that includes the dogs.

Happy holidays, my friends.

Robyn

UNDER THE CHRISTMAS TREE

For all of the fans who have embraced the spirit of Virgin River

1

During the Christmas holidays a side trip through Virgin River was a must; the town had recently begun erecting a thirty-foot tree in the center of town, decorated in red, white, blue and gold and topped with a great big powerful star. It dominated the little town, and people came from miles around to see it. The patriotic theme of the decorations set it apart from all other trees. Local bar owner Jack Sheridan joked that he expected to see the three wise men any minute, that star was so bright.

Annie McKenzie didn't pass through Virgin River very often. It was out of her way when driving from Fortuna, where she lived, to her parents' farm near Alder Point. It was a cute little town and she liked it there, especially the bar and grill owned by Jack Sheridan. People there met you once, maybe twice, and from that point on, treated you like an old friend.

She was on her way to her folks' place when, at the last moment, she decided to detour through Virgin River. Since it was the week after Thanksgiving, she hoped they'd started on the tree. It was a calm and sunny Monday afternoon and very cold, but her heart warmed when she pulled into town and saw that the tree was up and decorated. Jack was up on an A-frame ladder straightening out some trimmings, and standing at the foot of the ladder, looking up, was Christopher, the six-year-old son of Jack's cook, Preacher.

Annie got out of her truck and walked over. "Hey, Jack," she yelled up. "Looking good!"

"Annie! Haven't seen you in a while. How are your folks?"

"They're great. And your family?"

"Good." He looked around. "Uh-oh. David?" he called. Then he looked at Christopher as he climbed down the ladder. "Chris, you were going to help keep an eye on him. Where did he go? David?" he called again.

Then Chris called, "David! David!"

They both walked around the tree, checked the bar porch and the backyard, calling his name. Annie stood there, not sure whether to help or just stay out of their way, when the lowest boughs of the great tree moved and a little tyke about three years old crawled out.

"David?" Annie asked. He was holding something furry in his mittened hands and she got down on her knees. "Whatcha got there, buddy?" she asked. And then she yelled, "Found him, Jack!"

The child was holding a baby animal of some kind, and it looked awfully young and listless. Its fur was black-and-white, its eyes were closed, and it hung limply in little David's hands. She just hoped the boy hadn't squeezed the life out of it; boys were not known for gentleness. "Let me have a look, honey," she said, taking the creature out of his hands. She held it up and its little head lolled. Unmistakably a puppy. A brand-new puppy.

Jack came running around the tree. "Where was he?"

"Under the tree. And he came out with this," she said, showing him the animal very briefly before stuffing it under her sweater between her T-shirt and her wool sweater, up against the warmth of her body. Then she pulled her down vest around herself to hold him in place. "Poor little thing might be frozen, or almost frozen."

"Aw, David, where'd you find him?"

David just pointed at Annie. "*My* boppie!" he said.

"Yeah, he's right," Annie said. "It's a boppie…er, puppy. But it's not very old. Not old enough to have gotten out of a house or a yard. This little guy should've been in a box with his mom."

"David, hold Chris's hand," Jack ordered.

And David said something in his language that could be translated into *I want my puppy!* But Jack was on his belly on the cold ground, crawling under the tree. And from under there Annie heard a muffled "Aw, crap!" And then he backed out, pulling a box full of black-and-white puppies.

Annie and Jack just stared at each other for a moment. Then Annie said, "Better get 'em inside by the fire. Puppies this young can die in the cold real fast. This could turn out badly."

Jack hefted the box. "Yeah, it's gonna turn out badly! I'm gonna find out who would do something so awful and take him apart!" Then he turned to the boys and said, "Let's go, guys." He carried the box to the bar porch and Annie rushed past him to hold the door open. "I mean, there are animal shelters, for God's sake!"

The fire was ablaze in the hearth and there were a couple of guys dressed like hunters at the bar, sharing a pitcher of beer and playing cribbage. She patted the place by the hearth and Jack put down the box. Annie immediately began checking out the puppies. "I'm gonna need a little help here, Jack. Can you warm up some towels in the clothes dryer? I could use a couple more warm hands. There's not enough wriggling around in this box to give me peace of mind." Then suddenly, she herself began wriggling. She smiled a big smile. "Mine's coming around," she said, patting the lump under her sweater.

Annie knelt before the box, and David and Chris squeezed in right beside her. She took the wriggling puppy out from under her sweater, put him in the box and picked up another one. At least there was a blanket under them and they had their shared warmth, she thought. She put another one under her sweater.

"Whatcha got there?" someone asked.

She looked over her shoulder. The hunters from the bar had wandered over to the hearth, peering into the box. "Someone left a box of newborn puppies under the Christmas tree. They're half-frozen." She picked up two more, made sure they were moving and handed them over. "Here, put these two inside your shirt, warm 'em up, see if they come around." She picked up two more, checked them and handed them to the other man. The men did exactly as she told them, and she stuffed one more under her sweater.

Then she picked up a puppy that went limp in her palm. "Uh-oh," she muttered. She jostled him a little, but he didn't move. She covered his tiny mouth and nose with her mouth and pushed a gentle breath into him. She massaged his little chest gently. Rubbed his extremities, breathed into him again and he curled up in her palm. "Better," she murmured, stuffing him under her shirt.

"Did you just resuscitate that puppy?" one of the hunters asked.

"Maybe," she said. "I did that to an orphaned kitten once and it worked, so what the heck, huh? Man, there are eight of these little guys," she said. "Big litter. At least they have fur, but they are so *young*. Couple of weeks, I bet. And puppies are so vulnerable to the cold. They have to be kept warm."

"Boppie!" David cried, trying to get his little hands into the box.

"Yup, you found a box full of boppies, David," Annie said. She picked up the last puppy—the first one she'd warmed—and held it up to the hunters. "Can anyone fit one more in a warm place?"

One of the men took the puppy and put it under his arm. "You a vet or something?"

She laughed. "I'm a farm girl. I grew up not too far from here. Every once in a while we'd have a litter or a foal or a calf the mother couldn't or wouldn't take care of. Rare, but it happens. Usually you better not get between a mother and her babies, but sometimes... Well, the first thing is body temperature, and at least these guys have some good fur. The next thing is food." She stuck her hand into the box and felt the blanket they'd been snuggled on. "Hmm, it's dry. No urine or scat—which is not so good. Besides being really cold, they're probably starving by now. Maybe getting dehydrated. Puppies nurse a lot and they were obviously taken from the mother's whelp box."

Jack reappeared, Preacher close on his heels. Preacher was tall enough that he was looking over Jack's shoulder into the empty box. "What's up?" Preacher asked.

"Dad! David found a box full of puppies under the tree! They're freezing cold! They could be *dying!*" Christopher informed him desperately.

"We're warming 'em up," Annie said, indicating her and the hunters' lumpy shirts. "About half of them are wriggling and we'll know about the other half in a little bit. Meanwhile, we need to get some fluids and nourishment into them. They shouldn't be off the tit this young. Infant formula and cereal would be ideal, but we can make due with some warm milk and watered-down oatmeal."

"Formula?" Jack asked. "I bet I can manage that. You remember my wife, Mel. She's the midwife. She'll have some infant formula on hand."

"That's perfect. And if she has a little rice cereal or baby oatmeal, better still."

"Do we need bottles?" he asked.

"Nah," Annie said. "A couple of shallow bowls will

work. They're young, but I bet they're awful hungry. They'll catch on real quick."

"Whoa," one of the hunters said. "Got me a wiggler!"

"Me, too!" the other one said.

"Keep 'em next to your body for a while," Annie ordered. "At least until we get those warm towels in the box."

Because of a box full of cold, hungry, barely moving puppies, Annie had all but forgotten the reason she'd ended up in Virgin River. It was three weeks till Christmas and her three older brothers, their wives and their kids would descend on her parents' farm for the holiday. Today was one of her two days off a week from the beauty shop. Yesterday, Sunday, she'd baked with her mom all day and today she'd gotten up early to make a couple of big casseroles her mom could freeze for the holiday company. Today, she'd planned to cook with her mom, maybe take one of her two horses out for a ride and say hello to Erasmus, her blue-ribbon bull. Erasmus was very old now and every hello could be the last. Then she'd planned to stay for dinner with her folks, something she did at least once a week. Being the youngest and only unmarried one of the McKenzie kids and also the only one who lived nearby, the task of looking in on Mom and Dad fell to her.

But here she was, hearthside, managing a box of newborn puppies. Jack rustled up the formula and cereal and a couple of warm towels from the dryer. Preacher provided the shallow bowls and mixed up the formula. She and Chris fed a couple of puppies at a time, coaxing them to lap up the food. She requisitioned an eyedropper from the medical clinic across the street for the pups who didn't catch on to lapping up dinner.

Jack put in a call to a fellow he knew who was a veterinarian, and it turned out Annie knew him, too. Old Doc Jensen had put in regular appearances out at the farm since before she was born. Back in her dad's younger days, he'd kept a thriving but small dairy farm. Lots of cows, a few horses, dogs and cats, goats and one ornery old bull. Jensen was a large-animal vet, but he'd be able to at least check out these puppies.

Annie asked Jack to also give her mom a call and explain what was holding her up. Her mom would laugh, knowing her daughter so well. Nothing would pry Annie away from a box of needy newborn puppies.

As the dinner hour approached, she couldn't help but notice that the puppies were drawing a crowd. People stopped by where she sat at the hearth, asked for the story, reached into the box to ruffle the soft fur or even pick up a puppy. Annie wasn't sure so much handling was a good idea, but as long as she could keep the little kids, particularly David, from mishandling them, she felt she'd at least won the battle if not the war.

"This bar has needed mascots for a long time," someone said.

"Eight of 'em. Donner, Prancer, Comet, Vixen, and… whoever."

"Which one is Comet?" Chris asked. "Dad? Can I have Comet?"

"No. We operate an eating-and-drinking establishment," Preacher said.

"Awww, Dad! Dad, come on. *Please,* Dad. I'll do *everything.* I'll sleep with him. I'll make sure he's nice. *Please.*"

"Christopher…"

"*Please.* Please? I never asked for anything before."

"You ask for everything, as a matter of fact," Preacher corrected him. "And get most of it."

"Boy shouldn't grow up without a dog," someone said.

"Teaches responsibility and discipline," was another comment.

"It's not like he'd be in the kitchen all the time."

"I run a ranch. Little hair in the potatoes never put me off." Laughter sounded all around.

Four of the eight pups were doing real well; they were wriggling around with renewed strength and had lapped up some of the formula thickened with cereal. Two were trying to recover from what was certainly hunger and hypothermia; Annie managed to get a little food into them with an eyedropper. Two others were breathing, their hearts beating, but not only were they small, they were weak and listless. She dripped a little food into their tiny mouths and then tucked them under her shirt to keep them warm, hoping they might mistake her for their mother for now, all the time wondering if old Doc Jensen would ever show.

When yet another gust of wind blew in the opened front door, Annie momentarily forgot all about the puppies. Some of the best male eye candy she'd chanced upon in a long while had just walked into Jack's Bar. He looked vaguely familiar, too. She wondered if maybe she'd seen him in a movie or on TV or something. He walked right up to the bar, and Jack greeted him enthusiastically.

"Hey, Nate! How's it going? You get those plane tickets yet?"

"I took care of that a long time ago." He laughed. "I've been looking forward to this forever. Before too long I'm going to be lying on a Nassau beach in the middle of a hundred string bikinis. I dream about it."

"One of those Club Med things?" Jack asked.

"Nah." He laughed again. "A few people from school. I haven't seen most of them in years. We hardly keep in touch, but one of them put this holiday together and, since I was available, it sounded like an excellent idea. The guy who made the arrangements got one of those all-inclusive hotel deals—food, drinks, everything included except activities like deep-sea fishing or scuba diving—for when I'm not just lying on the sand, looking around at beautiful women in tiny bathing suits."

"Good for you," Jack said. "Beer?"

"Don't mind if I do," Nate replied. And then, like the answer to a prayer she didn't even know she'd uttered, he carried his beer right over to where she sat with the box of puppies. "Hello," he said.

She swallowed, looking up. It was hard to tell how tall he was from her sitting position, but certainly over six feet. Annie noticed things like that because she was tall. His hair was dark brown; his eyes were an even darker brown and surrounded with loads of thick black lashes. Her mother called eyes like that "bedroom eyes." He lifted his brows as he looked down at her. Then he smiled and revealed a dimple in one cheek.

"I said hello," he repeated.

She coughed herself out of her stupor. "Hi."

He frowned slightly. "Hey, I think you cut my hair once."

"Possible. That's what I do for a living."

"Yeah, you did," he said. "I remember now."

"What was the problem with the haircut?" she asked.

He shook his head. "Don't know that there was a problem," he replied.

"Then why didn't you come back?"

He chuckled. "Okay, we argued about the stuff you wanted to put in it. I didn't want it, you told me I did. You won and I went out of there looking all spiky. When I touched my head, it was like I had meringue in my hair."

"Product," she explained. "We call it product. It's in style."

"Yeah? I'm not, I guess," he said, sitting down on the raised hearth on the other side of the box. He reached in and picked up a puppy. "I don't like *product* in my hair."

"Your hands clean?" she asked him.

He gave her a startled look. Then his eyes slowly wandered from her face to her chest and he smiled slightly. "Um, I think you're moving," he said. "Or maybe you're just very excited to meet me." And then he grinned playfully.

"Oh, you're funny," Annie replied, reaching under her sweater to pull out a tiny squirming animal. "You make up that line all by your little self?"

He tilted his head and took the puppy out of her hands. "I'd say at least part border collie. Looks like mostly border collie, but they can take on other characteristics as they get older. Cute," he observed. "Plenty of pastoral breeds around here."

"Those two are the weakest of the bunch, so please be careful. I'm waiting for the vet."

He balanced two little puppies in one big hand and pulled a pair of glasses out of the pocket of his suede jacket. "I'm the vet." He slipped on his glasses and, holding both pups upside down, looked at their eyes, mouth, ears and pushed on their bellies with a finger.

She was speechless for a minute. "You're not old Doc Jensen."

"Nathaniel Junior," he said. "Nate. You know my father?" he asked, still concentrating on the puppies. He put them in the box and picked up two more, repeating the process.

"He...ah... My folks have a farm down by Alder Point. Hey! I grew up there! Not all that far from Doc's clinic and stable. Shouldn't I know you?"

He looked over the tops of his glasses. "I don't know. How old are you?"

"Twenty-eight."

"Well, there you go. I'm thirty-two. Got a few years on you. Where'd you go to school?"

"Fortuna. You?"

"Valley." He laughed. "I guess you can call me old Doc Jensen now." And there was that grin again. No way he could have grown up within fifty miles of her farm without her knowing him. He was too delicious-looking.

"I have older brothers," she said. "Beau, Brad and Jim McKenzie. All older than you."

At first he was startled at this news, then he broke into a wide smile. Then he laughed. "Are you that skinny, fuzzy-haired, freckle-faced, tin-mouthed pain in the neck who always followed Beau and Brad around?"

Her eyes narrowed and she glared at him.

"No," he said, laughing. "That must have been someone else. Your hair isn't pumpkin orange. And you're not all that…" He paused for a second, then said, "Got your braces off, I see." By her frown, he realized he hadn't scored with that comment.

"Where is your father? I want a second opinion!"

"Okay, you're not so skinny anymore, either." He smiled, proud of himself.

"Very, very old joke, sparky," she said.

"Well, you're out of luck, *cupcake.* My mom and dad finally realized a dream come true and moved to Arizona where they could have horses and be warm and pay lower taxes. One of my older sisters lives there with her family. I've got another sister in Southern California and another one in Nevada. I'm the new old Doc Jensen."

Now it was coming back to her—Doc Jensen had kids,

all older than she was. Too much older for her to have known them in school. But she did vaguely remember the son who came with him to the farm on rare occasions. One corner of her mouth quirked up in a half grin. "Are you that little, pimply, tin-mouthed runt with the squeaky voice who came out to the farm with your dad sometimes?"

He frowned and made a sound. "I was a late bloomer," he said.

"I'll say." She laughed.

Nate was now checking out his third set of puppies.

"Why don't I remember you better?" she mused aloud.

"I went to Catholic school down in Oakland my junior and senior year. I wasn't going to get into a good college without some serious academic help, and those Jesuits live to get their hands on a challenge like me. They turned me around. And I grew five inches my first year of college." He put down the puppies he'd been holding and picked up the first one. He became serious. She noticed a definite kindness, a softness, in his expression. "Annie, isn't it? Or do you go by Anne now?"

"Annie. McKenzie."

"Well, Annie, this little guy is real weak. I don't know if he'll make it."

A very sad look came into her eyes as she took the puppy from him and tucked him under her sweater again.

Nodding at her, Nate said, "As much incentive as that is to live, I don't know if it'll do. How long were these guys outside before someone found them?"

"No one knows. Probably since before sunrise. Jack was in and out all day, fussing with the tree, and he never saw anyone. His little boy crawled under the tree and came out holding a puppy. That's how we found them."

"And what's the plan now?"

"I don't know," she said, shaking her head.

"Want me to drop them off at a shelter for you? Then you don't have to witness the bad news if one or two don't make it."

"No!" she exclaimed. "I mean, that's probably a bad idea. Some of the shelters over on the Coast are excellent, but you know what it's like this time of year. All those people adopting cute puppies for Christmas presents and then returning them in January. And returning them is the *good* scenario. All too often they're neglected or abused. Wouldn't it be better to take care of them until reliable homes can be found?"

"Who, Annie?" he asked. "Who's going to take care of them?"

She shrugged. "I have a small house in Fortuna and I work all day."

"What about the farm?" he asked.

She was shaking her head before he finished. "I don't

think so. My dad's arthritis is bad enough that he slowly sold off the stock and my mom runs around like a crazy woman taking care of all the things that wear him out."

"Your dad's Hank McKenzie, right? He gets around pretty good for someone with bad arthritis."

"Yeah, he's proud. He doesn't let on. But it would fall to my mom and I can't ask her to take on eight puppies. And the whole family is coming home to the farm for Christmas. All thirteen of 'em."

"Well, Annie, I can't think of many options here," he said. "I know a few vets in the towns around here and I don't know one that would take this on. They'd put 'em in a no-kill shelter."

"Can't you help? You and your wife?"

He smiled at her. "No wife, Annie McKenzie. I have a real nice vet tech who's going to keep an eye on the stable while I'm out of town over Christmas, but that's the only help I have out there, and she doesn't have time to add eight puppies to her roster."

"Jack!" Annie called. She stood up. "Can you come here?"

Jack ambled over, wiping his hands on a towel.

"We have a situation, Jack," Annie said. "Dr. Jensen can't take the puppies and get them through this rough patch. He offered to drop them off at a shelter, but really, that's not a great idea." A couple of people had wandered over to listen in to the conversation, eavesdropping and making no bones about it. "I've volunteered at some of those shelters and they're awesome, but they're really, really busy at Christmastime. A lot of animals get adopted for presents, especially the really young, cute ones like these. You have no idea how many people think they want a fluffy pet for little Susie or Billie—until the first time the dog thinks the carpet is grass."

"Yeah?" Jack said, confused. A couple more people had wandered over from the bar to listen in to the conference.

Annie took a breath. "It's bad enough animals get returned. The worst case is they're not taken care of properly, get neglected or abused or get sick and aren't taken to the vet because the vet costs money. Sometimes people are embarrassed to return them and admit it was a mistake. Then they just take them to animal control, where they're on death row for three days before…" She stopped. "It can be a bad situation."

"Well, what are you gonna do?" Jack said. "Better odds than freezing to death under a Christmas tree."

"We could take care of them here, Jack," she said.

"We?" he mimicked, lifting a brow. "I see you about four times a year, Annie."

"I'll drive up after work every day. They're kind of

labor-intensive right now, but I'll tell you exactly what to do and you can get—"

"Whoa, Annie, whoa. I can't keep dogs in the bar!"

An old woman put a hand on Jack's arm. "We already named 'em, Jack," she said. "After Santa's reindeer. At least the ones we could remember. Little Christopher already asked Preacher if he could have Comet. 'Course no one knows who Comet is yet, but—"

"There's no mother to clean up after them," Nate pointed out. "That means puppy excrement. Times eight."

"Aw, that's just great," Jack said.

"Don't panic," Annie said. "Here's what you do. Get a nice, big wooden box or big plastic laundry basket. You could even put a wooden border around a plastic pad from an old playpen, then toss an old blanket or a couple of towels over it. Pull the blanket back to feed 'em the formula and cereal every few hours. Or feed a couple or three at a time outside the box so you can wipe up the floor. Trade the dirty towels for clean ones, wash one set while you use the other, and vice versa. Oh, and at least two of these little guys need a lot of encouragement to eat—the eyedropper gets 'em going. I could take the littlest, weakest ones to a vet but, Jack, they're better off with their litter mates."

"Aw, f'chrissake, Annie," Jack moaned.

"You can just grab someone at the bar and ask them to take a couple of minutes to coax some food into a sick puppy," she said hopefully.

"Sure," the old woman said as she pushed her glasses up on her nose. "I'll commit to a puppy or two a day."

"Annie, I can't wash towels with puppy shit on 'em in the same washer we use for napkins for the bar."

"Well, we did at the farm. My mom sterilized a lot," she said. "Bet you washed shitty baby clothes in the same... Never mind. If you just get the towels, bag 'em up in a big plastic bag, I'll do it. I'll come out after work and spell you a little, take home your dirty laundry, bring back fresh every day."

"I don't know, Annie," he said, shaking his head.

"Are you kidding?" Annie returned. "People will love it, keeping an eye on 'em, watching 'em plump up. By Christmas, all of them will be spoken for, and by people who know what to do with animals. These little guys will probably turn into some outstanding herders around here."

"Nathaniel, did you put her up to this?" Jack asked.

Nate put up his hands and shook his head. He didn't say so, but she did have a point. Adopted by a town, these puppies would get looked after.

"I can't say yes or no without Preacher," Jack said, going off to the kitchen.

Annie smiled crookedly as she listened to the people who had followed Jack to the hearth, muttering to each other that, sure, this plan could work. They wouldn't mind holding a puppy every now and then, maybe donating a blanket, getting a puppy to eat, wiping up the floor here and there.

When Preacher trailed Jack back to the box of puppies, his six-year-old son was close on his heels. Jack tried to speak very softly about what all this would entail, but Christopher didn't miss a syllable. He tugged at Preacher's sleeve and in a very small voice he said, "Please, Dad, please. I'll help every day. I'll feed and hold and clean up and I won't miss anything."

Preacher pulled his heavy black brows together in a fierce scowl. Then, letting out an exasperated sigh, he crouched to get to eye level with the boy. "Chris, there can never be a dog in the kitchen. You hear me, son? And we have to start looking for homes right away, because some may be ready to leave the litter sooner than others. This has to be real temporary. We prepare food here."

"Okay," Chris said. "Except Comet. Comet's going to stay."

"I'm still thinking about that. And I'll have to look up on the computer how you take care of a bunch of orphaned pups like these guys," Preacher added.

Annie let a small laugh escape as she plucked the

smallest, weakest puppy from under her sweater and put him back in the box. "Well, my work here is done," she said with humor in her voice. "I'll try to cut my day as short as I can at the shop, Jack. I'll see you tomorrow."

"Annie, they're not your responsibility," Jack said. "You've already been a huge help. I don't really expect you to—"

"I'm not going to turn my back on them now," she said. "You might panic and take them to the pound." She grinned. "I'll see you tomorrow."

Christmas Eve, they had ham and potatoes au gratin, while on Christmas Day, it would be stuffed turkey. The clan started to gather at about four and the house throbbed with noise and laughter. They ate, drank and gathered in the family room; *stuffed* themselves into the family room; and sang carols. The men sang too loudly and off-key, and the women, to the last one, had to drive home.

SHELTER MOUNTAIN

2

The puppies were found on Monday and Nate managed to stay away from the bar on Tuesday, but by Wednesday he was back there right about dinnertime. He told himself he had a vested interest—they might be about a hundredth the size of his usual patients, but he had more or less treated them. At least he'd looked at them and judged the care Annie recommended to be acceptable. In which case he didn't really need to check on them. But Jack's was a decent place to get a beer at the end of the day, and that fire was nice and cozy after a long day of tromping around farms and ranches, rendering treatment for horses, cows, goats, sheep, bulls and whatever other livestock was ailing.

But then there was Annie.

She was no longer a skinny, flat-chested, fuzzy-haired metal-mouth. Something he'd been reminding himself of for more than twenty-four hours. The jury was still out on whether she was a pain in the butt. He suspected she was.

She was tall for a woman—at least five-ten in her stocking feet—with very long legs. That carrot top was no longer bright orange—maybe the miracle of Miss Clairol had done the trick. In any case, her hair was a dark auburn she wore in a simple but elegant cut that framed her face. It was sleek and silky and swayed when her head moved. Her eyes were almost exotic—dark brown irises framed by black lashes and slanting shapely brows. And there was a smattering of youthful freckles sprinkled over her nose and cheeks, just enough to make her cute. But that mouth, that full, pink, soft mouth— that was gonna kill him. He hadn't seen a mouth like that on a woman in a long time. It was spectacular.

She was a little bossy, but he liked that in a woman. He wondered if he should seek therapy for that. But no—he thrived on the challenge of it. Growing up with three older sisters, he'd been fighting for his life against deter-mined females his entire life. Meek and docile women had never appealed to him and he blamed Patricia, Susan and Christina for that.

The very first thing Nate noticed when he walked

into the bar on Wednesday was that Annie was not there. He smiled with superiority. Hah! He should have known. She talked Jack and Preacher into keeping eight tiny puppies—a labor-intensive job—promising to help, and was a no-show. He went over to the box and counted them. Seven. Then he went up to the bar.

"Hey, Jack," he said. "Lose one?"

"Huh?" Jack said, giving the counter a wipe. "Oh, no." He laughed and shook his head. "Annie took one back to Preacher's laundry room for a little fluff and buff. He mussed his diaper, if you get my drift. It's the littlest, weakest one."

"Oh," Nate responded, almost embarrassed by his assumption. "He hanging in there?"

"Oh, yeah. And wouldn't you know—Christopher has decided that that one is *his*. Comet. Annie tried to talk him into falling in love with a stronger, heartier pup, but the boy's drawn to the one most likely not to make it."

Nate just laughed. "It was that way for me," he said. "I was older, though. We had the most beautiful Australian Kelpie—chocolate brown, silky coat, sweet face, ran herd on everything. My dad had her bred and promised me a pup. Out of her litter of six, I picked the runt and practically had to hand-feed him for weeks. The other pups kept pushing him off the tit. I was fifteen and, probably not coincidentally, also small for my age.

I named him Dingo. He was big and tough by the time I was through with him, and he lived a long life for a hardworking Kelpie. We lost him just a few years ago. He lived to be fifteen. 'Course, he spent his last four years lying by the fire."

"You'd think a boy would pick the strongest in the pack."

"Nah." Nate snorted. "We don't feel that strong, so we empathize. Can I trouble you for a beer?"

"Sorry, Nate—I wasn't thinking. Fact is, I've been sitting on our nest on and off all day. I have a whole new appreciation for what you do."

"Have they been a lot of trouble?"

"Well, not really, just time-consuming," Jack said. "They eat every three hours or so, then their bedding has to be changed, then they nap, then they eat. And so on. Kind of like regular babies. Except there are eight of them and half of them need encouragement to eat. Plus, every so often, you have to check that they're not too warm or too cold. I don't want to freeze 'em or cook 'em. And the bar's getting lots more company during the day—visitors to the litter. Since they're here, they decide to eat and drink—more serving, cooking and cleanup than usual. Other than that, piece of cake. And if I ever find the SOB that left 'em under the tree, I'm going to string him up by his—"

"Well, hey, Doc Jensen," a female voice sang out.

Nate turned to see Annie come out the back of the bar, Christopher trailing so closely that if she stopped suddenly, he'd have crashed into her. She carried a furry ball of black-and-white that fit perfectly into her palm. Looking at her, he realized he hadn't remembered her quite accurately. Or rather, quite *enough*. Tall, curvaceous, high cheekbones, soft dark auburn hair swinging along her jaw, long delicate fingers… She was beautiful. And her figure in a pair of snug jeans and turquoise hoodie with a deep V-neck just knocked him out. Where the heck had this girl been hiding?

And why was he, a man who could appreciate cleavage and tiny bikinis, suddenly seeing the merits in jeans, boots and *hoodies?*

Then he remembered she'd been hiding in a little hair salon in Fortuna, under a pink smock.

He picked up his beer and wandered over to the hearth. Christopher and Annie sat on opposite sides of the box, which left no place for him, so he stood there in the middle.

Annie passed Chris the puppy. "Hold him for just a minute, then snuggle him back in with his brothers and sisters," she said. "It's good for him to be part of his family. They give him more comfort than we can right now."

"A little maintenance?" Nate asked.

Annie looked up at him and smiled. "This is the part that gets to be a bother—without a mother dog to change their diapers and keep them clean, by the end of the day they're looking a little worse for wear. Some of them actually needed washing up. My dad always used to say a little poop never hurt a puppy, but you let that go long enough and it will. Gets them all ugly and matted and sick."

"You bathed him?"

"Four of them, without dunking them," she said. "Can't let them get cold. Preacher's wife loaned her blow-dryer to the cause. Okay, Chris, he's been away from home long enough now." She reached into the box and pushed some puppies aside to make room, and Chris gently put his puppy into the pile. "They'll be ready to eat again in about an hour. Why don't you get back to your homework, or dinner, or chores, or whatever your folks have in mind."

"Okay, Annie," he said.

And Nate fought a smile as Chris vacated his place on the hearth. But before he sat down he asked Annie, "Can I buy you a beer? Or something else?"

She tilted her head and smiled at him. "I wouldn't mind a beer, thanks." He was back with a cold one for her in just moments and sat down opposite her. "I think they're doing okay here," she said to him.

He wasn't a hard-hearted guy, but he only pretended

interest in the pups, picking one up and then another, looking at their little faces. He'd rather be looking at her, but didn't want to seem obvious. "Were you here yesterday?" he asked, studying a puppy, rather than her.

"Uh-huh," she said, sipping her beer. "Ah, that's very nice. Thanks."

"You planning to come every day?" he asked.

"If I can swing it," she said. "I kind of made a deal—if they wouldn't hand them over to some shelter, I'd do my part. These little guys are just too cute and vulnerable. They could turn into impetuous Christmas presents, no matter how carefully the shelter volunteers screen the potential owners. And look at their markings—I'd say Australian-shepherd-and-border-collie mix. Outstanding herders. They should find good homes around here, and they'll be glad to work for a living."

Nate lifted his eyebrows. "Good guess," he said. "You get off work before five?" he found himself asking.

"Not usually. I have a small shop in Fortuna—six chairs. It's a franchise—my franchise. So I'm responsible, plus I have a large client list and it's Christmastime. But I'm moving appointments around the best I can—a few of my clients will take another stylist in a pinch. And I've been training an assistant manager, so she's getting thrown into the deep end of the pool because of these

puppies. And I'm doing my puppy laundry and paperwork at midnight."

"What kind of paperwork?" he asked.

"The kind you have with a small business—receipts,
receivables, bills, payroll. Jack and Preacher are managing real well during the day when it's sort of quiet
around here, but when it gets busy at the dinner hour,
they need a hand. And you heard Jack—he's not washing
puppy sheets with his napkins." She smiled and sipped
her beer. "We should all take comfort in that, I guess."

"I guess." He smiled. "How'd you end up with a
beauty shop?"

"Oh, that's not interesting. I'd rather hear about what
you do. I grew up around animals and being a vet is my
fantasy life. You're living my dream."

"Then why didn't you pursue it?" he asked.

"Well, for starters, I had exactly two years of college
and my GPA was above average, but we both know it
takes way more than that to get into veterinary college.
Isn't it harder to get into veterinary college than medical school?"

"So I hear," he said. "So, after two years of college…?"

She laughed and sipped her beer. "One of my part-
time jobs was grooming dogs. I loved it. *Loved* it. The
only thing I didn't love was going home a grimy, filthy
mess and not exactly getting rich. But I saw the poten-

tial and needed to make a living. I couldn't focus on a course of study in college, so I went to beauty school, worked a few years, hit my folks up for a loan to buy a little shop, and there you have it. I do hair on two-legged clients now. And it's working just fine."

"And your love of animals?"

"I stop by this little bar every evening and babysit a bunch of orphaned puppies for a few hours," she said with a laugh. "I still have a couple of horses at the farm. My dad got rid of the livestock years ago except for Erasmus, a very old, very lazy, very ill-tempered bull who my dad says will outlive us all. They're down to two dogs, my mom keeps some chickens and their summer garden is just amazing. But it was once a thriving dairy farm, plus he grew alfalfa and silage for feed."

"Why isn't it still a thriving farm?" he asked.

"No one to run it."

"Your brothers don't want the farm life?"

"Nope," she said. "One's a high-school teacher and coach, one's a physical therapist in sports medicine and one's a CPA. All married with kids and working wives. All moved to bigger towns. And the closest one lives a few hours away."

"What about you?" he asked.

"Me?"

"Yeah, you. You sound like you love the farm. You

love animals. You still have a couple of horses at your parents' farm...."

She smiled. "I'd be real happy to take on the farm, but that's not a good idea. Not the best place for me."

"Why not? If you like it."

She cocked her head and smirked. "Single, twenty-eight-year-old woman, living with Mom and Dad on the farm, building up the herd and plowing the fields. Picture it."

"Well, there's always help," he said. "Hired hands for the rough stuff."

She laughed. "Rough stuff doesn't scare me, but I can't think of a better way to guarantee I'll turn into an old maid. My social life is dull enough, thanks."

"There are ways around that," he pointed out. "Trips. Vacations. Visitors. That sort of thing. Something to break up the isolation a little."

"That's right—that's what I heard. Before I knew who you were, I heard Jack ask you if you had your plane tickets yet and you said something about Nassau, a Club Med vacation and lots of string bikinis. Right?"

For some reason he couldn't explain, that embarrassed him slightly. "No, no. I don't know anything about that Club Med stuff. A buddy of mine, Jerry from vet school, set up a get-together over Christmas with our old study group. We've only been in touch by email and haven't been together since graduation. The Nassau part is fact, the string-bikinis part is fantasy. I'm planning to do some scuba diving, snorkeling, some fishing. I haven't been away in a while." He laughed. "Frankly, I haven't been warm in a while."

"You don't get together with your family over the holidays?" she asked.

"Oh, they were gracious enough to invite me to join them all on a cruise. *All* of them," he stressed. "My folks, three sisters and brothers-in-law, four nephews and two nieces. It's going to be hell to give up all that shuffle-board, but I'll manage somehow."

"Do they ever come back here?" she asked. "You know—to the old homestead? Where you all grew up?"

"Frequently. They move in, take over, and I move out to the stable and take up residence in the vet tech's quarters."

"You and the tech must be on very good terms."

He grinned at her. "She's married and lives in Clear River, but we keep quarters for her for those times we have cases that are going to need attention through the night. She was my dad's assistant before he retired. She's like a member of the family." Then he studied her face. Was that relief? "The family was all home for Thanks-giving," he went on to explain. "It was great to see them all, and boy was I glad when they left. It's madness. I have really good brothers-in-law, though. At least my sisters did that much for me."

She sipped her beer. "You must be looking forward to your vacation. When do you leave?"

"The twenty-third. Till the second of January. I plan to come home tanned and rested." And with any luck, he thought, sexually relaxed. Then he instantly felt his face grow hot and thought, *Why the hell did I think that?* He wasn't typically casual about sex. He was actually very serious about it.

Annie peered at him strangely. "Dr. Jensen, are you blushing?"

He cleared his throat. "You don't have to be so formal, Annie. Nate is fine. Is it a little warm by this fire?"

"I hadn't noticed, but—"

"Have you eaten?" he asked.

"No. I hadn't even thought about it."

"Let's grab that table, right there close by, before anyone else gets it. I'm going to tell Jack we want dinner. How about that?"

"Fine," she said. "That sounds fine. By the time we're finished, Chris will be back, ready to feed his puppy."

Through the rest of that first week the puppies seemed to do just fine. Thrived in fact. So did Annie, and she hoped it didn't show all over her face. There was no particular reason for Nate to show up day after day; the pups weren't sick, didn't need medical care and he hadn't made the commitment to help that she had. Yet he returned on Thursday, Friday and Saturday. She'd love to believe he was there to see her, but it seemed such a farfetched idea. So highly unlikely that she could interest a man like him through this odd doggie-day-care-in-a-bar that she wouldn't allow herself to even think about it.

But he was there by six every day, right about the time she finished her puppy chores. He always bought her a beer, then Jack provided dinner, which they ate together at a table near the hearth. They talked and laughed while catching up on their families and all the locals they knew, getting to know each other in general. Although she knew this friendship would probably fade and disappear by the time the puppies were adopted, and even though traipsing out to that bar every day was wearing her out, she was enjoying his company more than she could admit even to herself.

"Did you always plan to come back here? To take over your father's practice?" Annie asked him one evening.

"Nope," he said. "Wasn't part of my plan at all. First of all, I prefer Thoroughbreds to cows. I wanted to treat them, breed them, show them, race them. I did a couple of years' residency in equine orthopedics, worked in a big practice in Kentucky, then in a real lucrative prac-

tice outside Los Angeles. Then my dad wanted to re-
tire. He'd put in his time—he's seventy-five now. Years
back, he and my mom bought a horse property in a nice
section of Southern Arizona, but they wanted to keep
the house and stable, not to mention the vet practice, in
the family. You have any idea how hard it is to build a
practice with these tough old farmers and ranchers?" He
chuckled. "The name Nathaniel Jensen goes a long way
around here, even though I am the upstart."

"So here you are...back at the family practice?" she
asked. But she was thinking that he'd been rubbing elbows with big-money horse people. Society people,
whom she'd seen at a distance at certain competitions
and fairs, but knew none of. She'd been riding since she
could walk, took lessons and competed in dressage, and
so was more than a little familiar with the kind of wealth
associated with breeding, racing and showing Thoroughbreds. The well-to-do could send their daughters to Europe for lessons, fly their horses to Churchill Downs in
private planes and invest millions in their horse farms.
Humboldt County farm girls couldn't compete with that.
She swallowed, feeling not a little out of her league.

"I said I'd give it a chance. My plan was to put in a
year or two, save some money, maybe break in a new guy
with an interest in the stable and practice. But I haven't
gotten around to that and it's been two years."

"I see," she said. "You're still planning to leave?"

"I don't have to tell you what's great about this place." He smiled. "And I think I don't have to tell you what's missing. It's kind of a quiet life for a bachelor. Remember that dull social life you mentioned?"

"How could I forget?" she threw back at him.

"You seeing someone?" he asked suddenly, surprising her.

"Hmm? No. No, not at the moment. You?"

"No. Date much?" he asked.

Startled, she just shook her head. "Not much. Now and then." She thought for a moment and then said, "Ah. The vacation. Getting away to see if you can jump-start your social life a little bit?"

He just smiled. "Couldn't hurt. And it'll be nice to catch up with friends. We were real tight in vet school. We got each other through a lot of exams."

"How many of you are going?" she asked.

"Five men, including me, two of them married and bringing wives. Two women vets."

"Women vets? Married?"

"One's still single and one's divorced."

"Gotcha," she said. "I bet one's an old girlfriend."

"Nah," he said.

"Come on—didn't you ever date one?"

"I think I dated both of them. Briefly. We worked out

better as study partners than…well, than anything else."
He took a drink. "Really, I want to fish."

She took a last bite of her dinner. "Fishing is real good
around here," she said.

"I fish the rivers here. A little deep-sea fishing sounded
like a good idea. Some sun would be acceptable. I have
golf clubs," he said with a laugh. "I used to play a lot of
golf in L.A. Yeah," he mused, "a little sunshine won't
hurt."

After a moment she reminded him with a smile, "And
soon you'll be lying on a beach in the middle of a hundred string bikinis."

"Maybe you're right," he said with a grin. "Maybe I
should do more fishing around here if I want to catch
the big one."

By the time Sunday rolled around, Annie was back at
the farm. She went early in the day so she could drop by
the bar later that afternoon. Today, so close to Christmas, she was baking with her mother all day—breads,
pastries, cookies to be frozen for the barrage of company—but she would have her dinner at the bar. Because
of the puppies, of course.

"You're very quiet, Annie," her mother said. "I think
you're letting this adventure with the puppies wear you
out. You've always had such a tender heart."

"I am tired," she admitted, rolling out cookie dough. "I'm getting up extra early, starting at the shop earlier so I can leave earlier, staying up late to finish work. And you know I won't leave my house alone—I'm decorating for Christmas. I've been doing a little here and there, before and after work."

"Then you shouldn't be out here two days a week," Rose McKenzie said. "Really, I appreciate the help, but I'm not too old to do the holiday baking."

"I count on our baking as gifts," Annie said. "So I'm glad to help.

"I didn't realize we had a new and improved Doc Jensen," she went on, changing the subject. "I thought it was still old Doc Jensen who came for the horses and Erasmus when you needed a vet. But when he stopped to look at the puppies, he explained he was Nathaniel Junior. You never mentioned."

"Oh, sure we did, honey. His coming home was good gossip there for a while. He had some woman living with him, but she took off like a scalded cat. I don't think we talked about anything else for months."

"A woman? When was that?"

"A couple years ago. Some fancy young Hollywood girl," Rose said with an indulgent laugh. "We ran into them a few times—at the fair, the farmers' market, here and there." Her mother was kneading dough as she chattered. "You know, you don't run into people that often around here. They could've been here a year before anyone met her, but Nathaniel had her out and about. Probably trying to help her get acquainted. But it didn't work too well, I guess."

"I'm sure I would have remembered, Mom. I don't think you ever mentioned it."

Rose looked skyward briefly, trying to remember. "That might've been about the time you were preoccupied with other things. Like buying the Clip and Curl shop. And then there was Ed, and that ordeal with Ed. You might've had other things on your mind."

Ed. Yes, Ed. She hadn't exactly been engaged, thank God, but they'd been an item for about a year and she'd expected to be engaged. They *had* talked about marriage. She laughed humorlessly. "That could have distracted me a little," Annie agreed.

"The bum," Rose McKenzie muttered, punching dough more aggressively than necessary. "He's a pig and a fool and a liar and a...a bum!"

Loving it, Annie laughed. "He's really not a bum. He works hard and earns a good living, which it turned out he needed for all the women he had on a string. But I concede to pig, liar and fool, and I'm certainly not missing him. The louse," she added. "I can't remember now—why was it we didn't let the boys shoot him in the head?"

"I can't remember exactly, either," Rose said. "I knew all along he wasn't right for you."

"No, you didn't," Annie argued. "You had me trying on your wedding dress about once a month, asking me constantly if we'd talked about a date. You expected him to give me a ring."

"I just thought *if…*"

Ed was in farm-equipment sales and had a very broad territory in Northern California, a job that had him on the road most of the week. Then she learned that for the entire time they'd dated, Ed was involved with another woman in Arcata. About six months ago he'd decided it was time to make a choice, and he chose the other woman.

Ouch.

Annie's pride was hurt, but worse than hurt pride was her embarrassment. How had this been going on without her getting so much as a whiff of it? When she hadn't seen him, she had talked to him every single day. He never betrayed the slightest hint that she was not the only female in his life. And it made her furious to think he'd been with another woman while he was with her. She even drove to Arcata to sneak a look at her, but she couldn't figure out, based on looks, just what it was that won her the great prize that was Ed.

Before she could ponder that for long, that Arcata woman found *her,* looked her up, informed her they weren't the only two. Ed, as it happened, was quite the dabbler. He had at least one other steady girlfriend to spend the nights with.

Her tears had turned to fumes. She threw out everything that reminded her of him. She bought all new bedding and towels. Went to the doctor and got a clean bill of health. But at the end of the day when she grieved, it wasn't so much for Ed as for the *idea* of Ed; she had invested a year in a man she thought would give her the stability of marriage and family, a settled life. The dependence of love. Security. When she thought about Ed, she wanted to dismember him. She wanted her brothers to go after him and beat him senseless. But not only would she never take him back, she'd cross the street to avoid him. So maybe Rose was right—maybe they both really knew all along he just wasn't the one.

But neither was anyone else. She hadn't been out on five dates since the breakup a little more than six months ago, and the number of boyfriends she'd had before Ed had come along were too few to count. She went out with her girlfriends regularly, but the best part of her life was spending a couple of days on the farm, riding, cooking or baking or putting up preserves with her mom.

The farmhouse had a wide porch that stretched the length of the house, and from that porch you could watch the seasons come and go. The brightness of spring, the lushness of summer, the burnt color of fall, the white of winter. She watched the year pass from that porch, as she had since she was a little girl. But lately it seemed as though the years were passing way too quickly and she wondered if she'd ever find the right partner to sit there with rather than alone.

A Hollywood woman? A fancy Hollywood woman? That would explain things like Caribbean vacations. Nate was drawn to flashy, sexy women. Or maybe the kind of women found in the private boxes at races or horse shows; Annie had seen enough of those televised events to know the type—model gorgeous, decked out in designer clothes, hand-stitched boots, lots of fringe and bling. Or the type seen at the fund-raisers and society events attended by the wives, daughters and sisters of Thoroughbred breeders, the kind of women whose horses were entered in the Preakness. Or perhaps he preferred medically educated women, like another vet who could appreciate his professional interests—the kind of women who also rubbed elbows with the well-to-do because of their profession.

But probably ordinary, sensible-shoes farm girls didn't do anything special for a man like Nate.

Annie's thoughts were broken when her father walked into the kitchen and refilled his coffee cup. He put a hand on the small of his back and stretched, leaning back, rolling his shoulders.

"Are you limping, Dad?"

"Nah," he said. "Got a little hitch in my giddyup is all."

"As soon as I'm through with this puppy project, I'll make it a point to get out here more often to help."

"The doctor says the best thing is for him to keep moving," Rose said. "You do enough to help already."

"You don't remember that fancy Hollywood woman?" Hank asked, going back to the conversation he had overheard. Without waiting for an answer, he added, "Breeze woulda blown her away. Skinny thing. Could see her bones. Not at all right for Nathaniel." He took a sip of coffee and lifted his bushy brows, looking at her over the rim of his mug. "You'da been more his speed, I think. Yeah, better Nathaniel than that son of a so-and-so you got yourself mixed up with."

"I didn't even know Nate Jensen was here until a few days ago, remember?" Annie pointed out. "And before that, I was with the so-and-so, and Nate was taken."

"Yeah, you'da had to kill that skinny thing, but she

looked near death, anyhow." Then he grinned at her and left the kitchen.

"Will Nathaniel have his family for Christmas?" Rose asked.

"Actually, he said his parents, sisters and their families are going on a cruise. I gathered, from the way he said it, he'd throw himself off the boat if he were along. He said something sarcastic, like it would be hell to give up all that shuffleboard, but he'd manage."

"Oh, you must invite him to join us for the holiday dinners, Annie. As I recall, he was friendly with one of your brothers when they were kids."

"Mom, he's not hanging around. He's going on some highfalutin Caribbean vacation, meeting up with some old classmates from veterinary college, hoping to get lost in a sea of very tiny bikinis on the beach. Apparently his taste in women hasn't changed much."

"Really?" Rose asked. "Now to me, that sounds dull."

"Not if you're a single guy in your thirties, Mom."

"Oh. Well, then take him some of these cookies."

"I'm sure he couldn't care less about home-baked cookies." *Not if what he prefers is some fancy, skinny, rich girl,* she thought.

"Nonsense. I don't know the man who doesn't like home-baked cookies. Reminds them of their mothers."

"Just the image I'd most like to aspire to," Annie said.

"Being here with you three is Christmas enough for me," he said, meaning it.

MIKE FROM *SHELTER MOUNTAIN*

3

Rose McKenzie insisted that Annie take a plate of Christmas cookies to Dr. Jensen, but it made Annie feel silly, farm girlish, so she left them in the car when she went into Jack's Bar later that afternoon.

She gasped in pleasure when she walked in—the place had been decorated for Christmas. A tree stood in the corner opposite the hearth, garlands were strung along the bar and walls, small evergreen centerpieces sat on the tables, and the buck over the door wore a wreath on his antlers. It was festive and homey, and the fresh pine scent mingled with wood smoke and good cooking from the kitchen to complete the holiday mood.

It took her less than two seconds to see that Nate

wasn't there, which made her doubly glad she hadn't trotted in her plate of baked goods. Maybe this was the day he wasn't going to show. It wasn't as though he had any obligation here. In fact, besides giving the puppies a cursory look and asking Annie if there was anything wrong with any of them, he didn't do anything at all.

She gave Jack a wave and went directly to the puppies, which, in the past week, had gotten surprisingly big. Boy, if those weren't all border collies, she was no judge of canines. Out of the eight, two were solid black with maybe a little silver or gray or perhaps a mere touch of white—the only indication another breed might've been involved. But they had grown so much! And they were doing so beautifully—plump and fluffy and adorable. Just like everyone else who passed by that box, she couldn't resist immediately picking a puppy up and cuddling it against her chin.

Jack came over to the hearth and she grinned at him. "The bar looks wonderful, Jack. All ready for Santa."

"Yeah, the women got it ready for their hen party. Cookie exchange tomorrow at noon—you should come."

"Nuts, I'll be at work. But tell them the decorations are beautiful."

"Sure," he said. "Annie, we've got a situation. We're going to have to come up with another plan here."

Instinctively she picked up Comet to judge his size

and strength; he wriggled nicely. "Why's that, Jack?" she asked.

He was shaking his head. "This isn't going to work much longer. I can go another day, two at the most, while you figure something out, but the puppies have to find a new home. They're getting bigger, more energetic, and giving off the kind of odor reminiscent of a box full of puppy shit. This is an eating-and-drinking establishment, Annie."

"Are people complaining?" she asked.

"Just the opposite," he said, shaking his head. "We're drawing a nice crowd on account of the big tree and the cute little puppies. But you know puppies, Annie. They're wetting on a lot of laps while they're being held and snuggled. This is going to go from cute and fun to a big problem real soon."

"Oh," she said, helpless. "Oh." Well, it wasn't as though she had trouble understanding. It was different when the litter was in your downstairs bathroom or under the laundry sink in a home, or when there was a mother dog around tending the nursery. You just didn't realize how hard that mother dog worked unless you had to care for the puppies yourself. Even when there were eight of them, as long as they were nursing, good old Mom licked them from head to toe, keeping them clean and dry. The second you started giving them solid food, Mom stopped cleaning up after them and it took no time at all for them to get a little stinky and messy. But under normal circumstances, that came at about six weeks, right about the time they were ready to leave the nursery anyway.

In this case, there'd been no mom, and the formula and cereal that went in one end came out the other. Their bedding couldn't be changed fast enough or their cute little bottoms washed often enough to avoid a smell.

"What am I going to do?" she asked herself.

"We've got homes for some of them figured out," Jack said. "I'm not sure any of them are ready to be out of the box yet, but we've got a few adoptions worked out. There's Christopher, of course. He's not letting Comet get away."

"Comet's not ready to be the responsibility of a six-year-old. He needs a couple more weeks. And good as Chris is with him, he'll have to be supervised," Annie said.

"I know. And I'm sunk," Jack said. "David keeps babbling about his 'boppie.' I've been thinking about getting a dog, anyway, something to clean up the spills around my place. But…"

"And, Jack, you can't turn a puppy this size over to a three-year-old boy any more than you can put him in charge of eggs and ripe tomatoes."

"Yeah, yeah, when it's time, we'll be careful. And Buck Anderson, sheep rancher, says it's about time to get a couple of new herders ready. He's got a little child of his own and seven grandchildren. He can speak for two—his sons can help get 'em grown before they turn them over to the other dogs and the sheep. He'd like them to be Christmas dogs, though. Now, I know you don't trust people looking for puppies as Christmas gifts, but you can count on Buck. He knows the score." Jack took a breath. "I don't like their chances if they won't herd sheep, however."

"Okay, that's four taken care of," she said.

"Couple of other people have been thinking about it, but that's the progress so far. Did you realize everyone in town has named them after the reindeer?"

"Yeah, cute, huh? Jack, I don't have a place for them. I guess I could take them to my house and run home between haircuts to make sure they're fed and watered, but to tell the truth, I don't have that kind of time. At Christmastime, everyone wants to be beautiful. And I try to spend as much time at the farm as I can—the whole family's coming."

"Maybe we need to rethink that shelter idea. Couldn't they just look after them for a couple of weeks? Then we'll take at least a few off their hands...."

Just then Nathaniel blew in with a gust of wind. He

pulled off his gloves and slapped them in his palm. He looked around the recently decorated bar and whistled approvingly. "Hey," he said to Annie and Jack. "How's everything?" Silence answered him. "Something wrong?"

Annie stepped toward him. "Jack can't keep the puppies here anymore, Nate. They're starting to smell like dogs. It is a restaurant, after all."

Nate laughed. "I think you've hung in there pretty well, Jack. Lasted longer than I predicted."

"Sorry, Nate. If Annie hadn't been so convincing, these guys would have gone to a shelter right off the bat. Or someplace way worse. At least we've figured out homes for a few—when they're old enough and strong enough to leave the litter."

"Yeah, I understand," Nate said good-naturedly. "Well, if Annie promises not to bail on me, I'll take 'em home. I'm pretty busy most days, but I have a vet tech at the clinic to help. And they don't need quite as much hands-on care as they did a week ago—at least they can all lap up their meals without an eyedropper now. I can put 'em in the laundry room and close the door so they don't keep me up all night."

"Will they be warm enough?" Annie asked. "Are they strong enough?"

"They'll be fine, Annie. Jack—what's for dinner?"

"Chili. Corn bread. Really? You'll take them out of here?"

Nate laughed. "Can we mooch one more meal before we cart them away? I'm a bachelor—there's hardly ever any food in the house." He draped an arm around Annie's shoulders. "This one is spoiled now—she's used to getting fed for her efforts. And two beers."

"Yeah," Jack said, lifting a curious eyebrow. "Coming right up."

"After we eat, you can follow me home," he said to Annie, as if the matter was settled.

Annie knew approximately where the Jensen clinic, stable and house were, but she couldn't remember ever going there. You might take your poodle or spaniel to the small-animal vet, but the large-animal vet came to you, unless you had a big animal in need of surgery or with some condition that required long-term and frequent care. His stable also provided occasional short-term boarding for horses. And he had breeding facilities, but that also was most often done at the farm or ranch by the farmers and ranchers. Some owners of very valuable horses preferred to leave their prefoaling mares with the vet.

Nate transported the puppy box in the covered bed of his truck. They were bundled up with extra blankets and wouldn't get too cold on the short ride. Annie followed in her own truck. They made a left off the main road at the sign that said Jensen Stables, Dr. Nathaniel Jensen, DVM. The road was paved, which was high cotton in this part of the world. It was tree-lined and the snow-covered brush was cut back from the edge. The road had to be at least half a mile long. Then it opened into a well-lit compound. The stable was on the left of a large open area, with a corral surrounding it on the side and back. The clinic itself was attached to the stable. There were Christmas lights twinkling in one of the windows. On the right was a sprawling, modern one-story house with a brick sidewalk that led up to double front doors of dark wood set with beveled-glass windows. Not a single Christmas light or ornament on the house at all. Annie wondered if the vet tech had decorated the clinic.

Between the house and stable were two horse trailers. One could hold six horses, the other two, and both were so fancy they probably came with a bar and cabin attendants.

The garage door at one end of the house opened automatically, and Nate pulled in. Annie parked outside and walked through the garage. She carried the formula and baby cereal while he carried the box, managing to open the door into the house and flick on lights with his elbow as he walked through the kitchen and then disappeared. The kitchen was the kind Annie's mother would have died for—large new appliances, six-burner stove, double oven, work island with a sink. It was gorgeous. It looked newly remodeled.

Annie moved more slowly, peering past a long breakfast bar into a spacious family room with big, comfy-looking furniture and a beautiful fireplace. On each side of the fireplace were floor-to-ceiling bookcases filled with leather-bound volumes.

"Annie? Where are you?"

She stopped gawking and followed the voice. She passed a very long, old oak table in a large breakfast nook inside bay windows that looked out on the back of the property. A sharp left and down a short hall took her past a bathroom, a bedroom and into a laundry room. In addition to cabinets, there was a stainless-steel washer and dryer, along with a deep sink. This was not an old farmhouse, that was for sure.

"I'll use linens from the clinic to line their box," Nate said. "They'll be fine in here. Listen, I know you signed on for this duty, but I don't want you to feel like you have to rearrange your schedule to get out here the first minute you can escape work every day. Virginia, my tech, can help during the day and I get called out sometimes, but this time of year, no one's breeding or birthing, so it's not usually too hectic. But—"

"Okay," she said. "I won't come. I'll leave a number. If you need me."

"Well, could you still come sometimes?" he asked with a laugh. "If you give me a hand feeding and cleaning up, I'll thaw a hunk of meat to throw in the broiler or something. Nothing like Preacher's, but edible. Just let me know when you can be here."

"You have your tech...."

"I don't like to ask Virginia to stay after five unless we have special patients—she wants to get home, have dinner with her husband. I'll fix you up with a key, in case I'm tied up on a case and you beat me home."

"Sure. Tell me exactly what you want," she said.

He put his hands on his hips. "I want to know what's wrong. Why are you frowning like that? You've been frowning since I walked into Jack's."

Mentally, she tried to smooth out her eyebrows, but she could still feel the wrinkle. She'd been trying to picture him with a trophy girl on his arm, that was what. Or with an equestrienne from a high-muck-a-muck ranch who raced or showed horses all over the world. Or maybe a mature and attractive woman his age who was as smart and successful as he was. And he was so damn handsome it wasn't hard to imagine all this. But she said, "You're downright chipper. This is *exactly* what you didn't want, but you're almost thrilled about having the puppies here. What's up with that?"

He laughed. "Nah. I knew it was going to come to this. I'm glad Jack and Preacher handled them for that first week for two reasons—they had to be fed, dried and checked frequently, and I enjoyed stopping by the bar on the way home every day. Don't know when I've eaten so well," he added, rubbing a flat belly. "Now that it's apparent they're all going to make it, they only have to be checked and fed every few hours, something Virginia and I can handle during the day. I agree with you about the shelter. They'd probably be just fine—those folks are devoted, and they interview and screen efficiently before they let a tiny, orphaned animal out of there. But why take chances? If we have to use the shelter, we'll just do so after Christmas."

"That's it? You knew all along you'd get stuck with them?"

He just laughed. "Come on, I'll show you the house I grew up in, we'll put on some coffee, feed the pups and put 'em down for the night. How about that?"

"You don't have to show me the house. I'm not going to be poking around in here."

He grabbed her hand. "I'm not worried about you poking around. Come on," he said again, pulling her back through the kitchen. He took her through a spacious great room, where he said, "Many fights between my sisters happened here. When I grew up, there was old, floral, ratty furniture in here, but once everyone got educated and off Mom and Dad's payroll, new things began to appear around the house. Things got updated and remodeled." He pulled her down the hall, showed her where the master bedroom and three others were located. "I got the bed-and-bath on the other side of the kitchen. Kept me away from the girls." Then he took a right turn off the great room. "Formal living room, used only on family holidays like Christmas, and dining room, used for overflow at big family dinners." And then they were back in the huge kitchen.

"It's enormous," she said breathlessly. "It's very beautiful. What must it have been like to grow up in a house so large?"

"I probably took it for granted, like any kid would," he said with a shrug. "It's still my parents' house, though I doubt they'll ever move back here. Come on, I'll put on coffee."

"You don't have to entertain me, Nate."

"Maybe I'm entertaining myself. I don't have much company out here."

The moment they had the coffee poured Annie remembered. "Damn," she said. "Don't move. I have something for you." She dashed out the garage door to her car, retrieved the cookies and brought them in. In typical country fashion, they were arranged on a clear, plastic plate with plastic wrap covering them. "For you," she said. "They should be warm, but now they're nearly frozen. My mother insisted."

"She baked them for me?" he asked, surprised, as he peeled off the wrap and helped himself.

"Well, kind of."

"Kind of?"

"We baked together today. All day. We do that for the holidays. Stuff for the freezer, gifts for neighbors and for my girls at the shop. We bake on my days off for weeks right up to Christmas."

"You bake?" he asked, looking mesmerized, maybe shocked.

She smirked. "All farm girls bake. I also know how to quilt, garden, put up preserves and chop the head off a chicken. I couldn't butcher a cow by myself, but I know how it's done and I've helped."

"Wow."

She was not flattered by his response. She'd hardly led a glamorous life and she'd much rather have told him she'd gone to boarding school in Switzerland and dressage training in England. "I bet I remind you of your mother, huh?"

He chuckled. "Not exactly. Do you fish? Hunt?"

"I've been fishing and hunting, but I prefer the farm. Well, I shot a mountain lion once, but that was a long time ago and I wasn't hunting. The little bastard was after my mother's chickens, and the boys had already moved away, so I—"

"How old were you?" he asked.

She shrugged. "I don't know—thirteen or fourteen. But I'm not crazy about hunting. I like to ride. I miss the cows. I loved the calving. Ice cream made from fresh cream. Warm eggs, right out from under the chicken. I have more 4-H ribbons than anyone in my family. Erasmus, that mean old bull? He's mine. Blue ribbon—state fair. I was fifteen when he came along—he's an old guy now, and the father of hundreds. I have a green thumb like my mother—I can stick anything in the ground and it grows. I once grew a rock bush." He threw her a shocked expression and she rolled her eyes. He recovered. "Just one of those plain old farm girls. Size-ten boot and taller than all the boys till I was a senior in high school. My dad calls me solid. Steady. Not the kind of girl men are drawn to. I attract…*puppies*. That's what."

He smiled hugely, showing her his bright white teeth and that maddening dimple. "Is that a fact?"

"Not *your* type, certainly. I've never had a string bikini. I wouldn't know what to do with one. Floss your teeth? Is that what you do?"

He laughed. "There are sexier things than string bikinis," he said.

"Really?" she asked. "The minute I heard you describe being lost in the middle of a hundred string bikinis, I got a picture in my mind that I haven't been able to get rid of. It's like having a bad song stuck in your head."

"Oh, Jesus, don't you just have a giant bug up your ass," he said, amused.

"I have no idea what you mean," she said, though she knew *exactly*. She was a terrible liar. "I didn't even know you weren't your father, you know. I had no idea you were the vet until you showed up at Jack's. And today while we were baking, my folks told me that when you came up here to take over the practice, they'd talked about nothing else for months. I guess you brought your girlfriend with you. A beautiful, fancy, Hollywood woman."

Shock widened his mouth and eyes. "Get outta here," he said. Then he erupted into laughter. "Is that what they're saying?"

A little embarrassed, she shrugged. "I don't know that anyone's saying anything anymore, and I don't know who besides my folks saw it that way."

He laughed for a long time, finally getting himself under control. "Okay, look. She was my fiancée, okay? But it was my mistake, bringing her up here, because she was far too young. I must have been out of my mind. She wasn't ready to get married. Thank God. And she wasn't a Hollywood woman, although she really wanted to be. Maybe she is by now, for all I know. Susanna was from Van Nuys. The only thing she knew about horses was that they have four legs and big teeth. She was twenty-four to my twenty-nine, had never lived in a small town and really didn't want to."

"And thin," Annie added. "Very thin."

He put his hands in his pockets, rocked back on his heels, lifted expressive dark brows and with a grin he said, "Well, not all over."

"Oh, that's disgusting," she returned, disapproval sounding loud.

"Well, it's not nice to talk meanly about past girlfriends."

"I bet she looked great in a string bikini," Annie said with a snort.

"Just unbelievable," he said, clearly taunting her. "Now, why would you be so jealous? You don't even know poor, thin Susanna. For all you know, she's a sweet, caring, genuine person and I was horrible to her." And he said all this with a sly smile.

"I am certainly not jealous! Curious, but not jealous!"

"Green as a bullfrog," he accused.

"Oh, bloody hell. Listen, I'm shot. Long day. Gotta go." She grabbed her purse and jacket and whirled out of the kitchen. And got lost. She found herself in the wide hall that led to the bedrooms. She found her way back to the great room, then to the kitchen. "Where the hell is the door?"

He swept an arm wide toward the door that led to the garage, still wearing that superior smile. What an egomaniac, she thought, heading for the door.

When she got to her car, she thought, well, that was perfectly awful. What's more, he saw right through her. She was attracted to him, and because she knew there had probably been many beautiful women in his past, she'd let it goad her into some grotesque and envious remarks about the only one she knew of, Susanna. The child-woman who obviously had a little butt and nice rack. Why in the world would she do that? What did she care?

It probably had something to do with touring a four-thousand-square-foot custom home, beautifully furnished, across the compound from a spacious stable with a couple of horse trailers her dad would have killed for. Well, what was one to expect from a veterinary practice that served so many, over such a wide area? And not a new practice, either, but a mature one—probably forty years old. Established. Lucrative.

She'd grown up in a three-bedroom, hundred-year-old farmhouse. Her three brothers shared a bedroom and never let her forget it for a second. They *all* shared one very small bathroom. But she loved the way she'd grown up and had never been jealous a day in her life— why would she be now? Could it be that in addition to all that, she'd never gone to special, private schools, never worn custom-tailored riding gear, never could afford the best riding lessons or most prestigious competitions? Also, she had wide hips, big feet and a less-than-memorable bustline. "Oh, for God's sake, Annie," she said to herself. "Since when have you even thought about those things!"

How long had she been sitting here in her car? Long enough to get cold, that was how long. Well, it was time to suck it up. She'd go back in there and just tell him she was cranky, that being one of those "sturdy" farm girls who owns exactly one pair of high heels she can barely walk in, it just rubbed her the wrong way hearing about the kind of woman who could get the attention of one of the county's few bachelors. Not that *she* wanted his attention, but just the same… She'd apologize and promise never to act that way again. She wasn't usually emotional. Or irrational.

She walked back into the still-open garage, up to the back door and gave a short tap. It flew open. He reached out and grabbed her wrist, pulled her roughly into the house, put his arms around her, pressed her up against the kitchen wall just inside the door, and *kissed* her! His mouth came down on hers so fiercely, with such dominance and confidence, her eyes flew open in shock. Then he began to move over her mouth while he held her against the wall with his wide, hard chest, his big hands running up and down her rib cage, over her hips.

She couldn't move. She couldn't raise her arms or let her eyes drift closed or even kiss back. She held her breath. What the hell…?

He finally lifted his lips off hers and said, "You like me. I knew it."

"I don't like you that much. Never do that again," she said.

"You want me," he said, smiling. "And I'm going to let you have me."

"You're conceited. I do not want you."

He kissed her again, and again her eyes flew open. This time she worked her arms free and pushed against his chest.

"Well, hell, just kiss me back and see if I start to grow on you," he said.

"No. Because you think this is funny. I came back in here to apologize for being crabby. I don't care about that skinny woman. Girl. I'm just a little tired."

"You don't have to apologize, Annie. I think it's kind of cute. But you don't have to be jealous of Susanna. She's long gone and I hardly even missed her. We weren't right for each other. At all."

"That's what my dad said."

"Hank said that?"

She nodded.

"What did he say? Exactly?" Nate wanted to know.

She shouldn't. But she did. "He said I'd be more your type, but I'd have had to kill the skinny blonde first. He said she looked near death, anyway."

Nate thought that was hilarious. He laughed for a long time, but he didn't let go of her. "Good thing she left, then. She couldn't hold her own in any kind of fight. She cried if she broke a nail."

"I bet she was just one of many."

He withdrew a little, but the amusement stayed in his eyes. "You think I'm a player."

"How could you not be? It's not like I don't know about those rich horse people. And you're the *doctor!* Of course you've had a million girlfriends."

The smile finally vanished. "No," he said. "I'm not that guy, Annie. Just 'cause I've been around those folks doesn't mean I'm that kind of guy."

"Well, there are the girl vets you're going to the islands with," she reminded him.

"Tina and Cindy," he said with a laugh. "Shew. I hate to brag, but I'm thirty-two, Annie, and there have been a couple of women in my past. But I bet there are a couple of guys in yours, too. Tina and Cindy are just friends of mine."

"Uh-huh. I'm sure. Old friends and a hundred string bikinis."

"Come back in and finish your coffee," he said with a tolerant chuckle.

"I have to go. I have to get home to Ahab."

"Who's that?" Nate asked.

"My cat. Ahab. Tripod. He has a lot of names. He's three-legged."

"What happened?" Nate asked.

"I don't know. I adopted him from the shelter when it was clear no one else would ever take him. He's got a bad attitude, but he loves me. He's very independent, but he does like to eat. I have to go."

"Are you coming back tomorrow after work?"

"Are you going to be a gentleman?" she asked.

He lifted one of those handsome brows. "You want me to?"

No. "Absolutely. Or I'm leaving the puppies all to you without helping."

"Just come tomorrow after work. Swing by home and feed your cat first so you don't have to be in a hurry to leave." He gave her a very polite kiss on the cheek that just oozed with suggestiveness. "I'll see you then."

The first night in town was a relatively quiet one, with Brie and Jack's sisters and spouses dropping in to say hello and welcome, heading back to their homes early. But on Christmas Eve, it grew wild with everyone present at once. The street outside looked like a parking lot, dinner was big and messy, and the dishes took forever to clean up, but the evening was young.

WHISPERING ROCK

4

Christmastime in a beauty shop was always frantic and the Clip and Curl was no exception. There were less than two weeks till Christmas and Annie's clientele, the clientele of the whole shop, wanted to look their best for parties, open houses, family visits, neighborhood gatherings. Appointments were one after the other. There was a lot of gossip, a lot of excited chatter. Annie was pretty quiet the next day, but there was plenty of talk in the place to cover the void.

Pam, who was older than Annie by a few years and had been married for ten, was training to be the assistant manager. While Annie was applying foil to strips of hair for highlighting, Pam approached with the appointment book in her hands. "We have three choices. We can turn away some of our best regular customers, stay open till nine a couple of nights or open up the next two Mondays to fit them in."

"Why don't people schedule ahead of time?" Annie asked.

"As you taught me, they expect to be accommodated and we can either do that or lose them to another shop."

"Staying late is hard for me and you have a family. I don't want to stick you with that duty," Annie said. Then after thinking about it, she said, "Maybe I should work nights. That would settle that."

"Settle what?" Pam asked, holding the large appointment book in her crossed arms, against her chest.

"Oh, that guy. The vet. You know."

"Know what?"

"The guy at the bar, Jack, he said they couldn't keep the litter of puppies there anymore. The dogs are doing very well, growing, which means they'll soon be up to their eyeballs in puppy poop. Not a real appetizing prospect for a restaurant. So Jack said that's it, they have to go. Dr. Jensen took them to his house, which is part of the whole stable-and-vet-clinic operation. And since I made a commitment to help…he's counting on me coming over after work."

"To his house?"

"Yeah. He said if I'd help, he'd thaw something for us to eat. We've been having a beer and dinner at that bar."

"Listen, it's up to you, Annie. It's your shop. My husband's on board to get the kids from school and take care of their dinner and homework. You know I need whatever hours…"

"Then *you* make the decision," Annie said.

Pam lowered the appointment book and held it against her thigh. "Annie, I don't need you to stay if the shop is open till nine or open Mondays for a couple of weeks. Two of the girls are willing to work a little extra to help pay for Christmas. But you have to feel comfortable about leaving me in charge. And I don't want to push you to do that before you're ready. You've run a pretty tight, one-woman show here."

"Have I?"

Pam nodded. "But I don't blame you, Annie. This is your shop, your investment, your responsibility. Whenever you think I'm ready, I'm glad to help."

"Thing is, he kissed me."

It became very quiet in the shop. Pam's mouth dropped open.

"Nuts," Annie said. There were no ears gifted with supersonic hearing like those found in a beauty shop, despite the noise of dryers and running water. She looked around the small shop. It was tiny—three chairs on each side of the room. Two dryers and two deep sinks in back. Behind that was their break room and Annie's little office.

In the salon now were women in various stages of beautifying, rods, rollers, foils or back-combed tresses blooming from their heads. Beauticians with blow-dryers, curling irons, combs and brushes in their hands, poised over those heads. All silent. All waiting. "Talk among yourselves," Annie instructed.

"Lotsa luck," Pam said. "Is this guy, this vet, in any way appealing?"

Annie's cheeks got a little rosy.

"Is he cute?" Pam asked.

Annie leaned toward Pam and whispered, "You'd wet yourself."

And Pam's cheeks got a little pink. "Whew."

"Well, tell us about him," someone said.

"Yeah, what kind of guy is he?"

"Should you call the police or wear something with a real low neckline?"

"How old is he? How many times has he been married? Because that's key. Believe me!"

"Listen, I can't talk about this," Annie said. "I've known the man barely a week! And only because of these puppies! Honestly, if it weren't for these puppies, we wouldn't even know *about* each other. He's a large-animal vet. He was just doing the bartender, Jack, a favor by looking at the orphaned litter."

"Um, Annie, don't *you* have large animals? Who's your vet?"

"Well, *he* is, but I didn't *know* that. I mean, my folks keep an eye on the horses and Erasmus. My bull," she clarified for those confused stares in the room. "When they said they called Doc Jensen to the farm, I thanked them and paid the bill. I mean, it hardly ever happens that the horses or the bull needs something. I thought he was the same Doc Jensen who'd been looking after our animals since I was in diapers. But it turned out to be his son. Doc Jensen Junior." She cleared her throat. "He's thirty-two. And never been married."

"Whoa," someone said. Another woman whistled.

"He's had girlfriends," Annie said. "Not from around here. But when he came up here to take over his dad's practice a couple of years ago, he brought a young buxom blonde fiancée with him and it didn't work out, but—"

"Low neckline," someone advised.

"Tight jeans. Snug, anyway. I mean this in the nicest way, but if you could think about a little extra makeup, like eyeliner and lip liner," someone said.

"You don't need that," Pam said quietly.

"I was thinking that maybe being unavailable would be a good—"

"No!" three women said at once.

"Why would you do that?" Pam asked.

"He's just too damn sure of himself," Annie answered.

"Well, how about this," Pam said. "Maybe you could try being sure of *your*self?"

Annie thought about that for a second. "See, that's the hard part."

Usually Annie was very confident. She knew she was intelligent; she was a small-business owner and it was going well. She was independent and doubted that would ever change, even once she partnered up. And as for her modest upbringing, she had not yet met the person she'd trade places with. Life on the farm was rich in many ways. She might've had a moment of shallow jealousy over the skinny, fancy, city girl who could attract not only Nathaniel's attention, but acquire a big engagement rock, as well, but all that had passed pretty quickly.

There was one area in her life where her confidence was a little shaky, however. She'd barely recovered from Ed. She'd put a lot of faith and trust in a man who'd clearly been using her. If this new guy, the big-shot vet, was really interested in her, he'd have some proving to do. She wasn't going to be played for a fool. And she certainly wasn't going to be the only available two-legged female he'd run across lately.

Later that day after work, she fed Ahab, dug around in her refrigerator and fluffed up a nice green salad, fixed a plate of frosted brownies and headed for.

Nate's place.

When she pulled up to his house, a woman was just leaving the clinic, locking the door behind her. She was a tiny thing with salt-and-pepper hair cut supershort, and when she might have headed for the only car parked outside the clinic, she stopped and waited for Annie with a smile on her lips.

Annie approached her. "You must be Virginia," she said.

"And you would be Annie McKenzie," the older woman said. "Nice to meet you. I met your parents some years ago, but I think all you kids were either at school or had maybe already left home. Nate's not home yet, but you have a key, right?"

"I do," she said. "Thanks for helping with those puppies. These are for you," she added on a whim, passing Virginia the plate of brownies.

"You shouldn't have, but I'm glad you did. Annie, tell Nathaniel to give you both the clinic and my home phone numbers and to leave your phone number for me. If we run into a situation when he's stuck out at a farm or ranch, we can work together to cover for him. I live in Clear River and he tells me you're in Fortuna. It's about the same distance for both of us to get here."

"Sure. And I'll tell him to call me first. I don't have a husband to irritate by running off somewhere to take care of puppies."

Virginia tilted her head, regarding her. "He doesn't talk about women, you know," she said.

"Your husband?" Annie answered, confused.

Virginia laughed. "Nathaniel. Can't get a word out of him about his love life. And I've known him since he was this high," she said, her hand measuring about midthigh.

"Maybe it's not much of a—"

"But he's talked about you for a week now. Annie this, and Annie that."

Annie's eyes grew round and maybe a little panicked. "This and that *what?*" she asked.

"I think he finds you delightful. Maybe amazing. You knew exactly what to do with the puppies because, raised by Hank and Rose, you were trained to know. And you're tall. For years he's been asking me if I've always been this short. I think he likes tall women. When you were little, he said, you had a big batch of curly, carrot-orange hair, but you obviously outgrew it. You shot a mountain lion, butchered a cow, raised a blue-ribbon bull. Oh, and you're beautiful. But a little crabby, which he finds humorous." Virginia shook her head. "Nathaniel likes to try to find his way around a difficult woman," she said with a grin. "Being the youngest of four with three bossy older sisters, he can't help it, so don't let down your guard."

Annie laughed. No problem there—her guard was up.

"It's nice that you two have renewed your friendship," Virginia added.

"But, Virginia, we were never friends," Annie said. "We barely recall each other from childhood. He knew my older brothers, but not that well. We all went to different schools and might've run into each other at fairs, 4-H stuff, that sort of thing. Really—a long time ago. A couple of decades ago."

But the woman only flashed her friendly grin. "Isn't it great when you renew an acquaintance with someone you have that kind of history with?"

That kind of history? Annie wondered. That wasn't much history. "But we don't know each other as adults. Not at all."

Virginia laughed. "Bet that'll be the fun part. Now, you call me if you need me," she said, moving toward her car. "And thanks for the brownies! My husband will be as thrilled as I am!"

"Sure," Annie said. "Of course."

Virginia paused at her car door. "Annie, if you need anything other than puppy care, don't hesitate to call on me."

"Thanks," she said.

★ ★ ★

It wasn't long after Annie had spoken to Virginia and let herself into Nate's house that he came home. She heard his truck enter the garage, and when he walked in the door to the kitchen, his face lit up. "Hey," he said. "I thought I'd beat you here."

"Just got here," she said. "And something smells good."

"I just hope it also tastes good. I admit, Virginia gave me a hand."

"No shame in that, Nate." Then she smiled at him. Standing in the kitchen like that, waiting as he walked in the door after work, felt very nice. And then she told herself not to fantasize. Just one day at a time.

They fed the puppies and while a roast simmered in the Crock-Pot, complete with potatoes, carrots, onions and whole mushrooms, they let the puppies loose in the family room. They sat on the floor with them, a roll of paper towels handy, and laughed themselves stupid trying to keep track of the little animals, which escaped under the sofa, down the hall, behind furniture. They kept grabbing the puppies, counting, losing count, temporarily misplacing one. Nate estimated they were just over four weeks old because they were starting to bark, and every time one did, he or she fell over. It was better than television for entertainment.

After the puppies were put away again, dinner eaten,

dishes cleaned up, Annie made noises about leaving, and Nate talked her into sitting down in the family room. "It's early," he said. "Let's just turn on the TV for a while."

She plopped onto the couch. "Oh, God," she said weakly. "Don't let me get comfortable. I really have to go home. You have no idea how early I start my day."

"Oh, really?" he asked. "Do you have eight whiny, hungry puppies in your laundry room? I start pretty early myself. Besides, I want you comfortable. This is such a great make-out couch."

"How do you know that?" she asked.

He shrugged like it was a stupid question. "I've made out on it."

"You said you'd be a gentleman!"

"Annie, you just have to try me out—I'm going to be very gentlemanly about it. Come on, don't make me beg."

She grinned at him. "Beg," she said. "I think that's what it's going to take."

He got an evil look in his eye and said, "Come here." He snaked his fingers under her belt and tugged, pulling her down into the soft sofa cushions. "Let's put a little flush on your cheeks."

The next night Annie took eight lengths of ribbon in eight different colors to Nate's house. They tied the ribbons around the puppies' necks, so they could be identifiable. They weighed them, made a chart, had dinner—and Nathaniel was more than happy to put a flush on her cheeks again.

Night after night, she fed Ahab right after work so she'd be free to—ahem—help with the puppies. And talk and play and kiss. The kissing quickly became her favorite part. Greedy for that, she trusted Pam to hold the shop open two nights a week and a half day on Monday. In exchange for that, Annie insisted Pam take a little comp time to get her own Christmas baking and shopping done; she came in late a few days to compensate.

There was more contributing to that flush of happiness on Annie's cheeks than just the kissing. Minor though it might seem, getting to know him when he had his shirt pulled out of his jeans and his boots off seemed so much more than casual. Of course her boots were off, also, and while they necked, their feet intertwined and they wiggled their toes. They wiggled against each other, too. It was delicious.

When they were feeding or cleaning up after puppies, preparing a meal together, they were also getting to know each other. Annie had never really thought about it before, but that was what courtship was all about—figuring out if you had enough in common after the spark of desire to sustain a real relationship.

Nathaniel had wanted to work with Thoroughbreds since he was a kid. He owned a couple of retired race-horses, good for riding. "One good stud can set you up for a great side business," he said. The initial investment, however, could be major. "In the next year or two, I'm going to invest. See what I can do."

"Why not show horses?" she asked.

"That's good, too, but I like the races."

"I love horses," she said. "You knew that. But did you know this? I've competed in dressage events all over the state. When I was younger, of course. Eventually it became too expensive for me. The best training was never in my neighborhood and the biggest competitions, including for the Olympics, were out of my reach. But if I could ever do anything, I would teach beginner dressage. Maybe even intermediate."

She told him she had thought about inviting him out to the farm to meet her parents and horses, but realized he already knew them. He knew them before he knew her, in fact. So she invited him to see her little Fortuna house and she made him dinner there. "I don't have a great make-out couch, however," she warned him.

"Doesn't matter anymore," he said. "I needed that couch to get you going, but now that you're all warmed up, we can do it anywhere. The floor, the chair, against the wall, the car..."

"I was so right about you. You're just arrogant."

He was also sentimental. Nathaniel was charmed by her two-bedroom house with a detached garage. The decorating was not prissy like a little dollhouse, but dominated by strong colors and leather furniture. The best part was, she had it completely decorated for Christmas, a garland over the hearth, lights up on the outside eaves. She had drizzled glitter on her huge poinsettia, had a Christmas cactus as big as a hydrangea bush, lots of what his mother had always called gewgaws. Ribbons, candles, potpourris, a Santa collection and, of course, a tree. A real tree, decorated to match the house—in burgundy, green, cream and gold. "And you're not even spending Christmas at home," he said.

"But I live here," she reminded him.

"It just doesn't make sense for me to put up decorations," he said. "Mother left a ton of them in the garage cabinets, but I'm leaving before Christmas. And I didn't think anyone would be around to see them."

"I do it for myself," she said. "I'm having holidays, too. I'll spend nights here since it gets so crowded at the farm. In years past, I've been known to loan the house to one of the brothers and sisters-in-law and kids and just take the couch. Brad brings an RV, which the teenage boys pretty much commandeer. During summer visits, the kids stake out the barn and front porch."

"Sounds like fun. I think I would have liked that, growing up," he said. "When they all get here, will you let me meet them? Or re-meet them? I haven't seen the boys since junior high."

"Sure, but you have to be prepared."

"For what?"

"They're going to treat you like you're my boyfriend."

He smiled and pulled her against him. "What makes you think I'd have a problem with that?"

"I don't think we're in that place," she informed him. "I think we just eat, talk, take care of puppies and kiss."

"Annie," he said as if disappointed. "What do you think a boyfriend is?"

"Um, I never really…"

"Tomorrow is Sunday, your day at the farm with your folks," he said. "Get done with whatever it is you do by early afternoon. Come for a ride with me. Let me show you my spread—it's so peaceful in the snow. Bring a change of clothes so you can freshen up before we have dinner."

"I can do that," she said. "I'd like that."

Annie had seen herself as plain and sturdy, until she'd been under the lips and hands of Nathaniel Jensen, because he was so much more than she'd ever reckoned with. Handsome, smart, funny, compassionate, independent, strong, sexy—the list was endless. And he made her feel like so much more than a solid, dependable farm girl. When he kissed her, dared to touch her a bit more intimately than she invited, pulled his hands back when she said *not yet,* she felt sexy and pretty and adored. This was a man she looked forward to exploring, and she was taking him in slowly, with such pleasure.

So she told Rose she had a date to go riding with the vet and was, of course, excitedly excused from Sunday baking and dinner at the farm. "Please don't get all worked up," Annie told her mother. "This isn't anything special. We've become friends on account of those puppies."

"Right," Rose said. "Still, could you wear a little color to bring out your hair and eyes?"

"I said, take it easy," Annie stressed. "And don't mention it to anyone. I don't want to be the talk of the county the way that skinny Hollywood woman was."

But Annie wasn't taking it lightly—she was almost sizzling with pleasure. And she tried dressing up a little more. For riding, she wore her best jeans, newest boots and oldest denim jacket over a red turtleneck sweater. She added a black scarf. She brought along attractive slacks and high-heeled boots with a silk blouse and her best suede blazer to wear for dinner afterward. They talked about horses while they rode two of Nate's favorite mounts, a couple of valuable, albeit retired, Thoroughbreds, disciplined and with just the right amount of spirit. The conversation about breeding, training, racing and showing horses was so stimulating she could almost forget for a while that she was trying not to fall in love with him.

"I'm not around horse people enough anymore," she said. "When I was riding in competition as a girl, that was enough to keep me occupied twenty-four hours a day. No wonder I didn't have fun in college—I wasn't riding."

"You're good on a horse," he said. "You should ride every day. So should I—it's the best part of what I do."

They rode into the foothills behind Nate's stables along a trail that, although covered by a layer of snow, had been well used. The trees rose high above them and the sun was lowering in the afternoon sky. They talked about growing up as the youngest in their families, and the only one of their gender. While Annie's brothers treated her like a football, Nathaniel's older sisters played with him as if he were a baby doll they could dress up at will. "It's amazing I'm not weirder than I am," he said. "The next oldest is Patricia, who's thirty-seven. Then Susan, and the oldest is Christina—one every two years. My parents had decided to quit while they were ahead and then, bingo." He grinned. "Me. I upset the balance in a big way."

"I think a similar thing happened at the farm," she said. "The boys are thirty-three, thirty-four and thirty-seven. Then I came along and upset the bedroom situation. My parents decided I had to have my own, which left one for the boys. And then I raised a bull—did I mention he won a blue ribbon?"

"Several times, I believe."

"We actually needed him. We had a couple of old bulls who just couldn't step up to the plate anymore, y'know? But Erasmus was Ready Freddy. I'm real proud of that old bull." She smiled. "My brothers had their shot at raising animals and they did all right, but Erasmus was the blue-ribbon baby. I blew my brothers out of the 4-H water with that guy." She sighed wistfully. "I think having a daughter was harder on my dad and brothers than being the only girl was on me. And being the only girl wasn't easy. They were ruthless."

"Yet protective?" he asked.

"It's an uncomfortable place sometimes, to be tossed around like a beanbag and hovered over like a china doll."

"Did they make it hard on your boyfriends?" he asked.

"There weren't very many boyfriends," she said.

"I don't believe you," he replied with a grin. "You're lying to make me feel better."

So she told him about Ed. She hadn't planned to, but this was a perfect segue to explaining that she might have an issue or two with trust. Not only had the man in the only really serious relationship of her adult life cheated on her, horribly, but she had never had a clue. That bothered her. After it was over, it was so obvious, but while it was going on, she was oblivious. Not good.

They were headed back toward the stables when she told him. She expected him to be sympathetic and sweet. Instead, he was fascinated. "Are you *serious?* He had about three women going at once? Scattered around? Telling each one he was in love with only her? Really?"

"Really," she said, annoyed.

"How in the world did he manage that?" Nate asked.

"Well, a lot of phone calls while he was working. He talked to each one of us every day, sometimes several times a day. But with very few exceptions, we were assigned certain nights. We thought those were the days he didn't have to leave town. I should have known where I stood in the line. I was getting Mondays and Tuesdays. The woman he decided was the real one in his life was getting the weekends—Saturdays and Sundays. She dumped him, of course, when she discovered Ms.

Wednesdays, Thursdays and Fridays. Three days a week must be the trump, huh?"

"Holy cow," Nate said. "He didn't even need a house or apartment! He had all his nights covered!"

"You know, I'm not impressed by his ability to pull it off."

"Of course you're not," Nate said. "But if you just think about it, he had quite a scam going. Did he take you lots of places? Buy you nice things?"

"He couldn't do either," she explained. "First of all, he couldn't risk being seen out and about with a woman, since one of the other women or their friends might run into him. So he said he was so tired, and after a week of being on the road and eating in restaurants, he enjoyed staying home."

"Where you could cook for him," Nate stated.

She pursed her lips, narrowed her eyes and nodded. "He did buy me a hot-water heater when mine went out," she admitted. "He might've needed that hot shower," she muttered.

"The man's a genius," Nate said. Then upon studying her face, he said, "Oh, he's a bastard, but you have to give him some credit for all the planning and subterfuge that—"

"I give him no credit," she said harshly.

He grabbed her hand then, pulled her closer and said,

"Of course not. No credit. He should be killed. But I'm glad he didn't choose you. What if he'd chosen you? Can you imagine? We'd never meet and fall in love!"

She was so stunned that she pulled back on the reins and stopped her horse. "Are we in love?" she asked.

"I don't know about you, but I'm just getting started here—there's lots of potential. And he doesn't deserve you. I, however, deserve you. And will take you any-where you want. And I'm going to hold your hand the whole time. I'll feed you cookies and kiss your neck in public."

"People will think I'm your girlfriend."

"That's what I want people to think. I'm going to start right away. We're going to go out. We'll drive into town to look at Christmas decorations, go to Virgin River to check out the tree and have some of Preacher's dinner, and then I'm going to take you to a nice restaurant on the weekend. And anything else you feel like doing."

"Why?" she asked.

"I want everyone to know you're with me. I want everyone to know you're not Sundays and Mondays—you're every day."

Again she pulled back on the reins and stopped her horse. "What's sexier than a string bikini, Nathaniel?"

"Are you kidding me?" He reined in beside her. His voice grew quiet and serious. He rubbed a knuckle down her cheek, over her jaw, gazing into her dark eyes. "Denim turns me on. Long legs in jeans and boots astride a big horse, making him dance to subtle commands. A rough work shirt under a down vest, feeding a newborn foal with a bottle because the mare isn't responding." He threaded his fingers into her hair and said, "Silk, instead of cotton candy. A fire on a cold, snowy night. A woman in my arms, soft and content, happy with the same things that make me happy. Help making homemade pizza—that turns me on. A woman who knows how to deliver a calf when there's trouble—that blows my horn. A woman who can muck out a stall and then fall into the fresh hay and let me fall right on top of her. I'd like to try that real soon."

Her eyes clouded a bit. "Are you just leading me on? Because when Ed pulled his trick, my brothers wanted to kill him, but I wouldn't let them. You? If you're lying, I'm going to let them. You'll suffer before you die."

"I'm not lying, Annie. And you know it."

"Well, okay, then answer this—if you like me, why haven't you liked someone before me? Because these hills are full of girls just like me—sturdy farm girls who have pulled their share of foals from the dams, fed them and kept them warm and—"

"No, there aren't," he said. "I've been looking. Just like you, I haven't had a whole lot of dates because there really wasn't anyone like you. You're one of a kind, Annie McKenzie. I'm sorry you don't seem to know that. But now that I've found you, we need to date... and a whole lot more."

"Be warned," she said. "I'm not casual about this stuff."

"Me, neither," he said.

After they put up the horses' tack and brushed them down, when it was time to change for dinner, he suggested they share a shower.

"I don't think so, Nate. Not yet," she said. "Does my door lock?" And he laughed at her.

On the way to Arcata they enjoyed the multicolored Christmas lights all along the coastal towns and up into the mountains. The Arcata square was decorated with lights, lit-up trees and a life-size nativity scene. Many of the shop windows were also decorated and filled with Christmas ornaments, gaily dressed mannequins and animated toys. Just as he'd promised, he held her hand everywhere they went. He had chosen an Italian restaurant on the square, and as it happened, it was one of her favorites. It boasted homemade pasta, robust red wine and excellent tiramisu.

"When are your brothers and their families arriving?" he asked over dinner.

"Tomorrow," she said. "By the way, you're invited to dinner. Please be cool around my brothers and don't give anything away. They haven't grown up at all since you knew them, despite the fact they have sons of their own."

"I'll be cool, all right," he promised. "Don't you worry." And then he grinned.

On Christmas morning, a beautiful snow fell, dusting the pines and the trails, and they took a couple of the horses out for a ride.

WHISPERING ROCK

5

It was a successful date, proved by the way they were in each other's arms, kissing deeply, before they were even in his house. It was still early enough to get in a good, long session of kissing on that soft, deep, inviting couch, and they fell on it together, taking turns helping each other out of boots and jackets without hardly breaking the kiss. Within moments they were in their favorite position on that great sofa, lined up against each other, exploring the inner softness of their mouths. Her body grew predictably supple and soft while his grew more urgent and hard.

Nathaniel whispered, "Annie. Come to my bed."

And she said, "No."

"No?" he answered weakly. "Annie, you don't mean that."

"I do mean it. No."

"But you kiss me like you're ready. Why not?"

She pushed herself up on the couch just slightly so she could look at his eyes. "We've only known each other three weeks, for starters."

"I've kind of known you my whole life, even if I haven't known you since you got your braces off. But I've known you *intensely* for three weeks."

"We knew each other superficially for one week and intensely for the next two weeks. I might require a little more than that."

"Why?"

"Because I just broke up with Ed. Six months ago. It isn't that long."

"It's forever," he said. "I should have made you forget he ever existed by now."

"I think in another couple of weeks, I will have forgotten. And I'd kind of like to know how you feel after you've had your chance to lie on the beach surrounded by beautiful bodies in very small bathing suits."

"Oh, that. Listen, that's not even part of the equation," he said. "Really. That trip has nothing to do with how I feel."

"It has to do with how *I* feel," she said.

"Annie, if I hadn't made arrangements for this vacation long before I met you, I sure wouldn't plan it now. And it was a lot more than wanting to be lost in bikinis, believe me. It was a very convenient, very convincing plan, so I wouldn't find myself held hostage on a cruise ship with all my sisters and their kids. I explained—my brothers-in-law are great, but when their wives are around…"

"They have to act like husbands and fathers?"

"As opposed to regular guys," he clarified with a nod. "We've been on a couple of fishing trips together and I'm telling you, these guys are the best. They *are* my brothers. But when my sisters and the kids are around…"

"Husbands and fathers," she said helpfully again.

"But I'm not," he said. "I'm bored out of my mind. The only reprieve I get is a brandy and cigar with my dad and a conversation about veterinary medicine. Come on, don't you feel sorry for me? It's murder."

"So, you're not looking forward to seeing all your old buds?" she asked.

"That? Sure, that'll be great. We used to study together several nights a week. And then after graduation, we went off in all directions. This was a great idea Jerry had, but I can think of things I'd rather do." He lifted one eyebrow and grinned lasciviously.

She laughed at him. "Still, I'm not ready. Not till after your Club Med vacation."

"It's not Club Med, I told you. Are you waiting for me to say I love you, because if you're waiting for that, I—"

She put a finger to his lips and shushed him. "Don't go out on a limb here, Nathaniel."

"I'll call the travel agent in the morning and get you a ticket," he said. "Come with me."

She laughed, actually pleased by the offer. "My goodness, you'll go to a lot of trouble and expense for sex."

"For *you*," he clarified. "Not just for sex, for *you*."

"I am kind of impressed, but no thank you."

"Why not?"

"Ordinarily, if it were another time of year, I would, but not this time. Plus, I don't get to be with the whole family that often. The boys have it worked out that they do either Thanksgiving or Christmas with our side, the other holiday with their wives' side. So it's been a couple of years since we've all done Christmas together and I love that. My mom and I knock ourselves out to make it great."

He kissed her deeply. He pressed her down into the sofa with his body and held her hands at her sides, entwining his fingers with hers. "How about if I decide not to go on that vacation?"

"That you've paid for? To see your old best friends from school? Don't be ridiculous."

"Then come with me."

"No."

"Then I won't go," he said.

"You have to go. This is important, Nathaniel. You should get away, broaden your horizons. You've probably forgotten how much you miss your friends, how much you'd like to see a hundred tiny bikinis on perfect women. You have to go. I'm kind of interested in what you'll be like when you come back."

He thought about this for a few seconds. "Okay, then," he whispered. "A compromise."

"Hmm?"

"I'll go to the stupid beach without you, my virtuous girlfriend, you'll have Christmas with your family, and tonight you come to my bed."

She laughed. "No. Not till you've passed your time with the bikinis. And the women vets you used to date. Are they pretty?"

"Tina and Cindy? Oh, yeah, very pretty, but like I said, we were better as study partners. Honey, I've completely lost interest in bikinis. Unless you want to put one on for me just for fun."

"I don't know that that will ever happen."

"Annie, I'm not interested in bikinis. Not now. I'm only interested in you. Hey! This doesn't have anything to do with skinny Susanna, does it? Because I'm not all weirded out by Ed, who's really much stranger than Susanna."

She shook her head. "The only thing about Susanna that I still have to get over is that she was beautiful, feminine, small—except for her apparently exceptional boobs—and fancy, while I'm flat-footed and can cut the head off a chicken. But I'm working on that."

"They weren't real," he said. "She bought herself a pair for her twenty-first birthday. I'd much rather touch smaller real ones."

She kissed him, a short one on the lips. "Well, Nathaniel, if this works out, I like your chances." Then she grinned at him.

He was quiet for a moment and his eyes were serious, burning into hers. "You know, if I hadn't already paid for the whole damn thing, I'd cancel that trip. It's not what I want right now."

"Hey, I want you to go, and you'll have a good time. I'm not really worried about the bikinis. Not that much."

He pressed himself against her, proof that he was still all turned on. "It turns out three weeks is enough time for me," he said. "I'd rather just not go."

She put a hand against his cheek and smiled at him. "Even a grand gesture like that wouldn't get you lucky tonight."

He shook his head. "I don't want to be away from you for ten days. I barely found you. What if stupid Ed comes around and somehow proves to you that he's worth another chance?"

"Can't happen," she said. "I hardly remember what he looks like. I'll be right here when you get back."

"What if I get so lonely and distraught I make love to some big-breasted nymphomaniac while I'm down there and come back to you all innocent, lying about it, just to teach you a terrible lesson?"

"I'd know."

"You didn't know with Ed," he reminded her.

"I know. I've been thinking about that a lot because it's been a real issue with me, that somehow I didn't know. I think Ed wasn't that important to me, or I would have been upset we had so little time together, and I wasn't. Wouldn't I have known something was *off* if he'd meant more to me? I don't think I cared as much as I wanted to. Lord, I think I would have married him even knowing he'd only spend two nights a week with me." She took a breath. "Maybe I would've married him *because* he'd only spend two nights a week with me." She ran her fingernails through the hair at Nate's temple. "But much as I fight it, Nathaniel, it's different with you." Then she smiled.

"In only three weeks?" he asked softly.

She was shaking her head. "It didn't take three whole weeks."

He took a breath, then groaned deeply just before he covered her mouth in a deep, hot, wet kiss that went on and on and on. When he finally lifted his lips from hers, he said, "Okay. We'll do this your way. We'll wait until you're ready. And when it's over and we're together forever, don't think you can boss me around like this."

"You've got a deal," she said, laughing.

Nathaniel called Annie twice before noon on Monday. First he wanted to know if there was anything he could bring to the farm. "I think we're throwing a couple of big pans of lasagna in the oven for dinner, and Mom is busy making bread. How about bringing some good red wine?"

The next time he called, he said, "I know you work on Tuesday. I'm leaving Tuesday afternoon. So tonight, if I pass the brother test, will you come home with me for just a little while?"

"For just a little while. And don't try that 'I'm going into battle and you have to show your love before I leave' trick. Okay?"

And he laughed.

That was the best part about Annie—her sense of humor. No, he thought—it was her beauty. Her dark red hair, her creamy, freckled complexion, her deep brown eyes. But then a smile came to his lips as he recalled

how good she was on a horse. An accomplished equestrienne. And while she would not find the term *sturdy*
at all complimentary, he admired that about her. Forti-
tude had always appealed to him. Sometimes when he
was holding her, he felt like he was clinging to her as if
she anchored him to the ground. She had no idea how
unattractive flighty, timid, weak women were to him.
Did such women make some men feel strong and capable? Because for Nathaniel, to be chosen by a woman
of strength and confidence met needs he didn't even
know he had.

He had calls to make, ranches to visit, patients to see,
inoculations to administer, a couple of cows who had a
fungus to look in on, breeding animals who would deliver early in the year to check. He phoned the vet from
Eureka who would cover for him while he was away, paid
a visit to a local winery to select a few bottles of good red
and finally made his way to the McKenzie farm.

When he pulled in, the place almost resembled a fair
in progress. Not one but two RVs were parked near the
back of the house, which probably eliminated the need
to borrow Annie's house for the family. There were also
trucks and snowmobiles on trailers. A bunch of cross-
country skis leaned up against the back porch. The Mc-
Kenzies were here to play. Kids ran around while several
sat on the top rail of the corral. Inside the corral, Annie

had a couple of young children mounted on her horses. She held the reins and led them around the corral while they held the saddle pommels. Four men—her brothers and father—leaned on the rail, watching.

Nate wandered up to the fence and leaned his forearms on the top rail with the rest of them. "So," he said. "I'm here for the inspection."

The man next to him turned and his mouth split into a huge grin. "Hey, man," Beau McKenzie said. "I heard a rumor you were dating my sister. Good to see you, buddy." He stuck out his hand. "This true? You and Annie? Because I can tell you things that will give you ultimate control over her!"

"Nathaniel Jensen," the next man said. Brad McKenzie stuck out his hand. "I don't think I've seen you in twenty years! You finally made it over five foot six, good for you."

"Yeah, and beat the acne." Nate laughed. "How you doing, pal?"

"Jim, any chance you remember this clown?" Beau asked his oldest brother.

"I just remember this squirt from football," Jim McKenzie said, sticking out a hand. "Couldn't tackle worth shit, but you sure could run."

"I had to run," Nate said. "If anyone had caught me, I'd be dead. I was the smallest kid on the team."

"You take steroids or something? You caught up."

"Nah, I just got old like the rest of you," he said. "Thanks for letting me invade the family party. Annie's been looking forward to it so much."

"This is true, then?" Beau asked, Brad and Jim and even Hank looking on with rather intense gazes.

What had she said? That he'd have to be cool? Maybe she expected him to joke around the way they did? One side of his mouth tilted up in a sly smile. He supposed it wasn't cool, but could they beat him up for being honest? "She knocks me out," he said. "Where have you been hiding her? I didn't even know she was here! I bumped into her in a bar!"

"That's our Annie," Beau said. "Out tying one on."

Nate laughed again. "Actually, she rescued eight orphaned puppies. Mostly border collie, we think. Cute as the devil. How many you want?"

Beau put a hand on his shoulder. "Pass on the puppies, my friend. But we got beer, Nathaniel. And seriously, we can give you stuff on her that will give you years worth of control. Power. Mastery. Don't we, guys?"

"We do," said Brad.

"Indeedy," said Jim.

It was an amazing day for Nathaniel, though not exactly a brand-new experience. The venue was a little smaller and more crowded than his family gatherings, but the family interaction was pretty much the same as in his family. The men got a little too loud, the kids ran wild and had to be rounded up several times, the women had a little tiff about kitchen things like whether the bread should have garlic butter or not and whether the salad should be dressed or not. There was a lot of furniture moving to accommodate a dinner for seventeen. They needed the dining-room table extended, and two card tables. The youngest child present at dinner was three and the oldest fourteen, and they sat at the kid table, as it was known in both the Jensen and McKenzie households. Nathaniel felt at once a special guest and right at home.

The McKenzie boys had married well; their wives were attractive, fun, energetic, and there was a lot of family rapport—which always helped. The kids were mostly well behaved, just a couple of small problems that the mothers foisted off on the fathers. Mrs. McKenzie fussed over Nate in a welcoming fashion, maybe a hopeful fashion, showing her approval. Mr. McKenzie, whom Nate had only known as Hank for the couple of years he'd been practicing here, handed Nate his jacket and took him out to the front porch during the after-dinner cleanup. Hank gave him a cigar. None of the brothers joined them, so Nate knew this was the father-and-man-in-his-daughter's-life talk.

Hank lit Nate's cigar. "I don't have a whole lot to say about this. Always got along with you just fine, so I don't have any basic complaint," Hank said.

"That's good," Nate said, puffing. Coughing. He smoked about a cigar a year and never remembered to take it easy.

"Just a couple of things I want to say."

"I'm ready."

"I like Annie," her father said. "She's good people." He puffed. "Now that might not seem like much of a recommendation, but in my book, it's the best there is. She's just plain good. She'd never in a million years hurt a soul. But don't get lazy on her, because she's nice but she's tough. She can hold her own if there's some injustice, and she's not afraid of a fight. And smart? She could've run this dairy farm single-handed, she's that smart. That strong-willed. I offered it to her, too. Boys didn't want it, so I said, 'Annie, you could do it just fine, even if I dropped dead tomorrow,' and she said, 'Dad, if I stick myself out here with the cows, I'll never leave and never do anything else and I think maybe there's got to be more to my life. At least more people in my life.' That's what she said. So that's how it was. She bought that beauty shop and I sold off the Holsteins. You better be nice to her."

"Yes, sir," he said.

"Don't even think about hurting her, Nathaniel. I can handle about anything but seeing my girl, who I admire and respect, hurt."

"I promise," Nate said.

"Because if you do…"

"You'll shoot me?" Nate asked.

"Aw, hell, why would I do that? I'm not a violent man. I'll just spread the word that as a vet, you're not worth a crap."

Nate couldn't help it, he burst out laughing.

"The boys, though," Hank went on, "they're a tad violent. When it comes to Annie. So be nice."

Nate hadn't had a lot of dates in the past couple of years, but in the past ten he'd had quite a few. When he was tending Thoroughbreds in Kentucky and then in Los Angeles County, plenty of women were attracted to him. Socialites, daughters of rich breeders, women he'd met at parties, on ranches, at races. He'd never been talked to by a father, however. Not even Susanna's, not even when he'd given her a rock and carted her up to Humboldt County with the misguided notion of marrying her.

As father talks went, Hank's hadn't been stunning.

But Nate liked it. It made him feel like a man with a job to do.

"It's probably way too early to talk about intentions," Hank said.

"No, sir, it's not," Nate replied. "I like Annie even more than you do. It's my intention to treat her very well while we're dating, and I think it might be a good match for both of us. I also think we might have a future, me and Annie. But you know what? She's a smart, stubborn girl—it's going to be up to her."

"Yeah, I reckon," Hank said.

"So. Could you at least wish me luck?" Nathaniel asked.

"You bet," Hank said, sticking out his hand. "Best of luck there, Nathaniel. Try not to screw this up."

"You bet, sir. Nice cigar, by the way."

"Yeah, not bad, huh? Have no idea where I got 'em. One of the boys, probably."

Nate wasn't sure, but he didn't think his own father had ever had one of these talks with his brothers-in-law or he would've heard about it. But right there, right then, he decided that if he ever had a daughter, he was going to do that. It was a good idea—take the young man aside, expound on the girl's wonderful qualities, threaten his life a little. It had merit.

A few minutes later Beau joined them, clipping off the

tip of a cigar. Then Brad, then Jim. Nate leaned close to Beau's ear. "How'd you know he was done with me?" Nate asked.

"If he wasn't done, you weren't going to work out," Beau said with a shrug.

"Just out of curiosity," Nate asked, "has he had many of these talks?"

"I think you're the first."

"What about that loser, Ed?"

"Ah, Ed. I don't think Annie brought him around all that much. From what we heard, he was very busy. I met him once, I think, and not on a holiday. He did sell a couple of things to my dad, though. Farm things. Before he and Annie hooked up. Dad? We didn't like Ed much, did we?"

Hank just snorted and said something derisive under his breath.

"Just out of curiosity, why didn't you like him?" Nate asked.

"He swindled me on a hay baler," Hank said. "Said he had the best price in the county. Took me about a month to find all kinds of better deals."

"So, it didn't have anything to do with how he treated her?" Nate asked.

"Son, you really think if a man will swindle you on a hay baler, you can trust him with your kin?"

"I hadn't ever thought about it that way."

"I can't imagine another way to think about it," Hank said.

"Wow," Nate said, feeling more than a little privileged. *Yeah,* he thought. *I'm picking out my daughter's guy and giving him a talking-to.*

When the cigars were finished, the men wandered back inside where the women were sitting in the kitchen with coffee. Nate paused in the doorway and signaled Annie. "Got a second?" he asked her. When she stood before him, he said, "I'm going to get a head start. Spend as much time as you want with the family. I'll go home and make sure the puppies are fed and watered and their bedding is dry."

"I can come now."

"No, stay. I'll get the puppy chores done and when you get there, I'll have more time with you. By the way, are we all set on their care while I'm gone? We talked about it a little...."

"Not to worry, Nate. Virginia and I worked out the details. We're going to share the load and they'll be looked after. And if it's okay with you, I'll make sure the adopted ones are delivered on Christmas Eve. I think Pam from the shop is going to take one, which brings us down to three left to place. I'll make sure they're okay."

"Tell anyone you take a pup to that if they bring 'em by in a couple of weeks, I'll check them over and give them shots, free of charge."

"That's nice, Nathaniel."

"Then I'll see you in a little while," he said, giving her a platonic peck on the cheek. "Thank you, Mrs. McKenzie," he said to Rose. "Nice meeting you all."

"Have a great trip, Nate," someone said.

"Good meeting you."

"Travel safe."

He shook the men's hands and was on his way.

Two thoughts occupied him as he drove home. He couldn't wait to get his arms around Annie. And he didn't want to be away from her for ten days. He didn't think a beach full of naked women could make him more inclined to leave right now. But he had packed his bags earlier, not leaving it to the last minute, and he would get this over with. Then, as far as he was concerned, it was full steam ahead with her. And she'd better not give him the slip, either. He was thirty-two and had had plenty of girlfriends, but he couldn't remember ever wanting a woman like he wanted this one. Heck, he wanted her whole family. He wanted to bring her into his. He wanted them to merge and grow.

He'd even been engaged without wanting all that. It was eerie.

He was barely home, the puppies slopping up their dinner, when the pager on his belt vibrated. He recognized the phone number of a horse breeder whose animals he took care of. His favorite patients, Thoroughbreds. This family was not nearby—they were over the county line in Mendocino.

He answered the call. One of their valuable broodmares was miscarrying, and she was all freaked out, kicking at the stable walls.

He disconnected the line, but he held the phone. He took a deep, disappointed breath before he dialed the McKenzie farm and asked for Annie.

"Nate? What's up?" she asked when she came on the line.

"You don't know how much I hate to do this. I have to go out on an emergency. There's a mare miscarrying, and the stable is in the next county. It could be complicated. It could be late."

"Don't worry about the time, Nate. See about the horse," she said.

"Honey, you shouldn't wait here for me. I might be tied up until very late. There's a chance I'll be out all night with just enough time to come home, clean up, get ready to leave. But, Annie, I won't leave without seeing you—worst case, I'll stop by your shop on my way out of town tomorrow."

"You don't have to do that, Nate. If you find yourself pressed for time, just give me a call."

"But I *do* have to," he said softly. "I can't leave without holding you, without kissing you goodbye."

"That's so sweet. But if it doesn't work out that way, I understand. Drive carefully. I hope everything is all right with the mare."

Despite Nate's warning that he might not make it home until very late, she went to his house anyway. She could hear in his voice his desire to spend a little time with her, and what did she have to keep her away? If he wasn't back by early morning, she'd feed the puppies and go home to shower and get ready for work.

She was inexplicably drawn to the master bedroom, though she had no real reason to go there. It was the sight of a couple of suitcases open on the floor, filled with clothing, that saddened her so deeply she felt a small ache in her heart. Oh, she was going to miss him so much! Disappointment filled her—she had looked forward to an hour or two of cuddling before she had to give him up for his ten-day adventure. Now it was probably not to be.

Suck it up, Annie, she said to herself. And with that, she shucked her jacket and went to make sure the puppies were taken care of. "Well, my little loves," she said to the box of squirming, jumping, yelping, vibrating puppies. "Ew," she said, taking a sniff. "Time for a re-fresh, I see." And she set about the task of giving her little charges clean fur and dry bedding. "Yeah, you're ready for new homes. You have to be about six weeks by now. Close enough, as far as I'm concerned."

Her puppy chores didn't take long. She wandered into the family room and sat on that comfy sofa. That lonely sofa. She hated to leave prematurely; she wanted to give him time to get home, to catch up with her. As she looked around the family room, it seemed so barren. At least compared to the farmhouse, which was full to the brim with food, decorations, people, laughter and happiness.

She turned on the fire to make it more welcoming for him, and then on a whim she went to the garage and looked through the storage cabinets that lined the walls of the three-port garage. She smiled to herself. Nathan-iel's mother had certainly made it easy. One entire cabi-net held boxes that were neatly labeled. She skipped the one that said "ornaments" but opened another. And an-other. And another.

She really only meant to bring a touch of Christmas into the house for Nate, even if it was only for one night, or just an early morning. First was a centerpiece for that long, oak kitchen table, then a couple of fat, glittery can-

dles on a bed of artificial holly, which she put on the coffee table. She thought if she were decorating this house
for real, there would be lots of fresh stuff and the smell
of pine. And the aroma of hot chocolate and cookies.

She put her jacket on to go back into the garage and
soon she had a garland for the mantel, stockings and brass
stocking holders, and three-foot-tall nutcracker characters for a grouping in the corner. She found a large basket of red ceramic apples mixed with huge pinecones,
a poinsettia with little twinkling lights. That gave her
another idea, and she found some tiny tree lights in a
box, which she brought in and used to adorn the house
plants—a couple of tall ficus trees and a couple of lush
philodendron and ivy. She tied thick, red velvet bows
to the backs of the kitchen chairs.

A box labeled "Christmas dishes" was just too much
to resist. Inside were some festive plates and cups. So
she turned on the oven and poked around in the pantry,
laughing to herself. Hadn't she said she wouldn't poke
around? Well, Nathaniel obviously didn't do a lot of
baking, and who knew how long that canister of flour
had been there? And the brown sugar was like a brick.
But he did have butter, sugar and M&M's. It took only
thirty minutes to produce a plate of pseudo chocolate-
chip cookies. She found chocolate-milk mix and fixed
up a couple of cups with spoons in them, ready for fill-

ing. It was probably in her DNA—she covered the festive plate of cookies with plastic wrap.

"Christmas for a day," she said to herself, pleased.

She made sure all the boxes were stowed in the garage. Then she looked at the clock. Almost eleven, and she had to get up early for work. But it didn't take her a second to make her decision—a girl doesn't find a quality boyfriend every day. She turned down some lights in the house, took off her boots, reclined on the sofa in front of the fire with the throw over her legs and promptly fell asleep.

"Holy crap," she said. "Is this really happening?"

"Listen, Mel, I need a change. A temporary if not permanent one. If you find me qualified, I'll see you right after Christmas."

She was speechless for a minute. Then she said, "Ho ho ho," and he laughed.

CAMERON AND MEL FROM *TEMPTATION RIDGE*

6

Nate was physically tired and emotionally drained. By the time he reached the Bledsoe stables, the mare had miscarried a five-month foal and she was skittish. Frantic might be a better word. Indication was that the horse was sick, the cause of the miscarriage, though Nate had checked her over before she was bred and she'd been in good shape. Because he wasn't going to be around to follow up, he had called Dr. Conner, the Eureka vet. He tranquilized the mare to calm her, administered antibiotics, made sure the placenta was whole, and then transported the products of conception to Eureka so that Dr. Conner could follow up with a postmortem to try to determine the cause. Conner would probably choose to do an endometrial biopsy. Other horses in the stable would have to be examined immediately; Bledsoe had six breeding at the moment.

But that was not the hardest part. Not only was the mare valuable and the stud a champion, the owners' teenage daughter had raised this horse from a filly and it was her first foal. The girl was as distraught as the horse, and terrified her mare was going to die.

She wasn't going to die, but the jury was still out on whether she was a good broodmare. Some mystery problem or illness had taken its toll and caused her to drop the foal and suffer a considerable amount of bleeding. Time and follow-up would tell the story. But when Nate left the family, quite late at night, it looked as though the teenage girl was going to sleep in the stable with her horse.

Now that was something he could see Annie doing.

And to speak of the devil herself, when he pulled up to his house, it was dimly lit from inside and her truck was parked out front. The clock on the car console said two-fifteen. Lord, what was she doing? Half of him was so grateful he could burst, the other half wanted to spank her for staying up so late—he knew she had a long day in the shop ahead of her so that she could be closed the afternoon of the twenty-fourth and all day the twenty-fifth.

Annie, he had learned, was not afraid of hard work.

He entered the dimly lit house quietly. His first re-action was surprise, but pleasure quickly followed. On the breakfast bar a thick red candle flickered beside a plate of cookies and a couple of cups. There was choco-late powder in the cups, ready for hot milk to be added. Bows on the chairs, garlands strung around, table deco-rations, twinkling lights everywhere, and his girl, asleep in front of a fire. He chuckled to himself. Well, hadn't *she* been busy.

It was like really coming home. Holidays meant a lot to her. Her sense of love and family spilled over to ev-eryone around her, and he felt so…embraced inside, like it was his first Christmas. He smiled to himself. In an important way, it was.

He took off his boots, belt and jacket in the kitchen. He blew out candles, turned off all but the twinkling tree lights and fireplace, and knelt down by the sofa, softly kissing her beautiful lips.

"Mmm," she murmured, half waking. "You're home. I must've fallen asleep."

"You were probably exhausted, digging through the storage," he said with humor in his voice.

"I'll put it all away before you get back," she whis-pered. "I should go, now you're home…."

"Are you crazy?" he asked. He slipped one arm under

her knees, the other behind her back and stood with her in his arms. "We're going to get some sleep. It's almost morning, anyway. And this couch isn't going to do it. I want to hold you. I want to fall asleep with you in my arms. Now close your eyes and your mouth."

She hummed and snuggled closer to him. "Everything all right? With the mare?" she asked.

"It'll get sorted out. I'll tell you about it in the morning." He carried her to his bedroom and laid her gently on the bed. "Do you need the alarm?" he asked her. "I can set it for you."

"Nah. I haven't slept past seven in my life."

"Good," he said. He pulled back the comforter and crawled in, jeans and all, and she did the same. "Come close," he said. "All I want in life is to feel you against me. Mmm, just like that. Aaah, Annie, my Annie…"

Suddenly he knew that even as exhausted as he was, he wasn't going to sleep. He had a stunning thought— *this is what it feels like when you actually fall in love.* He'd thought that whole falling-in-love thing was some girl story that guys didn't experience. He was familiar with being attracted. Oh-ho, was he familiar with that! And of course he had known desire in all sizes, from warm to boiling. Wanting a woman, yes, that was a fairly regular occurrence. But this was all those things mixed together and yet something completely different at the same time.

He wanted to be only with Annie; if he were allowed one friend for the rest of his life, he would choose her. He wanted to come home to the kind of warmth she could bring to a room. He wanted to crawl in beside her and feel the comfort of her body, which fit so perfectly against his. He didn't want to be away from her; he wanted her for life.

He began unbuttoning her blouse. In spite of the fact that she seemed to be asleep, he was undressing her, knowing he shouldn't. But then he felt her fingers working away at *his* shirt buttons and he sprang to life, hard and ready. His hands went to the snap on her jeans while hers worked at his. Like choreography, they were slipping each other's jeans down and off and he pulled her hard against him, his shorts to her dainties. "God," he said. "God, God, God."

She pulled away just enough to shrug out of her shirt and remove her socks. She left the panties for Nate to handle, which he did immediately. "Let me have these," he said, clutching them in his fist. "Let me keep these for the rest of my life. Can I?"

She laughed at him and tugged down his boxers. "Sure," she whispered against his lips. "And you can keep your underwear."

He moaned as if in pain, his hand finding a breast. "Why are you wearing a bra?" he asked.

"Because you've been undressing me for five seconds and haven't gotten to that yet?" she returned. She unsnapped the clasp and it fell apart, just in time for his lips on her breast. He rolled on top of her, probing. "Condom," she whispered. "Condom, Nate."

"Right," he said. "Got it." And he leaped out of bed, raced unceremoniously to the master bath, running back to the king-size bed with a packet in his hand, ripping it open as he went. He flopped on the bed and pulled her close. Then he froze. All motion stopped. Their thighs were pressed together, their lips straining toward each other, their hands pulling their bodies closer, and he said, "Annie? Are you ready for this?"

She didn't say anything and he couldn't see her face in the darkness of the room. She took his hand and captured the foil packet. She pulled his hand down between her legs where his fingers could answer his question.

He moved his hand up her inner thigh, opened her legs a bit, caressed her wonderfully wet folds. "Aaah," he said once more against her lips.

"Ready," she whispered. "Ready." And then she applied the protection.

"You know what, Annie?" he said. "Coming home to you, making love to you, it feels like the one thing I've always been ready for."

"Then let's not waste any more time," she said.

★ ★ ★

He fell asleep while still inside her, holding her close. Sometime in the night, they roused just enough to make love again. When he awoke in the morning, he was alone. There was a little puppy, whimpering, faint and distant.

He found her note in the kitchen:

Nate—you were so tired, you slept through puppy breakfast, which was noisy. I decided you should sleep. I want you to have the most wonderful time of your life on your trip. I'll take care of everything while you're gone and I'll put away the decorations. And thank you for last night. It was perfect. Love, Annie.

He picked up the note and read it again and again. "It's awful hard to leave you, Annie," he whispered. "Especially at Christmas."

Nathaniel booked his flights to coordinate with the rest of the group—they were all meeting for breakfast in Miami. From there they would fly together to Nassau. He had to take a commuter from Santa Rosa to San Francisco. That meant a two-hour drive south to pick up the first leg of his trip. From San Francisco he would take a nonstop red-eye to Miami. He would be there in early morning. He'd have breakfast in the airport with his old gang. It brought to mind the breakfasts they'd had together after all-night study sessions, right before a big exam. Then they'd get to the Bahamas early in the day to begin their ten-day vacation.

He didn't mind driving, which was a good thing, since his practice had him running around the mountains and valleys of three counties looking after livestock. The drive from Humboldt County to Santa Rosa was beautiful and calm. But rather than enjoy the rolling hills and snow-covered pines and mountains, all he thought about was Annie.

Before he left Humboldt County, he had called her at her shop. "I'll be leaving in a couple of hours. Sure you want to let me go without you?" he had asked.

"This is your trip, Nate. Not mine," she said. "You planned it, you've looked forward to it, you paid for it— now go and enjoy it. I have family things to do. And puppy things. When you get back all the decorations will be put away, the puppies will be distributed to their new homes and you'll be tanned and rested. And it will be a whole new year."

"I hear cell reception is terrible there, but I'll try to call you while I'm gone," he said. "I want to see if you have any regrets about turning down an all-expense-paid vacation. And there's a note for you on the kitchen counter—my hotel info. Call me if you need anything. Anything at all."

When he said that, he had been thinking, *Me. Call if you need me. Call me if you miss me.*

But Annie had laughed cheerfully. "Now, Nate, what are you going to do if I need something? Catch a flight home? You'll be on the other side of the country! And you'll be with your friends—a reunion, Nate. Now stop worrying about stuff you can't do anything about. Just have fun. Besides, I can manage just about anything."

A few weeks earlier Nathaniel had been looking forward to this vacation with such enthusiasm. He'd built a few fantasies about girls in bikinis and low-cut sundresses. He saw himself inviting a beautiful woman out to dinner; maybe he'd be taking some lovely young thing sailing. He envisioned staying up late with his buddies, laughing, drinking and smoking cigars. He figured he'd be needed to rub suntan lotion on a bare female back.

None of those mental images were working for him now. Now all he could think about was how long the next ten days were likely to be. He hoped he'd at least catch an impressive fish or two. That's what he'd like to take home to her—a big, mounted sailfish. Maybe they'd hang it over the bed and remember their first Christmas. And their last one apart.

★ ★ ★

Annie had laughed brightly while on the phone with Nate, but melancholy stole her laughter away the moment she hung up. She supposed it was a combination of being a little bit tired and sad that he'd be away. She'd been up late decorating his house and baking him those awful-tasting cookies; he just didn't have the right ingredients on hand, and what he had was far from fresh. Of course she hadn't slept much in his bed; he'd kept her busy. And so satisfied. He was such a wonderful lover, but instead of leaving her sated, it left her wanting more of him.

And then she had to get up very early—she had to go home, shower and dress for work and arrange the Christmas gift baskets for the girls in the shop.

She wondered if he had felt her lips press softly against his before she'd left him. Had he heard her say, "Goodbye, Nate. Be safe. Hurry home"? He hadn't stirred at all.

She had been happy to hold him close, warm him and put him to sleep. She wouldn't mind doing that every day for the rest of her life.

She knew her mood had plummeted and she didn't want anyone in the shop noticing, so she grabbed up the appointment book and walked to her small office at the back of the little shop. But sure enough, Pam followed her. Pam stood in the doorway, looking at her.

"Don't worry, Annie. He'll be thrilled to get home to you," Pam said.

"Sure. Of course. I didn't say anything otherwise, did I?"

"You didn't have to," Pam said. "You laughed and joked with him on the phone, but the second you hung up, you got real sober. Serious. Maybe a little worried."

"Do you think it was a mistake to let him go?" Annie asked.

"The time will fly by," Pam said. "It's nice to see you like this. You love him."

"I love him," she admitted. Because he was sensitive but also very confident and strong, she thought. He was a sucker for a bunch of puppies even though they were such a pain to take care of. He didn't even have to think twice about whether to be out till two in the morning because someone had a problem with an animal. The way Annie had been raised, she'd come to accept that people who cared for animals had a special kind of soul, a precious gift. You weren't likely to get much back from animals except a lick on the hand or maybe a good performance in a competition. And in her family's case—the animals provided milk and meat, their roof, their very beds and clothes, their land and legacy. She had been raised with deep respect for animals and the physicians who cared

for them. Those gifted doctors were men and women
who knew the meaning of unconditional love.

"I love him because he's tender and strong and smart,"
Annie said. She smiled sentimentally. "And he's so cute
he makes my knees wobble. But, Pam, I didn't tell him.
I tried to show him, but I didn't tell him."

Pam chuckled. "You'll have your chance very soon."
Pam stepped really close to Annie and made her voice a
whisper. "Sweetheart, you're beautiful and smart. And
I bet you make his knees wobble, too."

She smiled at her friend. "Thank you, Pam. That's
sweet. The sweetest part is it wasn't just a compliment—
I know you meant it. Did I tell you he asked me to go
with him?"

"Ah, no. You might've failed to mention that. And
you weren't tempted?"

"Sure I was tempted. But it's his trip and I have family things going on. But after this, if he feels for me what
I feel for him, it's the last time I'm letting him get that
far away from me without him knowing how I feel."

Pam gave her a fake punch in the arm. "Good plan.
I've worked with you for five years, Annie, since before
you bought the franchise on this little shop. Have you
ever been in love before?"

Annie let go a huff of laughter. "Don't be ridiculous—

I'm twenty-eight. I've been in love plenty of times, starting with Dickie Saunders in the second grade."

But never like this, she thought. Nothing even close
to this. She wanted to massage his temples when he was
stressed or worried, wanted to curl into him and bring
him comfort, wanted to trust him with every emotion
she had. She'd go into battle for him if he needed that
from her, or better still, laugh with him until they both
cried. It would feel so good to stand at his side and help
him with his work. Or argue with him for a while before
making up—she would have to promise never to have
PMS again and he would have to pledge not to be such
a know-it-all. *Green as a bullfrog,* he'd called her. She'd
never had a man in her life who could see right through
her so fast, who could read her mind, feel her feelings.

Realizing she'd been off in kind of a daze, she refo-
cused and looked at her friend. She shrugged.

"That's what I thought," Pam said with a smile.

Nathaniel was pressed up against the cold window of
a packed 747 all the way from San Francisco to Miami.
Over five hours of nighttime flying. Three or four times
he got up and walked around the dimmed cabin. Normally he could sleep on long flights, but not on this
one. When he arrived at his destination at 7:00 a.m. on
the morning of Christmas Eve, he had almost an hour

before meeting his friends for breakfast in a preselected restaurant in the international terminal.

By the time he got to the restaurant, Jerry, Ron, Cindy and Tina were there, surrounded by enough luggage to sink a cruise ship. Missing were Bob and Tom and their wives. Jerry spotted Nate first and called, "Hey, look who just dragged himself off the red-eye. You look like hell, man," he said, grinning, sticking out a hand. "Get this man a Bloody Mary!"

Nate shook hands, hugged, accepted the drink, complete with lemon wedge and celery stalk, and raised his glass. "Great to see you guys," he said. "We can't keep meeting like this."

"Beats not meeting at all." Jerry looked at his watch. "We have an hour and a half." He looked around and frowned. "Nathaniel, did you manage to get your luggage checked through?"

"Nah, I left it with a skycap."

There was some head shaking. "Always has been one jump ahead of us," Tina said.

"Thing is—I can't make it. Sorry, guys."

Confused stares answered him. "Um, don't look now, buddy—but you're in Miami. Almost at Bahama Mama heaven."

Nate chuckled and took a sip of his Bloody Mary. "This was a good idea," he said of the drink. "I left my luggage at the airline counter with the skycap. They're working on a flight for me, but it looks bleak. Who would travel on Christmas Eve on purpose? Why are they booked solid? I'd never travel on Christmas Eve if I didn't have to, but I told them I'd take anything. I might end up eating my turkey dinner right here."

"What the hell...?"

"It's a woman," Nate said. He was shaking his head and laughing at himself. "I gotta get back to a woman."

Jerry clamped a hand on his shoulder. "Okay, let me guess, you got drunk on the plane..."

"Why didn't you just bring her?" Cindy asked.

"She couldn't come," Nate said. "She had all kinds of family stuff going on and she couldn't miss it. She's real close to her family—great family, too. So I said I'd stay home, but she said no to that. She said I should have my vacation. She insisted. And I let her."

"All right, bud, keep your head here. Give her a call, tell her you're miserable without her and you'll be home soon. Hell, get a flight out in two or three days if you still feel the same way."

"I have to go," Nate said. "I don't want to be sitting in a bar with you losers if they find a flight for me." He took another swallow of his drink. He stared at it. "Really, this was a good idea. So was the trip. Anyone game to try this next year? I shouldn't have any complications next year—that I can think of."

"Nathaniel, if she's the right one, she's not going anyplace," Jerry attempted.

He grinned. "That's the best part. She's not going anyplace. But you have no idea how much Christmas means to Annie. She's like the Christmas fairy." He chuckled. "Listen, I don't expect you to get this, but as much as I was looking forward to spending a few days with you guys, it hit me on the plane—I'm going to feel alone without her. I'm going to be with the best friends I've ever had, and I'm not going to have much fun, because she's not with me." He shook his head. "I know where I'm supposed to be right now, and I better get there."

"Nathaniel, this will pass," Ron said. "How long have you known this woman?"

"Oh, jeez—about three weeks. About three of the best weeks of my life. When you find the right one, you don't fly away and leave her wondering how you feel. See, Jerry, in case you ever find some brain-damaged female willing to throw her lot in with you, you'll want to remember this—you better not let her out of your sight and you better not leave her without telling her you love her. Got that?"

Jerry looked confused. "Isn't that why they invented

florists? Don't you just dial up a big, expensive batch of flowers and—"

"Nathaniel, that is *so* sweet," Tina said. "I had no idea you were so sweet. Didn't we date once? Were you ever that sweet to me?"

With a laugh, Nate put down his drink, grabbed her, hugged her and gave her a kiss on the cheek. He gave his old pal Cindy a hug. He punched Jerry in the arm and gave Ron's hand a quick shake. "I'll be in touch. Have a good time on the beach. Thanks for the drink. Tell Bob and Tom I'm sorry I missed them. Merry Christmas." And he turned and strode away.

After closing the shop on the twenty-third, Annie had gotten right out to Nate's house to take care of the puppies. She'd gone back after dinner at the farm to make sure they were fixed for the night and then she'd stayed a while, enjoying her stab at Christmas decorations. Virginia had been good enough to check on the puppies on the morning of the twenty-fourth, as she had to look after the horses anyway.

Annie had purchased five decorated hat boxes at the craft store, and on Christmas Eve she took one little pup—a female, Vixen—to work with her for Pam. Pam's mom would keep the puppy safe and warm until Christmas morning. They closed the shop at noon and Annie headed back to Nate's before going to the farm.

There was a long-standing tradition on Christmas Eve at the farm—Hank covered a hay wagon with fresh hay, hooked up Annie's horses and took the kids for a hayride while the women finished dinner. The winter sun was setting early, so they would have their hayride before dinner. The snow had begun to fall, so the wagon would have to stick to the farm roads. Seven kids, their dads and grandpa set out, singing and laughing.

And in the kitchen, the traditional prime rib was being prepared. In years past, it was their own beef, but now they had to buy it. From the kitchen window, Annie watched the hay wagon pull away from the house. Telling herself not to be moody, she briefly fantasized about sending Nate out with the kids and her dad and brothers. Well, there were years ahead for that.

Rose came up behind her and slipped her arms around Annie's waist. "You can go with them if you want to," she murmured. "There is *more* than enough help in the kitchen. Too much, if you ask me!"

Annie laughed at her mom. "I'm staying in," she said. "After dinner I have puppies to deliver on behalf of Santa. We're down to three boys. I think after Christmas, when things are quieter at work, I'll advertise. And

I'll call the shelters to see if anyone they consider good potential parents are looking for a puppy."

Rose used a finger to run Annie's hair behind her ear. "Are you a little down this year?" she asked quietly.

"I'm fine," she said, shaking her head.

"It's okay to miss him, especially over the holidays," Rose said. "I like Nathaniel. He seems like a good boy."

Boy, Annie thought, amused. She couldn't tell her mother that he was all man. More man than she'd experienced in her adult life. And she hoped he pestered her as much when he came home as before he left. "Let's get everything on the table, Mom. They'll be back and freezing before we know it."

Of course the kids didn't want the hayride to end until they were blue with cold. Hank pulled right up to the back of the house to let the kids off so their mothers could fuss over them, warming them. Then with the help of his sons they unhooked the horses, took them to the barn and brushed and fed them. By the time everyone was inside, the house was bursting with noise and the smells of food, along with the scent of hay and horses. Stories from the ride, punctuated by laughter, filled the house while the meat was carved and dish after dish of delicious food was carried to the tables, then passed around.

The hayride wasn't meant for pure enjoyment; it was

calculated to wear out the kids who might otherwise stay up half the night. After the main course and dessert, the women headed to the kitchen for cleanup and coffee, while Grandpa, Annie's brothers and the kids got out a variety of board games. That was when Annie took her leave. She had to go back to Nate's house, gather up her Christmas puppies and make some deliveries.

Bundled up and on the way to her truck, she wandered around the house to the back. The moon was so high and bright it lit up the farm. The weathered barn in rusty red stood quiet. She remembered when it was teeming with life—cows, horses, goats, chickens, not to mention people. Every single one of the McKenzie kids had had big parties at the farm. Her dad would dig a hole and fill it with hot coals to cook corn; hot dogs would be turned on the grill, and Rose would put out a huge bowl of potato salad and deviled eggs to die for. The kids who came to the farm from town would run wild through the pastures, barn and woods. They'd swing from the rafters of the barn on a rope and fall into a pile of hay, ride the horses, chase the goats. She could remember it like it was yesterday as she looked over the rolling hills and pastureland.

Someday, she thought, my own children and their friends will play here.

She climbed up on the hay wagon and lay down in

the sweet hay, looking up at the sky. It was clear, black, speckled with stars. At the moment the house was throbbing with noise, but ordinarily it was so quiet in the country you could hear a leaf rustle a hundred yards away.

The sound of a car approaching caused her to sit up, and she recognized the Dicksons' truck, their nearest neighbors. Another country custom—people dropped in on each other, bringing homemade treats and staying for at least a cup of coffee. Of course the McKenzies didn't go visiting when the family was home—there were too many of them. A second truck trundled along behind the Dicksons'—looked like the whole fam-damn-ly was coming over. She plopped back down on the hay, hoping to be invisible. Once they all got inside, she'd take off. She wasn't feeling sociable.

There was only one person she wanted to be with right now. She hugged herself and tried to pretend his arms were—

"Annie? You out here?" Beau called from the back porch.

Don't answer, she told herself.

"Annie!"

But her truck was parked out front. "I'm looking at the stars, but I'm leaving in a second. What?"

"I just wanted to know where you are!" he yelled back.

"Well, go away and leave me alone! You're scaring the stars!" And then more quietly she muttered, "Pest."

Seconds later she felt the wagon move, heard it squeak and a large body flopped down next to her in the hay.

"Aw, Beau, you jerk!" she nearly yelled. She sat straight up, plucked straw out of her hair with a gloved hand and looked at the body next to her. Not Beau. Nathaniel lay facedown in the hay beside her. "What are you doing here?" she asked in confusion.

He turned his head to one side. "I came back to sweep you off your feet, but I've been either flying or driving or hanging around airports so long that I'm too tired to roll over, much less sweep you anywhere. And I didn't get much sleep the night before I left, either." He grinned. "Thank you very much."

"You didn't go?" she asked.

"I went. I made it all the way to Miami."

"And came *back?*"

He yawned hugely. "I realized halfway there that I couldn't go to the Bahamas without you, but they wouldn't turn the plane around."

She was quiet for a second. "You've lost your mind."

"Tell me about it," he said. "What have you done to me?"

"Like this is *my* fault? That you're a lunatic?"

He yawned again. "I was normal until three weeks ago,"

he said. "It's amazing how many people fly on Christmas Eve. I couldn't get a nonstop. I was up and down all day. I had to go from Miami to Lansing to Seattle to San Francisco. The last leg—I had to ride in the bathroom."

"You did not," she said with a laugh. She lay down in the hay beside him.

"Then I had to rent a car and drive to Santa Rosa to get my truck. Then drive home."

"Hey!" Beau called from the back porch. "You guys want the horses hitched up?"

Annie sat up again. "No, thank you," she yelled back. "Can you please go away?"

"You guys making out in the hay?"

"Go away!" they both yelled.

"Jeez." The back door slammed.

Annie lay back down. "Now, what do you have in mind?" she asked him.

"I had a plan," he said. "I was going to tell you I love you, then seduce you, put a really nice flush on your cheeks, but I'm not sure I have the strength. I do love you, however. And a little sleep tonight might give me a second wind, so brace yourself."

She giggled. "I have puppies to deliver," she informed him.

"Aw, you haven't done that already? I was so hoping we could just go home and go to bed...."

"Why don't I take you home to your house, then you can sleep and I'll deliver the puppies. I don't think you should be driving if you can't roll over."

"I'll be fine," he said, facedown in the hay. "You'll see. Any second now I'll perk right up."

"You love me?" she asked. "What makes you think so?"

He couldn't roll over, but he looped an arm over her waist and pulled her closer. "You are so under my skin, Annie McKenzie, I'll never be a free man again. Pretty soon now you'll probably want to say you love me, too. Hurry up, will you? I'd like to be conscious for it."

She laughed at him.

"Say it, damn it," he ordered.

"I love you, too," she said. "I can't believe you came back in the same day. Why didn't you just call? Or come back and tell me you had a miserable time? You could have had your vacation and then told me."

"Because, Annie—I realized if I stayed away from you, I'd be lonely. No matter how many people were around, I'd feel alone if I wasn't with you." He pulled her closer. "I wanted you to know how important it was to me, to be with you. I wanted you to know you were worth a lot of trouble. You aren't something I can put off till later. You're not the kind of woman I can send flowers to with a note to say how I feel—you have to be in my arms. I'm not looking for the easy way with you, Annie. I want the forever way. And I don't think that's going to ever change. Now can we please deliver the puppies and get some sleep?"

"Sure," she said, running her fingers through the short hair over his ear. "Merry Christmas, Nathaniel."

"Merry Christmas, baby. I brought you something. A diamond."

"You brought me a diamond?" she asked, stunned.

He dug in his pocket and pulled out a plastic diamond about the size of a lime, attached to a key chain. "Our first Christmas Eve together, and I shopped for your present in an airport gift shop. By the way, when I get the real diamond, I don't think it's going to be this big."

She laughed and kissed him. "You will never know how much I like this one."

"Wanna show me?" he asked, hugging her tight.

"I will," she promised. "For the next fifty years."

"Works for me, Annie. I love you like mad."

"You make my knees wobble," she said. "Let me take you home so you can start wobbling them some more."

"My pleasure." He kissed her with surprising passion for a man dead on his feet. "Let's go home."

★ ★ ★ ★ ★

MIDNIGHT
CONFESSIONS

For everyone who believes in the power of romance

1

Sunny Archer was seriously considering a legal name change.

"Come on, Sunny," her uncle Nathaniel said. "Let's go out on the town and see if we can't put a little of that legendary sunshine back into your disposition!"

Out on the town? she thought. In *Virgin River*? A town of about six hundred? "Ah, I think I'll pass…"

"C'mon, sunshine, you gotta be more flexible! Optimistic! You can't lick this wound forever."

Maybe it was cute when she was four or even fourteen to say things like "Sunny isn't too sunny today!"

But this was December 31 and she had come to Virgin River to spend a few quiet days with her uncle Nate and his fiancée Annie, to try to escape the reality of a heart that wouldn't heal. And if the hurt wasn't bad enough, her heart had gone cold and hard, too. She looked at her watch—4:00 p.m. Exactly one year ago at this time she was having her hair and makeup done right before slipping into a Vera Wang wedding gown, excited, blushing and oblivious to the fact that her fiancé, Glen, was getting blitzed and ready to run for his life.

"I'm not really in the mood for a New Year's Eve bash, Uncle Nate," she said.

"Aw, sweetheart, I can't bear to think of you home alone, brooding, feeling sad," Nathaniel said.

And feeling like a big loser who was left at the altar on her wedding day? she wondered. But that's what had happened. How was she supposed to feel?

"Nate," Annie said under her breath, "this might be a bad night to push the party idea...."

"Ya think?" Sunny said sarcastically, noting to herself that she hadn't been so irritable and sarcastic before becoming an abandoned bride. "Listen, you guys, please go. Party like rock stars. I actually have plans."

"You do?" they both asked hopefully.

"I do. I'm planning a ceremonial burning of last year's calendar. I should probably burn three years' worth of them—that's how much time and energy I invested in the scumbucket."

Nate and Annie were speechless for a moment; they

exchanged dubious looks. When Nate recovered he said,
"Well all righty, then! We'll stay home and help with
the ceremonial burning. Then we'll make some pop-
corn, play some monopoly, make some positive resolutions or something and ring in a much better new year
than the last."

And that was how Sunny, who wasn't feeling at all ac-
commodating, ended up going to the big Virgin River
blast at Jack's Bar on New Year's Eve—because she just
couldn't let her uncle Nate and sweet, funny Annie stay
home to watch her sulk and whimper.

There had been a long history in Sunny's family of
returning to the Jensen stables for a little rest and reju-
venation. Sunny and her cousins had spent countless vacations around the barn and pastures and trails, riding,
playing, inhaling the fresh clean air and getting a regular new lease on life. It had been Sunny's mother's idea
that she come to Virgin River for a post-Christmas re-
vival. Sunny's mom was one of Nate's three older sisters,
and Sunny's grandpa had been the original owner and
veterinarian of Jensen's Clinic and Stable. Now Uncle
Nate was the vet and Grandpa was retired and living in
Arizona.

Sunny was her mama's only child, age twenty-five; she
had one female cousin, Mary—who it just so happened

had managed to get *her* groom to the church. Since Uncle Nate was only ten years older than Sunny at thirty-five, she and her cousin had had tragic crushes on him. Nate, on the other hand, who had grown up with three older sisters, thought he was cursed with females.

Until he was thirty, anyway. Then he became a little more avuncular, patient and even protective. Nathaniel had been sitting in the church on New Year's Eve a year ago. Waiting, like everyone else, for the groom to show, for the wedding to begin.

The past year had passed in an angry, unhappy blur for Sunny. Her rather new and growing photography business had taken off—a combination of her kick-ass website and word of mouth—and rather than take a break after her personal disaster, she went right back to work. She had scheduled shoots, after all. The catastrophic twist was that she specialized in engagement, wedding, anniversary, belly and baby shots—five phases of a couple's life worth capturing for posterity. Her work, as well as her emotional well-being, was suffering. Although she couldn't focus, and she was either unable to sleep or hardly able to pull herself out of bed, she pressed on the best she could. The only major change she'd made in her life was to move out of the town house she had shared with Glen and back into her mom and dad's house until she could afford something of her own. She had her workroom in the basement of her parents' place anyway, so it was just a minor shift in geography.

During the past year at her parents', Sunny had a revelation. The driving reason behind most young women her age wanting their own space, their independence and privacy, was their being involved in a serious relationship. Since she was determined not to repeat past mistakes by allowing another man into her life, there was no need to leave the comfort, security and economy of her parents' house.

She was trying her hand at photographing sunrises, sunsets, landscapes, seascapes and pets. It wasn't working—her images were flat and uninteresting. If it wasn't bad enough that her heart was broken, so was her spirit. It was as if her gift was lost. She'd been brilliant with couples, inspired by weddings—stills, slide shows, videos. She saw the promise in their eyes, the potential for their lives. She'd brought romance to the fat bellies of pregnant women and was a veritable Anne Geddes with babies! But now that she was a mere observer who would never experience any of those things firsthand, everything had changed. Not only had it changed, it pierced her heart each time she did a shoot.

When she confessed this to Annie, Annie had said, "Oh, darling, but you're so young! Only twenty-five! The possibilities ahead are endless if you're open to them!"

And Sunny had said, "I'm not upset because I didn't make the cheerleading squad, Annie. My fiancé dumped me on our wedding day—and my age doesn't matter a damn."

The town was carpeted in a fresh blanket of pretty white snow, the thirty-foot tree was lit and sparkling as gentle flakes continued to fall, and the porch at Jack's Bar, strung with lights and garlands, was welcoming. There was a friendly curl of smoke rising from the chimney and light shone from the windows.

Nate, Annie and Sunny walked into the bar at 8:00 p.m. and found the place packed with locals. Jack, the owner, and Preacher, the cook, were behind the bar. There was a festive table set up along one whole wall of the room, covered with food, to which Annie added a big plate of her special deviled eggs and a dill-speckled salmon loaf surrounded by crackers.

"Hey, looks like the whole town is here," Nate said.

"A good plenty," Jack said. "But I hope you don't see anyone here you want to kiss at midnight. Most of these folks won't make it that long. We have a strong skeleton crew that will stay late, however. They're busy getting all the kids settled back at Preacher's house with a sitter—it's going to be a dormitory. Vanessa and Paul's two are bunking in with Preacher's little Dana, my kids are sleeping in Preacher's room, Cameron's twins are in the guest room, Brie and Mike's little one is borrowing Christopher's room because he's planning on sitting up until midnight with the sitter. Oh, and to be very clear, the sitter is there for all the *little* kids—not for Chris," Jack added with a smile. "He's eight now. All man."

"Jack, Preach, meet my niece Sunny. Sunny, this is Jack and Preacher, the guys who run this place."

She gave them a weak smile, a nod and a mumbled nice to meet you.

"Hop up here, you three. As soon as you contribute your New Year's resolution, you get service," Jack said. "The price of admission is a food item and a reso-lution."

Sunny jumped up on a bar stool, hanging the strap of her large bag on the backrest. Jack leaned over the bar and eyed the big, leather shoulder bag. He peered at her with one brow lifted. "Going on a long trip right after the party?"

She laughed a little. "Camera equipment. I never leave it behind. Never know when I might need it."

"Well, by all means, the first annual New Year's Eve party is your canvas," Jack said. He slid a piece of paper and pen toward her.

Sunny hovered over it as if giving it careful thought. She knew if she said her resolution was to get this over with as soon as possible, it would open up the conversation as to why she now and would forever more find New Year's Eve the most reprehensible of holidays.

"Make it a good one, Sunny," Jack said. "Keep it generic and don't sign it—it's anonymous. There's a surprise coming right after midnight."

Sunny glanced at her watch. God, she thought. *At least four hours of this? I'll never make it!* She wrote on her slip of paper. "Give up men."

Drew Foley was a second-year orthopedic resident at UCLA Medical and had somehow scored ten days off over Christmas, which he'd spent in Chico with his two sisters, Marcie and Erin, their guys Ian and Aiden and his new nephew. The three previous Christmases he'd spent with his family, and also his former fiancée, Penny. That somehow seemed so long ago.

When surgical residents got days off, they weren't *real* days off. They're merely days on which you're not required in surgery, clinic, class, writing reports or being verbally beaten to death by senior residents and attending physicians. But there was still plenty of studying to do. He'd been hitting the books straight through Christmas even with the distraction of family all around, including Marcie's new baby who was really starting to assert himself. With only a few days left before he had to head back to Southern California, he borrowed the family's isolated cabin on the ridge near Virgin River so he could study without distraction. He'd managed to focus completely for a couple of days and had impressed himself with the amount of academic ground he'd covered. As he saw it, that bought him a New Year's Eve beer or two and a few hours of satellite football on New Year's Day. On January 2 he'd head back to Erin's house in Chico, spend one more evening with the family, then throw himself back into the lion's den at UCLA Medical.

He grabbed his jacket. It was New Year's Eve and he'd spent enough time alone. He'd swing through town on his way to Fortuna to collect his beer, just to see what was going on. He'd be surprised if the only bar and grill in town was open, since Jack's Bar wasn't usually open late on holidays. In fact, the routine in Virgin River on regular days was that Jack's shut down before nine, open till ten at the latest, and that was only if there were hunters or fishermen in the area. This was a town of mostly farmers, ranchers, laborers and small-business owners; they didn't stay out late because farm chores and animals didn't sleep in.

But to his surprise, once in town he found that the little bar was hopping. It made him smile—this was going to save him some serious mountain driving and he'd get to have a beer among people. When he walked into the packed bar he heard his name shouted. "Ho! Doc Foley! When did you hit town?"

This was the best part about this place. He'd only been up here maybe a half dozen times in the past couple of years, but Jack never forgot anyone. For that matter, most of Jack's friends and family never did either.

He reached a hand across the bar in greeting to Jack. "How's it going, Jack?"

"I had no idea you were up here!" Jack said. "You bring the family along?"

"Nah, I was with the family over Christmas and came up to get a little studying done before I have to get back to residency. I thought I'd better escape the girls and especially the baby if I intend to concentrate at all."

"How is that baby?" Jack asked.

Drew grinned. "Red-headed and loud. I'm afraid he could be a little rip-off of Marcie. Ian should be afraid. Very, very afraid."

Jack chuckled. "You remember my wife, Mel."

"Sure," he said, turning toward the town's renowned midwife and accepting a kiss on the cheek. "How are you?"

"Never better. I wish we'd known you were up here, Drew—I'd have made it a point to call you, invite you."

Drew looked around. "Who knew you folks ripped up the town on New Year's Eve? Is everyone here?"

"Pretty good number," Jack said. "But expect this to change fairly quick—most of these folks will leave by nine. They start early. But I'm hanging in there till midnight," he assured Drew. "I bet I can count on one hand the number of Virgin River residents willing to stay up for a kiss at midnight."

And that's when he spotted her. Right when Jack said *kiss at midnight* he saw a young woman he'd be more than willing to accommodate when the clock struck twelve. She was tucked back in a corner by the hearth, swirling a glass of white wine, her golden hair falling onto her shoulders. She seemed just slightly apart from the table of three women who sat chatting near her. He watched as one of those women leaned toward her to speak, to try to include her, but she merely nodded, sipped, smiled politely and remained aloof. Someone's wife? Someone's girl? Whoever she was, she looked a little unhappy. He'd love to make her happier.

"Drew," Jack said. "Meet Nate Jensen, local vet."

Drew put out his hand, but didn't want to take his eyes off the girl. He said, "Nice to meet you," but what he was thinking was how long it had been since just looking at a beautiful woman had zinged him in the chest and head with almost instant attraction. Too long! Whoa, she was a stunner. He'd barely let go of Nate's hand, didn't even catch the guy's response because his ears were ringing, when he asked Jack, "Who is that blonde?"

"That's my niece," his new acquaintance said. "Sunny."

"Married? Engaged? Accompanied? Nun? Any-thing?"

Nate chuckled. "She's totally single. But—"

"Be right back," Drew said. "Guard my beer with your life!" And he took off for the corner by the hearth.

"But..." Nate attempted.

Drew kept moving. He was on automatic. Once he was standing right in front of her and she lifted her eyes to his, he was not surprised to find that she had the most beautiful blue eyes he could have ever imagined. He put out his hand. "Hi. I'm Drew. I just met your uncle." She said nothing, didn't even shake his hand. "And you're Sunny. Sunny Jensen?" he asked.

Her mouth fixed and her eyes narrowed. "Archer," she corrected.

Drew gave up on the shake and withdrew his hand. "Well, Sunny Archer, can I join you?"

"Are you trying to pick me up?" she asked directly.

He grinned. "I'm a very optimistic guy," he said pleasantly.

"Then let me save you some time. I'm not available."

He was struck silent for a moment. It wasn't that Drew enjoyed such great success with women—he was admittedly out of practice. But this one had drawn on him like a magnet and he was unaccountably surprised to be shot down before he'd even had a chance to screw up his approach. "Sorry," he said lamely. "Your uncle said you were single."

"Single and unavailable." She lifted her glass and gave him a weak smile. "Happy New Year."

He just looked at her for a moment, then beat a retreat back to the bar.

Jack and Nate were watching, waiting for him. Jack pushed the beer toward him. "How'd that work out for you?"

Drew took a pull on his beer. "I must be way out of practice," he said. "I probably should'a thought that through a little better...."

"What? Residency doesn't leave time for girls?" Jack asked with a twist of the lip.

"A breakup," Drew explained. "Which led to a break from women for a while."

Nate leaned an elbow on the bar. "That a fact? Bad breakup?"

"You ever been around a good one?" Drew asked. Then he chuckled, lifted an eyebrow and said, "Nah, it wasn't that it was so bad. In fact, she probably saved my life. We were engaged, but shouldn't have been. She finally told me what I should've known all along—*if we got married, it would be a disaster.*"

"Bad fit?"

"Yeah, bad fit. I should have seen it coming, but I was too busy putting titanium rods in femurs to pay attention to details like that, so my bad. But what's up with Sunny Archer?"

"Well," Nate said. "I guess you probably have a lot in common."

"Uh-oh. Bad breakup?"

"Let's just say, you ever been around a good one?"

"I should've known. She didn't give me a chance. And here I thought I'd bungled it."

"Gonna go for round two?" Jack asked him.

Drew thought about that a minute. "I don't know," he said with a shrug. "Maybe I should wait until she gets a little more wine in her."

Nate slapped a heavy hand on Drew's shoulder. "That's my niece, bud. I'll be watching."

"Sorry, bad joke. I'd never take advantage of her, don't worry about that," Drew protested. "But if she shoots me down twice, I could get a serious complex!"

During the month of December, Maureen was kept busy getting ready for a very special Christmas. While she shopped for gifts for Rosie and a new Riordan baby whose gender was still unknown, she kept thinking, *This is what Christmas is all about—children!*

MOONLIGHT ROAD

2

Drew nursed his beer slowly and joked around with Jack and Nate over a plate of wings, but the subject of breakups had him thinking a bit about Penny. There were times he missed her, or at least he missed the idea of what he thought they would be.

He had met her while he was in med school. She was a fellow med student's cousin and it had been a fix up. The first date had gone smoothly; the next seven dates in as many weeks went even better and before he knew it, he was dating Penny exclusively. They had so much in common, they grew on each other. She was an RN and he was studying medicine. She was pretty, had a good sense of humor, understood his work as he understood hers and in no time at all they had settled into a comfort zone that accommodated them both. And it didn't hurt that the sex was satisfying. Everything seemed compatible.

Penny had been in charge of the relationship from the start and Drew didn't have to think about it much, which suited him perfectly. He was a busy guy; he didn't have a lot of time for flirtation or pursuit. Penny was very well-equipped to fill him in on their agenda and he was perfectly happy to go along. "Valentine's Day is coming up," she would say. "I guess we'll be doing something special?"

Ding, ding, ding—he could figure that out easy. "Absolutely," he would say. Then he'd get a reservation, buy a gift. Penny thought he was brilliant and sensitive and all was right with his world.

It had been working out effortlessly until he asked her to go to Southern California with him, to live with him. His residency in orthopedic surgery was beginning, he'd dated Penny exclusively for a couple of years and it seemed like the natural progression of things. "Not without an engagement ring," she'd said. So he provided one. It had seemed reasonable enough.

But the move from Chico changed everything. It hadn't gone well for Penny. She'd been out of her element, away from her job, friends and family, and Drew had been far too stressed and overworked to help her make the transition. She was lonely, needed attention, time, reassurance. And he had wanted to give it to her, but it was like squeezing water out of a rock. It wasn't long before their only communication was in the form of arguing—make that fighting. Fights followed by days of not speaking or nights in which she cried into her pillow and wouldn't take comfort from him, if he could stay awake long enough to give it.

Drew shook off the memory and finally said to Nate, "So, tell me about Sunny, who, if you don't mind me saying, might be better named Stormy...."

"Well, for starters, jokes about her name don't seem to be working just now," Nate replied.

"Ahh," he said. Drew was distracted by a sudden flash and saw that it was none other than Stormy Sunny herself with the camera, getting a shot of a couple in a toast. "What's with the camera?"

"She's a photographer, as a matter of fact. A good one," Nate said. "She started out studying business in college but dropped out before she was twenty-one to start her own business. My sister Susan, her mother, almost had a heart attack over that. But it turned out she knew exactly what she was doing. There's a waiting list for her work."

"Is that a fact?" he said, intrigued. "She seems kind of young…"

"Very young, but she's been taking great pictures since she was in high school. Maybe earlier."

"Where?"

"She lives in L.A. Long Beach, actually."

Long Beach, Drew thought. Like next door! Of course, that didn't matter if she wouldn't even talk to him. But he wasn't giving anything away. "Is she a little artsy-fartsy?" Drew asked.

Nate laughed. "Not at all—she's very practical. But lately she's been trying some new stuff, shooting the horses, mountains, valleys, roads and buildings. Sunrises, sunsets, clouds, et cetera." Nate looked over at Sunny as she busily snapped pictures of a happy couple. "It's kind of nice to see her taking pictures of people again."

Drew watched Sunny focus, direct the pair with one hand while holding her camera with the other. Her face seriously lit up; her smile was alive and whatever it was she was saying caused her subjects to laugh, which was followed by several flashes. She was so animated as she took five or six more shots, then pulled a business card out of the pocket of her jeans and handed it to the couple. She was positively gorgeous when she wasn't giving him the brush. Then she retreated to her spot by the hearth and put her camera down. He noticed that the second she gave up the camera, her face returned to its seriousness. The sight of her was immediately obscured by partiers.

He wanted one of those business cards.

"Hey, buddy, you didn't make out your resolution," Jack said, passing him a slip of paper and pen. "That's the price of admission."

"I don't usually do resolutions," Drew said. "Well, except every morning when I resolve to fly under the radar of the senior residents."

"Because?" Jack asked.

Sometimes Drew forgot that few people knew what the life of a junior resident was like. "Because they're sociopaths with a mean streak."

"Ah," Jack said as if he bought that. "Maybe that's your resolution—to avoid sociopaths? When you've written one, it goes in the pot here."

"And then?" Drew asked.

"When you're getting ready to leave, you can draw one—maybe you'll get a better one than you wrote. Give you something new to strive for."

Drew laughed. "I dunno. This is such a crazy idea," he said. "What if the one I draw is to bike across the U.S.?"

Jack looked around. "Nah," he said. "No danger of that around here. You could draw one that says to remember your annual mammogram, however. Now get on it," he said, tapping the paper on the bar.

Chuckling, Drew wrote. Then he scratched it out. Thinking about the grumpy but beautiful woman in the corner he wrote "Start the new year by giving a new guy a chance." Then he folded it in half and shoved it in his pocket; he asked for a new piece of paper. On his second try he wrote "Don't let past hurts ruin future possibilities."

Then he took a bolstering swallow of his beer and said, "Excuse me a second." And off he went to the other side of the room.

He stood in front of Sunny, smiled his handsomest smile and said, "So. You're a photographer."

She looked up at him, her expression deadpan. "Yes," she said.

"You like being a photographer?" he asked.

Again there was that pregnant pause before she said, "Yes."

"What do you like best about it?"

She thought for a moment. Then she said, "The quiet."

He had to ask himself why in the world he was interested. She was beautiful, but Drew had never been drawn by beauty alone. He'd known lots of gorgeous women who fell short in other areas, thus killing his interest instantly. For a woman to really intrigue him she had to be fun, smart, good-natured, energetic, driven by something besides her looks and above all, *positive*.

So far this one, this Sunny, had only looks going for her and it was not enough. Still, for unknown reasons, he lingered. "The quiet," he repeated. "Anything else?"

"Yes. It doesn't require any other people. I can do it alone."

"Just out of curiosity, are you always this unapproachable, or is it just at New Year's Eve parties?"

She shrugged. "Pretty much always."

"Gotcha. One last question. Will you take my picture?"

"For what occasion?" she asked.

Nothing came to mind. "Passport photo?" he attempted.

"Sorry. I don't do passport photos."

He smiled at her. "Well, Sunny—you're in luck. Because that's all I got. You are, as you obviously wish to be, on your own."

Oh, I'm such a bitch, she thought as she watched Drew's back weave through the people to return to the bar. When he sat up on the stool beside her uncle, she cringed in embarrassment. She adored her uncle Nate and knew how much he cared about her, how it had hurt him to see her in pain on what was supposed to have been her wedding day, how it killed him to see her struggle with it for so long afterward. But while she knew Nate had nothing but sympathy for her, she realized he was running short on patience with her bitterness and what could only be described as attitude a full year later.

He wasn't the only one. Friends had tried to encourage her to let go of the heartache and move on. If she didn't want to date again, fine, but being pissed off all the time was not only wearing on friendships, it was hurting business. And she was hearing a lot about the fact that she was only twenty-five! She wasn't sure if twenty-five was so young it excused her for making such a mistake on Glen or if that meant she had decades left to find the right guy!

Then, right after she arrived in Virgin River, Annie had taken her aside, sat her down and said, "This rage isn't going to help you get on with your life in a positive way, Sunny. You're not the only one who's been dumped. I found out the man I was supposed to marry had three full-time girlfriends he lived with—each of us part-time, of course."

"How'd he manage that?" Sunny had asked, intrigued and astonished.

"He obviously kept a very careful calendar. He was in sales and traveled. When I thought he was selling farm equipment, he was actually with one of the other girlfriends."

"Oh, my God! You must have wanted to *kill* him!"

"Sure. I was kind of hoping my dad or one of my brothers would do it for me, but when they didn't I got past it. I realize I wasn't left at the altar with a very expensive, nonrefundable wedding to pay for, like you were. I can't imagine the pain and humiliation of that, but even so, I was very angry. And now I'm so grateful that I found a way to get beyond that because if I hadn't, I would never have given Nate a chance. And your uncle Nate is the best thing that ever happened to me."

What Sunny wanted to tell Annie was that the pain and humiliation wasn't the worst part—it was that her friends and family *pitied* her for being left. What was wrong with her, that he would do that?

She knew what was wrong, when she thought about it. Her nose was too long, her forehead too high, her chest small and feet big, her hips too wide, she hadn't finished college and she took pictures for a living. That they were good pictures didn't seem to matter—it wasn't all that impressive. She sometimes veered into that territory of "if I had been a supermodel with a great body, he'd never have left me." Intellectually she knew that was nonsense, but emotionally she felt lacking in too many ways.

Instead she said to Annie, "Did you know? Did you ever have a hint that something was wrong?"

She shook her head. "Only when it was over, when I

looked back and realized he never spent a weekend with me, and I was too trusting to wonder why he hadn't ever asked me to join him on a business trip to one of the other towns where he stayed overnight on business. Oh, after it was all over, I had lots of questions. But at the time?" She shook her head. "I didn't know anything was wrong."

"Me either," Sunny said.

"I probably didn't want to know anything was wrong," Annie added. "I don't like conflict."

Sunny didn't say anything. She was pretty well acquainted with her own denial and that hurt just about as much as the hard truth.

"Well, there was one thing," Annie corrected. "After it was all over I wondered if I shouldn't have been more desperate to spend every moment with *him,* if I loved him so much. You know—Nate gets called out in the middle of the night pretty often, and I never make a fuss about it. But we both complain if we haven't had enough time together. We need each other a lot. That never happened with Ed. I was perfectly fine when he wasn't around. Should have tipped me off, I guess."

No help there, Sunny thought. Glen had complained constantly of her Fridays through Sundays always being booked with shoots. There were times she worked a sixteen-hour day on the weekends, covering three weddings and receptions and a baptism. Slip in some engagement slide shows, photos of babies, whatever had to be done for people who worked Monday through Friday and who only had weekends available. Then from Monday through Thursday she'd work like a dog editing and setting up proofs.

Glen was a California Highway Patrolman who worked swing shifts to have weekends off and she was always unavailable then.

She revisited that old argument—wait a minute! Here was a clue she hadn't figured out at the time. Glen had a few years seniority with CHP, so why would he work swings just to have those weekends off when he knew she would be tied up with her clients the entire time? She'd been rather proud of the fact that it hadn't taken her long to develop a strong clientele, to make incredibly good money for a woman her age—weddings were especially profitable. But she'd had to sacrifice her weekends to get and keep that success.

So why? It would have been easy for him to get a schedule with a Tuesday through Thursday, her lightest days, off. In fact, if he had been willing to take those days off, and work the day shift regularly, they could have gone to bed together every night. He said at the time that it suited his body clock, that he wasn't a morn-

ing person. And he *liked* to go out on the weekends. He
went out with "the boys." The *boys?* Not bloody likely....

After being left at the church a couple of his grooms-
men had admitted he'd been having his doubts about the
big, legal, forever commitment. Apparently he'd worried aloud to them, but all he ever did was argue with
her about it. *We don't need all that! We could fly to Aruba,
get married there, take a week of sailing, scuba diving...* He
hadn't said the commitment was an issue, just the wedding—something Sunny and her mom were having a
real party putting together. So she had said, "Try not to
worry so much, Glen—you'll get your week in Aruba
on the honeymoon. Just be at the church on time, say
your lines and we'll be diving and sunning and sailing
before you know it."

Sunny shook her head in frustration. What was the
point in figuring it out now? She grabbed her coat, her
camera and headed out the door. The snow was still
gently falling and she backed away from the town Christmas tree, snapping photos as she went. She zoomed in
on some of the military unit patches used as decorations, caught snowflakes glistening against gold balls and
white lights, captured angles of the tree until, finally, far
enough away, she got the whole tree. If these came out
the way she hoped, she might use them for something
next Christmas—ads or cards or something.

Then she turned and caught a couple of good shots of the bar porch, the snow drifting on the rails and steps and roof. Then of the street with all the houses lit for holiday cheer. Then the bar porch with a man leaning against the rail, arms crossed over his chest—a very handsome man.

She lowered the camera and walked toward Drew. There was no getting around the fact that he was handsome—tall and built, light brown hair, twinkling brown eyes, and if she remembered right, a very sexy smile. He stood on the porch and she looked up at him.

"Okay, look, I apologize," she said. "It's not like me to be so rude, so 'unapproachable' as you call it. I got dumped, okay? I'm still licking my wounds, as my uncle Nathaniel puts it. Not a good time for me to respond to a come-on from a guy. I'm scared to death to meet a guy and end up actually liking him, so I avoid all males. That's it in a nutshell," she added with a shrug. "I used to be very friendly and outgoing—now I'm on guard a lot."

"Apology accepted. And I had a bad breakup, too, but it was a while ago. Water under the bridge, as they say."

"You got dumped?"

He gave a nod. "And I understand how you feel. So let's start over. What do you say? I'm Drew Foley," he said.

She took another step toward the porch, looking up at him. "Sunny Archer. But when? I mean, how long ago did you get dumped?"

"About nine months, I guess."

"About?" she asked. It must not have impacted him in quite the same way if he couldn't remember the date. "I mean—was it traumatic?"

"Sort of," he said. "We were engaged, lived together, but we were arguing all the time. She finally told me she wasn't willing to have a life like that and we had to go our separate ways. It wasn't my idea to break up." He shrugged. "I thought we could fix it and wanted to try, but she didn't."

"Did you know?" she asked. "Were you expecting it?"

He shook his head. "I should have expected it, but it broadsided me."

"How can that be? If you should have expected it, how could it possibly have taken you by surprise?"

He took a deep breath, looked skyward into the softly falling flakes, then back at her. "We were pretty miserable, but before we lived together we did great. I'm a medical resident and my hours were…still are hideous. Sometimes I'm on for thirty-six hours and just get enough time off to sleep. She needed more from me than that. She…" He looked down. "I don't like calling her *she* or *her*. *Penny* had a hard time changing her life in order to move in with me. She had to get a new job, make new friends, and I was never there for her. I should have seen it coming but I didn't. It was all my fault but I couldn't have done anything to change it."

"Where are you from?" she asked him.

"Chico. About four hours south of here."

"Wow," she said. "We actually do have some things in common."

"Do we?" he asked.

"But you're over it. How'd you get over it?"

He put his hands in his front pants pockets. "She invited me to her engagement party three months ago. To another surgical resident. Last time I looked, he was on the same treadmill I was on. Guess he manages better with no sleep."

"No way," she said, backing away from the bar's porch a little bit.

"Way."

"You don't suppose…?"

"That she was doing him when she was supposed to be doing me?" he asked for her. "It crossed my mind. But I'm not going there. I don't even want to know. All that aside, she obviously wasn't the one. I know that now. Which means it really *was* my fault. I was hooking up with someone out of inertia, not because I was insanely in love with her. Bottom line, Sunny, me and Penny? We both dodged a bullet. We were not meant to be."

She was speechless. Her mouth formed a perfect O.

Her eyes were round. She wished she'd been able to take her own situation in such stride. "Holy crap," she finally said. Then she shook her head. "I guess you have to be confident to be in medicine and all."

"Aw, come on, don't give the study all the credit. I might actually have some common sense." He took a step down from the bar porch to approach her, his heel slid on the step and he went airborne. While he was in the air, there were rapid flashes from her camera. Then he landed, flat on his back, and there were more flashes.

Sunny stood over him, camera in hand. She looked down at him. "Are you all right?"

He narrowed his eyes at her. It took him a moment to catch his breath. "I could be paralyzed, you know. I hope I was hallucinating, but were you actually taking my picture as I fell?"

"Well, I couldn't catch you," she said. Then she smiled.

"You are sick and twisted."

"Maybe you should lie still. I could go in the bar and get the pediatrician and the midwife to have a look at you. I met them earlier, before you got here."

He looked up at her; she was still smiling. Apparently it didn't take much to cheer her up—the near death of a man seemed to put her in a better mood. "Maybe you could just show them the pictures...."

She fell onto her knees beside him and laughed, her

camera still in hand. It was a bright and happy sound and those beautiful blue eyes glittered. "Seriously, you're the doctor—do you think you're all right?"

"I don't know," he said. "I haven't moved yet. One wrong move and I could be paralyzed from the neck down."

"Are you playing me?"

"Might be," he admitted with a shrug of his shoulders.

"Hah! You moved! You're fine. Get up."

"Are you going to have a drink with me?" he asked.

"Why should I? Seriously, we're a couple of wounded birds—we probably shouldn't drink, and we certainly shouldn't drink together!"

"Get over it," he said, rising a bit, holding himself up on his elbows. "We have nothing to lose. It's a New Year's Eve party. We'll have a couple of drinks, toast the New Year, move on. But give it a try not so pissed off. See if you can have some fun." He smiled. "Just for the heck of it?"

She sat back on her heels and eyed him warily. "Is this just more inertia?"

His grin widened. "No, Sunny. This is part chivalry and part animal attraction."

"Oh, God.... I just got dumped by an animal. So not looking for another one."

He gave her a gentle punch in the arm. "Buck up. Be a big girl. I bet you haven't let an interested guy buy you a drink in a long time. Take a chance. Practice on me. I'm harmless."

She lifted one light brown brow. "How do I know you're harmless?"

"I'm going back to sacrifice myself to the gods of residency in two days. They'll chew me up and spit me out. Those chief residents are ruthless and they want revenge for what was done to them when they were the little guys. There won't even be a body left. No one will ever know you succumbed to having a beer with me." And then he smiled with all his teeth.

She tsked and rolled her eyes at him.

He sat up. "See how much you like me? You're putty in my hands."

"You're a dork!"

He got to his feet and held out a hand to her, helping her up. "I've heard that, but I'm not buying it yet. I think if you dig deep enough, I might be cool."

She brushed off the knees of her jeans. "I'm not sure I have that kind of time."

There was a time when Becca had dreamed of a Christmas proposal and a beautiful ring under the tree. Christmas was her favorite season—the sparkling lights, the carols, the time with her family.

BRING ME HOME FOR CHRISTMAS

3

Once Drew got up and moved, he limped. He claimed a wounded hip and leaned on Sunny. Since she couldn't be sure if he was faking, she allowed this. But just as they neared the steps, the doors to the bar flew open and people began to spill out, laughing, shouting, waving goodbye.

"Careful there," he yelled, straightening up. "I just slipped on the steps. They're iced over. I'll get Jack to throw some salt on them, but take it slow and easy."

"Sure," someone said. "Thanks, Drew."

"Be careful driving back to Chico," someone else said.

"Say hello to your sisters," a woman said. "Tell them to come up before too long, we miss them."

"Pinch that cute baby!"

"Will do," Drew said in response, and he pulled Sunny to the side to make way for the grand exodus. The laughing, joking, talking people, some carrying their plates and pots from the buffet table, headed for their cars.

"What the heck," Sunny said. "It's not even nine o'clock!"

Drew laughed and put his arm back over her shoulder to lean on her. "This is a little town, Sunny. These folks have farms, ranches, orchards, vineyards, small businesses and stuff like that. The ones who don't have to get up early for work—even on holidays—might stay later. And some of the folks who are staying are on call—the midwife, the cop, the doctor." He grinned. "Probably the bartender. If anyone has a flat on the way home, five gets you ten either Jack or Preacher will help out."

"Do you know all these people?"

"A lot of them, yeah. I'll give you the short version of the story—my sister Marcie was married to a marine who was disabled in action and then later died. She came up here to find his best friend and sergeant—Ian Buchanan. She found him in a run-down old cabin up on the ridge, just over the county line, but the nearest town was Virgin River. So—she married him and they have a baby now. My oldest sister, Erin, wanted a retreat up here, but she couldn't handle a cabin with no indoor bathroom or where you'd have to boil your bath water and chop your wood for heat, so she got a local builder to renovate one into something up to her standards with electricity, indoor plumbing and a whirlpool tub." He laughed. "Really, Marcie's pretty tough, but if Erin risked breaking a nail, that would make her very cranky." He looked at Sunny and smiled. "It used to be a lean-to, now it should be in *Architectural Digest*. Anyway, I've been up here several times in the past couple of years, and Jack's is the only game in town. You don't have to drop into Jack's very many times before you know half the town. I'm hiding out in the cabin for a few days to get some studying done, away from my sisters and the baby. I have to go back on the second. I just swung through town for a beer—I had no idea there was a party."

They just stood there, in front of the porch, his arm draped across her shoulder. It was kind of silly—she was only five foot four and he was easily six feet, plus muscular. He didn't lean on her too heavily.

"Is it very hard, what you do? Residency?"

"It doesn't have to be. It could be a learning experience, but the senior residents pile as much on you as they can. It's like a dare—who can take it all and keep standing. That's the part that makes it hard." Then he sobered for a second. "And kids. I love working with the kids, making them laugh, helping them get better, but it's so tough to see them broken. Being the surgeon who puts a kid back together again—it's like the best and worst part of what I do. Know what I mean?"

She couldn't help but imagine him taking a little soccer player into surgery, or wrapping casting material around the arm of a young violinist. "Your sister was married to a soldier who was killed…?"

"She was married to a marine. Bobby was permanently disabled by a bomb in Iraq. He was in a nursing home for a few years before he died, but he never really came back, you know? No conscious recognition—the light was on but no one was home. They were very young."

"Were you close to him?"

"Yeah, sure. He was two years older and we all went to high school together. Bobby went in right after graduation. Ian was a little older, so I didn't know him until Marcie brought him home." He laughed sentimentally. "She's something, Marcie. She came up here to find Ian, make sure he was all right after the war and to give him Bobby's baseball card collection. She brought him home on Christmas Eve and said, 'This is Ian and I'm going to marry him as soon as he can get used to the idea.'"

"This is why," she said softly. "This is why you can move on after getting dumped by your fiancée. You've seen some rough stuff and you know how to count your blessings. I bet that's it."

He turned Sunny so she faced him. Of course he couldn't lean on her then, but he got close. "Sunny, my family's been through some stuff... Mostly my sisters, really—they had it toughest. But the thing that keeps me looking up instead of down—it's what I see at work everyday. I'm called on to treat people with problems lots bigger than mine—people who will never walk again, never use their arms or hands, and sometimes worse. Orthopedic pain can be terrible, rehab can be extended and dreary.... Tell you what, sunshine—I'm upright, walking around, healthy, have a brain to think with and the option to enjoy my life. Well, I'm not going to take that for granted." He lifted a brow, tilted his head, smiled. "Maybe you should spend a little time in my trauma center, see if it fixes up all those things you think you should worry about?"

"What about your chief residents?" she asked, showing him her smile.

"Oh, them. Well, I pretty much wish them dead. No remorse, either. God, they're mean. Mean and spiteful and impossible to please."

"Will you be a chief resident someday?"

His smile took on an evil slant. "Yes. But not soon enough. Watch yourself on these stairs, honey." Before opening the door for Sunny, he stopped her. "So—want to find a cozy spot by the fire and tell me about the breakup that left you so sad and unapproachable?"

She didn't even have to think about it. "No," she said, shaking her head. "I'd rather not talk about it."

"Fair enough. Want to tell me how you got into photography?"

She smiled at him. "I could do that."

"Good. I'll have Jack pour you a glass of wine and while he's doing that I'll scatter some salt on those icy steps." He touched her pink nose. "Your mission is to find us a spot in that bar where we can talk. If I'm not mistaken, we're the only two singles at this party."

Sunny went back to the place near the fire where she had left her camera bag and put her camera away. She glanced over at Drew. He stood at the bar talking with Jack; Jack handed him a large canister of salt.

And suddenly it was someone else standing at the bar, and it wasn't this bar. Her mind drifted and took her back in time. It was Glen and it was the bar at their rehearsal dinner. Glen was leaning on the bar, staring morosely into his drink, one foot lifted up on the rail. His best man, Russ, had a hand on his back, leaning close and talking in Glen's ear. Glen wasn't responding.

Why hadn't she been more worried? she asked herself in retrospect. Maybe because everyone around her had been so reassuring? Or was it because she *refused* to be concerned?

Sunny wasn't very old-fashioned, but there were a few traditional wedding customs she had wanted to uphold—one was not seeing her groom the day of her wedding. So she and her cousin Mary, who was also her matron of honor, would spend the night at Sunny's parents' house after the rehearsal dinner. Even still, she remembered thinking it was a little early when Glen kissed her good-night that evening.

"I'm going out with the boys for a nightcap, then home," he said.

"Is everything all right?" she asked.

"Sure. Fine." His smile was flat, she knew things were not fine.

"You're not driving, are you?"

"Russ has the keys. It's fine."

"I guess I'll see you tomorrow." She remembered so vividly that she laid her palm against his handsome cheek. "I can't wait for tomorrow."

He didn't move his head, but his eyes had darted briefly away. "Me, too."

When Russ came over to her to say good-night, she had asked, "What's bothering Glen?"

"Oh, he'll be fine."

"But what is it?"

Russ had laughed a bit uncomfortably. "Y'know, even though you two have been together a long time, lived together and everything, it's still a pretty big step for a guy. For both of you, I realize. But guys… I don't know what it is about us—I was a little jittery the day before my wedding. And it was absolutely what I wanted, no doubt, but I was still nervous. I don't know if it's the responsibility, the lifestyle change…"

"What changes?" she asked. "Besides that we're going to take a nice trip and write a lot of thank-you notes?"

"I'm just saying… I've been in a bunch of weddings, including my own, and every groom I've ever known gets a little jumpy right before. Don't worry about it. I'll buy him a drink on the way home, make sure he gets all tucked in. You'll be on your way to Aruba before you know it." Then he had smiled reassuringly.

"Will you ask him to call me to say good-night?" she asked.

"Sure. But if he's slurring by then, don't hold it against me!"

She'd been up late talking to Mary; they'd opened another bottle of wine. By the time they fell asleep it was the wee hours and they'd slept soundly. In the morning when she checked her cell phone, she found a text from

Glen that had come in at three in the morning. Going to bed. Talk to you tomorrow.

She wanted to talk to him, but she thought it would probably be better if he slept till noon, especially if there was anything to sleep off, so he'd be in good shape for the ceremony. All she wanted was for the wedding to be perfect! She had many bridely things to do and was kept busy from brunch getting a manicure and pedicure, surrounded by the women in her family and her girlfriends.

The New Year's Eve wedding had been Sunny's idea. It had been born of a conversation with the girls about how they'd never had a memorable New Year's Eve—even when they had steady guys, were engaged or even married. Oh, there'd been a few parties, but they hadn't been special in any way. Sunny thought it would be fantastic—a classy party to accompany her wedding, something for everyone to remember. An unforgettable event.

Little did she know.

She'd been so busy all day, she hadn't worried that she never heard from Glen. She assumed he was as occupied with his guys as she was with her girls. In fact, it hadn't really bothered her until about five, still a couple of hours till the wedding. She called him and when he didn't pick up, she left him a voice mail that she loved him, that she was so happy, that soon they would be married and off on a wonderful honeymoon.

It was very hard for a photographer to choose a photographer; almost no one was going to measure up to
Sunny's expectations. But the very well-known Lin Hui
was trying her best, and started snapping shots as soon as
the girls showed up at the church with hairdressers and
professional makeup artists in tow. Her camera flashed
at almost every phase of preparation and in addition
captured special memories—shiny, strappy heels against
flowers, female hands clutching white satin, mothers of
the bride and groom embracing and dabbing each other's
eyes. But the poor thing seemed very nervous. Sunny
assumed it was because of the challenge of shooting another professional. She had no idea it was because Lin
couldn't find the groom for a photo shoot of the men in
the wedding party.

It happened at six forty-five, fifteen minutes before
the ceremony was to start. Sunny's father came into the
wedding prep room with Russ. Both of them looked as
if someone had died and she immediately gasped and ran
to her father. "Is Glen all right?"

"He's fine, honey." Then he sent everyone out of the
room including Sunny's mom and the mother of the
groom. He turned to Russ and said, "Tell her."

Russ hung his head. He shook it. "Don't ask me what's
got into him, I really can't explain. There's no good rea-

son for this. He said he's sorry, he just isn't ready for this. He froze up, can't go through with it."

She had never before realized how fast denial can set in or how long it can last. "Impossible. The wedding is in fifteen minutes," she said.

"I know. I'm sorry—I spent all day trying to get through this with him. I even suggested he just show up, do it, and if he still feels the same way in a few months, he can get a divorce. Honest to God, it made more sense to me than this."

She shook her head and then, inexplicably, laughed. "Aw, you guys. This is not funny. You got me, okay? But this isn't funny!"

"It's not a joke, baby," her father said. "I've tried calling him—he won't pick up."

"He'll pick up for me," she said. "He always picks up for me!"

But he didn't. Her call was sent to voice mail. Her message was, "Please call me and tell me I'm just dreaming this! Please! You can't really be ditching me at the church fifteen minutes before the wedding! Not you! You're better than this!"

Russ grabbed her wrist. "Sunny—he left his tux in my car to return. He's not coming."

Sunny looked at her father. "What am I supposed to do?" she asked in a whisper.

Her father's face was dark with anger, stony with fury. "We'll give him till seven-fifteen to call or do something honorable, then we make an announcement to the guests, invite them to go to the party and eat the food that will otherwise be given away or thrown out, and we'll return the gifts with apologies. And then I'm going to kill him."

"He said he'll pay back the cost of the reception if it takes his whole life. But there's no way he can pay me back for what he asked me to do today," Russ said. "Sunny, I'm so sorry."

"But *why?*"

"Like I said, he doesn't have a logical reason. He can't, he said." Russ shook his head. "I don't understand, so I know you can't possibly."

Sunny grabbed Russ's arm. "Go tell his mother to call him! Give her your cell phone so he'll think it's you and pick up!"

But Glen didn't pick up and his mother was left to growl angrily into the phone's voice mail right before she fell apart and cried.

Before they got even close to seven-fifteen everyone nearby was firing questions at Sunny like it was her fault. *Why? Did he talk to you about this? Was he upset, troubled? Did you suspect this was coming? You must have noticed something! How can you not have known? Suspected? Were you having problems? Arguing about something? Fighting? Was his behavior off? Strange? Was there another woman?* It didn't take long for her to erupt. "You'll have to ask *him!* And he's not even here to ask! Not only did he not show up, he left me to try to answer for him!"

At seven-ten, right before her father made an announcement to the wedding guests, Sunny quietly got into the bridal limo. She took her bouquet—her beautiful bouquet filled with roses and orchids and calla lilies—made a stop at her parents' house for her purse and honeymoon luggage and had the driver take her home.

Home. The town house she shared with Glen. Her parents were frantic, her girlfriends were worried, her wedding guests wondered what went wrong. She wasn't sure why she went home, maybe to see if he'd moved out while she was having a manicure and pedicure. But no—everything was just as she'd left it. And typical of Glen, the bed wasn't made and there were dirty dishes in the sink.

She sat on the edge of their king-size bed in her wedding gown, her bouquet in her lap and her cell phone in her hand in case he should call and say it was all a bad joke and rather than pulling out of the wedding he was in the hospital or in jail. The only calls she got were from friends and family, all worried about her. She fended off most of them without saying where she was, others were forced to leave messages. For some reason she couldn't explain to this day, she didn't cry. She let herself fall back on the bed, stared at the ceiling and asked herself over and over what she didn't know about this man she had been willing to commit a lifetime to. She was vaguely aware of that special midnight hour passing. The new year didn't come in with a kiss, but with a scandalous breakup.

Sunny hadn't had a plan when she went home, but when she heard a key in the lock she realized that because she'd taken the bridal limo and left her car at her parents', Glen didn't know she was there. She sat up.

He walked through the bedroom door, grabbing his wallet, keys and change out of his pockets to drop onto the dresser when he saw her. Everything scattered as he made a sound of surprise and he automatically reached for his ankle where he always kept a small, backup gun. Breathing hard, he left it there and straightened. Cops, she thought. They like always having *something,* in case they happen to run into someone they put away…or a pissed-off bride.

"Go ahead," she said. "Shoot me. It might be easier."

"Sunny," he said, breathless. "What are you *doing* here?"

"I *live* here," she said. She looked down at the bouquet she still held. Why had she clung to that? Because it was sentimental or because it cost 175 dollars and she couldn't return it? "You can't have done this to me," she said almost weakly. "You can't have. You must have a brain tumor or something."

He walked into the room. "I'm sorry," he said, shaking his head. "I kept thinking that by the time we got to the actual date, the wedding date, I'd be ready. I really thought that."

"Ready for what?" she asked, nonplussed.

"Ready for that life, that commitment forever, that next stage, the house, the children, the fidelity, the—"

She shook her head, frowning in confusion. "Wait a minute, we haven't found a house we like and can afford, we agreed we're not ready for children yet and I thought we already had commitment..." His chin dropped. "Fidelity?" she asked in a whisper.

He lifted his eyes and locked with hers. "See, I haven't really done anything wrong, not really. I kept thinking, I'm not married yet! And I thought by the time—"

"Did you sleep with other women?" she asked, rising to her feet.

"No! No! I swear!"

She didn't believe him for a second! "Then what *did* you do?"

"Nothing much. I partied a little. Had drinks, you

know. Danced. Just went out and sometimes I met girls, but it didn't get serious or anything."

"But it did get to meeting, dancing, buying drinks. Talking on the phone? Texting little messages? Maybe having dinner?"

"Maybe some of that. A couple of times."

"Maybe kissing?"

"Only, maybe, twice. At the most, twice."

"My God, have I been brain damaged? To not know?"

"When were we together?" he asked. "We had different nights off, we were like roommates!"

"You could have fixed that easy! You could have changed your nights off! I couldn't! People don't get married or have fiftieth anniversary parties on Tuesday nights!"

"And they also don't go out for fun on Tuesday nights! I guess I'm just a bad boy, but I enjoy a ball game or a run on a bar or club on a weekend when people are out! And you were never available on a weekend! We talked about it, we *fought* about it! You said it would never change, not while you took pictures."

"This isn't happening," she said. "You stood up two hundred wedding guests and a trip to Aruba because I work weekends?"

"Not exactly, but... Well... Look," he said, shaking his head. "I'm twenty-six. I thought you were probably the best thing for me, the best woman I could ever hook up with for the long haul except for one thing—I'm not ready to stop having fun! And you are—you're all business. Even that wedding—Jesus, it was like a runaway train! Planning that astronomical wedding was like a second job for you and I never wanted anything that big, that out of control! Sunny, you're way too young to be so old."

That was one way to deliver what she could only describe as a punch to the gut. Of all the things she thought she knew about him, she hadn't given enough credence to the fact that even at twenty-six, he was younger than she. More immature. He wanted to have *fun.* "And you couldn't tell me this last month? Or last week? Or *yesterday?*" She stared at him, waiting.

"Like I said, I thought I'd work it out in my head, be ready in time."

Talk about shock and awe. "You're an infant. How did I not realize what a liability that could be?"

"Excuse me, but I lay my life on the line every day! I go to work in a bulletproof vest! And you're calling me an *infant?*"

"Oh, I'm so sorry, Glen. You're an infant with a dick. With a little, tiny brain in it." She took a breath. "Pack a bag. Take some things and see if you can find a friend who will take you in for a few days. I'll move home to my mom and dad's as soon as I can. I hope you can make the rent alone. If I recall, I was making more money with my boring old weekend job than you were with your bulletproof vest."

Sunny sat back on the bed, then she lay down. Still gowned in a very big wedding dress, holding her valuable bouquet at her waist, Sunny closed her eyes. She heard Glen rustling around, finding clothes, his shaving kit, the essentials. Her mind was completely occupied with thoughts like, *will the airline refund the money for the first-class tickets because the groom didn't show?* How much nonrefundable money had her parents wasted on a wedding that never happened? Would the homeless of L.A. be eating thousands of dollars worth of exquisite food discarded by the caterer? And since her name was also on the lease to this town house, would fun-man Glen stiff her there, too? Hurt her credit rating *and* her business?

"Sunny?" Glen said to her. He was standing over her. "Wake up. You look so... I don't know... *Funereal* or something. Like a dead body, all laid out." He winced. "In a wedding dress..."

She opened her eyes, then narrowed them at him. "Go. Away."

Sunny gave her head a little shake to clear her mind and looked up to see Drew standing in front of her. He held a glass of wine toward her. "I salted the steps, got you a wine and me a beer. Now," he said, sitting down opposite her. "About this photography of yours…"

"It happened a year ago," she said.

"Huh? The picture taking happened a year ago?" he asked.

"The wedding that never was. Big wedding—big party. We'd been together three years, engaged and living together for one, and all of a sudden he didn't show. I was all dressed up in a Vera Wang, two hundred guests were waiting, little sausages simmering and stuffed mushrooms warming, champagne corks popping…and no groom."

Total shock was etched into his features. "Get out!" he said in a shocked breath.

"God's truth. His best man told me he couldn't do it. He wasn't ready."

Suddenly Drew laughed, but not unkindly, not of humor but disbelief. He ran his hand through his hair. "Did he ever say *why?*"

She had never told anyone what he'd said, it was too embarrassing. But for some reason she couldn't explain, she spit it right out to Drew. "Yeah. He wasn't done having fun."

Silence reigned for a moment. "You're not serious," Drew finally said.

"Deadly. It was all so stunning, there was even a small newspaper article about it."

"And this happened when?" he asked.

"One year ago. Today."

Drew sat back in his chair. "Whoa," was all he could say. "Well, no wonder you're in a mood. Fun?" he asked. "He wasn't done having *fun?*"

"Fun," she affirmed. "That's the best explanation he could come up with. He liked to party, go to clubs, flirt, dance, whatever… He's a Saturday-night kind of guy and just wasn't ready to stop doing that and guess what? Photographers work weekends—weddings, baptisms, et cetera. Apparently I'm a real drag."

Drew rubbed the back of his neck. "I must be really backward then. I always thought having the right person there for you, listening to your voice mails and texting you to pick up her dry cleaning or saying she'd pick up yours, someone who argued with you over what sushi to bring home or what went on the pizza, someone who would come to bed naked on a regular basis—I always thought *those things* were fun. Sexy and fun."

She grinned at him. "You find dry cleaning sexy?"

"I do," he said. "I really do." And then they both laughed.

"I bought a couple of presents before Thanksgiving, but other than those, I don't have a thing," she said, thinking aloud. "I don't have anything for you and I'd like it to be a special Christmas."

He grinned. "You think it won't be? You don't need to put a bow on it, baby."

BECCA AND DENNY FROM
BRING ME HOME FOR CHRISTMAS

4

Sunny sat forward, elbows on her knees, a smile on her face and said, "I can't wait to hear more about this—the things you find sexy. I mean pizza toppings and dry cleaning? Do go on."

He took a sip of his beer. "There is a long list, Miss Sunshine, but let's be clear—I am a boy. Naked tops the list."

"Yes, there are some things all you *boys* seem to have in common. But if I've learned anything it's that showing up naked regularly apparently isn't quite enough."

"Pah—for men with no imagination maybe. Or men who don't have to push a month's worth of work into a day."

"Well, then...?" she asked. "What?"

"I like working out a budget you'll never stick to. There's something about planning that together, it's cool. Not the checkbook, that's not a two-person job—it's dicey. No two people add and subtract the same, did you know that? And the chore list, that turns me on like you wouldn't believe. Picking movies—there's a real skill to that. If you can find a girl who likes action, then you can negotiate three action movies to every chick flick, and you can eventually work up to trading chick flicks for back rubs." He leaned close to whisper. "I don't want this to get out, but I actually like some of the chick flicks. I'm picky, but I do like some."

"Shopping?" she asked.

"I have to draw the line there," he said firmly. "That just doesn't do it for me. If I need clothes or shoes I take care of it as fast as I can. I don't like to screw around with that. It's boring and I have no skills. But I get that you have to look at least half decent to get a girl to like you." He smiled. "A pretty girl like you," he added.

"Then how do you manage that? Because tonight, you weren't even aware there was a party and you don't look that terrible."

"Why, thank you," he said, straightening proudly. "I either ask my oldest sister, Erin, to dress me—the one who made the lean-to into a showplace—or failing that I just look for a gay guy working in clothing."

She burst out laughing, not realizing that Nate, Annie, Jack and a few others turned to look. "That's awful, shame on you!"

"Gimme a break—I have gay friends. You can say anything you want about them but the common denominator is—they have fashion sense. At least the guys I know do."

"Then why not ask a gay friend to go shopping with you?"

"I don't want to mislead anyone," he said with a shrug.

"Sure you're not just a little self-conscious about your...um...somewhat *flexible* status?"

He leaned so close she could inhale the Michelob on his breath. His eyes locked on hers. "Not flexible about that. Ab. So. Lutely. Not." Then he smiled. "I only swing one way."

She couldn't help it, she laughed loudly. Happily.

"You gotta stop that, my sunshine. You're supposed to be miserable. You were left at the altar by a juvenile idiot a year ago tonight. We're grieving here."

"I know, I know," she said, fanning her face. "I'm going to get back into depression mode in a sec. Right now, tell me another thing you find impossibly sexy, and keep in mind we've already covered that naked thing."

"Okay," he said. He rolled his eyes skyward, looking for the answer. "Ah!" he said. "Her lingerie in the bathroom! It's impossible. Hanging everywhere. A guy can't even pee much less brush his teeth or get a shower. I hate that!" And there was that wicked grin again. "Very sexy."

"Okay, I'm a little confused here. You hate it? And it's very sexy?"

"Well, you have to be a guy to get this. A guy goes into the bathroom—which is small like the rest of your house or apartment until you're at least an evil senior resident—and you put your face into all the satin and lace hanging all over the place. You rub it between your palms, wear a thong on your head for a minute, have a couple of reality-based fantasies, and then you yell, 'Penny! Get your underwear out of here so I can get a shower! I'm late.'"

She put her hands over her face and laughed into them.

His eyes glowed as he looked at her. "Be careful, Sunny. You're enjoying yourself."

She reached across the short space that separated them and gave him a playful slug. "So are you! And your breakup was more recent."

"Yeah, but—"

He was about to say *but not more traumatic*. At least he wasn't left in a Vera Wang gown hiding from two hundred wedding guests. But the door to the bar opened and in came the local Riordans—Luke, Shelby and little

Brett, their new baby. Luke was holding Brett against his chest, tucked under his jacket. Drew jumped to his feet. "Hey! Son of a gun!" Then he grabbed Sunny's hand and pulled her along. He turned to her and said, "Kind of family. I'll explain."

Leaving Sunny behind him a bit, he grabbed Shelby in a big hug and kissed her cheek. He grabbed Luke, careful of the baby and Luke scowled at him and said, "Do *not* kiss me!"

"All right, but gee, I'll have to really hold myself back," Drew said with a laugh. He winked at Sunny before he pulled her forward. "Meet Sunny, here visiting her uncle. Sunny, remember I told you about the sister who turned the shack into a showplace? That's Erin—and while she was up here finding herself, she also found Luke's brother Aiden. They're engaged. That makes me almost related to these guys and little Brett."

Shelby reached out to shake Sunny's hand. "I heard you'd be visiting, Sunny. We know Nate and Annie. I sometimes ride with Annie."

"Hey, I thought you said you weren't coming out tonight," Jack said from behind the bar. "Baby sleeping and all that."

"We should'a thought that through a little better," Luke said. "Brett prefers to sleep during the day and is a regular party animal at night."

Mel moved closer and said, "Aww, let me have him a minute." She pulled the little guy from Luke and indeed, his eyes were as big as saucers—he was wide-awake at nine-thirty. Mel laughed at him. "Well, aren't you something!"

Shelby said to Sunny, "Mel delivered him. She gets really invested in her babies."

"Let's have your resolutions," Jack said. "Then I'll set you up a drink and you can graze the buffet table."

"What resolutions?" Luke wanted to know.

Jack patted the fishbowl full of slips of paper on the bar. "Everyone has contributed their number one, generic resolution. You know the kind—quit smoking, lose ten pounds, work out everyday. We're going to do something fun with them at midnight. A kind of game."

"I don't do games," Luke said.

"Lighten up, it's not like charades or anything. It's more like cracking open a fortune cookie."

"I don't do resolutions," Luke said.

"I'll do his," Shelby said, sitting up at the bar. "I have some ideas."

"Easy, baby," Luke said. "You know you don't like me too perfect. Rough around the edges caught you in the first place."

Shelby glanced over her shoulder and smiled at him. Nate, who was sitting beside her, leaned in and pretended to read her resolution. "No more boys' nights out or dancing girls?" he said. "Shelby, isn't that a little strict for our boy Luke?"

Luke just laughed. So did Shelby.

Sunny took it all in. She had always liked to be around couples who were making that whole couple thing work—understanding each other, give and take, good humor, physical attraction. She'd done a lot of weddings. They weren't all easy and pleasant. A lot of the couples she photographed she wouldn't give a year.

Drew whispered in her ear. "Shelby is a full-time nursing student. She and Luke run a bunch of riverside cabin rentals and while Shelby goes to school and studies, Luke not only takes care of the cabins and house, but Brett, too. I think dancing girls are way in the past for Luke."

"Hmm," she said. She went for her camera and started taking pictures again, and while she did so she listened. Sunny could see things through the lens that were harder to see with the naked eye. For her, anyway.

She learned that Vanessa and Paul Haggerty were more conventional. She was home with the children while he was a general contractor who did most of the building and renovating around Virgin River, including the reconstruction of that old cabin for Drew's sister, the cabin Drew was staying in. Abby Michaels, the local doctor's wife, had a set of toddler twins and was overseeing the building of a house while her husband, Cam, was at the clinic or on call 24/7. The situation was a bit different for Mel and Jack Sheridan. The local midwife was always on call and Jack had a business that was open about sixteen hours a day—they had to shore each other up. They did a lot of juggling of kids and chores—Jack did all the cooking and Mel all the cleaning. If all the jokes could be believed, apparently Mel could burn water. Preacher and Paige worked together to raise their kids, run the kitchen and keep the accounting books at the bar. Brie and Mike Valenzuela had a child and two full-time jobs—she was an attorney, he was the town cop. And Sunny already knew that Uncle Nate and Annie were partners in running the Jensen's Clinic and Stable. Their wedding was scheduled for May.

Lots of interesting and individual methods of managing the realities of work, family, relationships. She wondered about a couple who would split up because one of them wasn't available to party on Saturday nights. She already knew that wasn't an issue among these folks.

While she observed and listened, she snapped pictures. She instructed Mel to hold the Riordan baby over her head and lower him slowly to kiss his nose. She got a great shot of Jack leaning on the bar, braced on strong arms spread wide, wearing a half smile as he watched his wife with a baby she had delivered, a proud glow in his eyes. Preacher was caught with his huge arms wrapped around his little wife, his lips against her head. Paul Haggerty put a quarter in the jukebox and danced his wife around the bar. Cameron Michaels was clinking glasses with Abby Michaels and couldn't resist nuzzling her neck—Sunny caught that. In fact, she caught many interesting postures, loving poses. Not only was there a lot of affection in the room, but plenty of humor and happiness. God, she never used to be the type that got dragged down.

When Sunny was focusing the camera, she didn't miss much. Maybe she should have been looking at Glen through the lens because clearly she missed a lot about him. Or had she just ignored it all?

She wondered if this was all about it being New Year's Eve, being among friends and the promise of a brand-new start, a first day of a new year. That's what she'd had in mind for her wedding—a new beginning.

Then she spotted Drew, apart from the crowd, leaning against the wall beside the hearth, watching her with a lazy smile on his lips. He had one leg crossed over the other, one hand was in his front jeans pocket and he lifted his bottle of Mich, which had to be warm by now since he'd been nursing it for so long. She snapped, flashed the camera, making him laugh. He posed for her, pulling that hand out of his pocket and flexing his muscles. Of course it was impossible to see his real physique given the roomy plaid flannel shirt. He put his leg up on the seat of a nearby chair, gave her a profile and lifted the beer bottle—she liked it. He grinned, scowled, stuck his tongue out, blew raspberries at the camera—she snapped and laughed. Then he crooked his finger at her for her to come closer and she took pictures as she went. When she got real close he pulled the camera away.

"Let's get out of here," he whispered. "Somewhere we can talk."

"Can't we talk here?" she asked.

He shook his head. "Listen," he said.

She listened—the jukebox. Only the jukebox. He turned her around. Every single eye was on them. Watching. Waiting. She turned back to Drew. "Everyone knows," she said. "We are the only single people, we're both single and miserable—"

"Single," he said. "I'm not miserable and I know you intended to be miserable, but that's not really working out for you. So?" he asked with a shrug. "Wanna just throw caution to the wind and see if you can enjoy the rest of the evening?"

"I can't enjoy it here?"

"With all of them watching you? Listening?" he asked with a lift of the chin to indicate the bar at large.

When she turned around to look, she caught everyone quickly averting their eyes and it made her laugh. She laughed harder, putting her hand over her mouth.

"Don't do that," he said, pulling her hand away. "You have an amazing smile and I love listening to you laugh."

"Where would we go?"

"Well, it's only ten. I could take you to Eureka or Fortuna—there's bound to be stuff going on, but I'd prefer to find somewhere there's not a party. I could show you the cabin Erin turned into a showplace, but I don't have any 'before' pictures. Or we could take a drive, park in the woods and make out like teenagers." He grinned at her playfully. Hopefully.

"You're overconfident," she accused.

"I've been told that. It's better than being underconfident, in these circumstances at least."

"I have to speak to Uncle Nathaniel," she said.

He touched her cheek with the knuckle of one finger. "Permission?"

She shook her head a little. "Courtesy. I'm his guest. Grab our coats."

The walk across the bar to her uncle was very short and in that time she realized that Drew wasn't overconfident—*Glen* was overconfident. He preened, and had always managed to strike a pose that accentuated his height, firm jaw, strong shoulders. Drew clowned around. Laughed. Drew seemed to be pretty easygoing and took things as they came. But she'd known him for two whole hours. Who knew what secrets he harbored?

But what the hell, Sunny thought. *I can experiment with actually letting a male person get close without much risk—I'm never going to see him again. Who knows? Maybe I'll recover after all.*

"Uncle Nate," she said. "I'm going to go with Drew to see if anything fun is happening in Fortuna or Eureka. If you're okay with that."

"Well," he said. "I don't actually know—*ow!*"

Annie slugged him in the arm. "That's great, Sunny," she said. "Will you come back here or have Drew take you home?"

She shrugged and shook her head. "I don't know. Depends on where we are, what's going on, you know. Listen, if the cells worked up here, I'd call, but…"

"Your cell from Fortuna or Eureka to my home phone works. Or to Jack's landline. We'll be here till midnight," Nate said. Then he glared briefly at Annie. "Jack, can you give her your number?"

"You bet," Jack said, jotting it on a napkin. "I've known Drew and his family a couple of years. You're in good hands, Sunny."

"Does he have four-wheel drive?" Nate asked.

Sunny grinned. "Oh, you're going to be a fun daddy,

yessir." Then she walked back to Drew and let him help her slip on her jacket.

"Where did you say we were going?" Drew asked.

"I said Fortuna or Eureka, but I want to see it—the cabin."

He grabbed his own jacket. "Hope I didn't leave it nasty."

"And is that likely?" she wanted to know.

"Depends where my head was at the time," he said. He rested her elbow in the palm of his hand and began to direct her out of the bar. As they were leaving he put two fingers to his brow and gave the gawkers a salute.

Sunny was trying to remember, what was the first thing Drew had said to her? She thought it was something simple, like "Hi, my name is Drew." And what had been Glen's opening line? With a finger in her sternum he had said, "Yo. You and me."

"Oh, God," he said. "What's this?"

"I'm your Christmas present!" she said on a laugh. "Do you have any idea how big the battery pack has to be to do this?"

How do you turn down a Christmas present? He snatched her against him and went after her mouth with every ounce of passion he felt inside. He didn't stop until they were both almost freezing from standing in the open doorway.

PATRICK AND ANGIE FROM
MY KIND OF CHRISTMAS

5

"I'm not sure that was the best thing to do," Nate Jensen said right after Sunny and Drew left. "I'm supposed to be looking after her, and I let her go off with some guy I don't even know."

"She was *laughing!*" Annie stressed. "Having fun for the first time in so long! She didn't need your permission, Nate. She was being polite, telling you where she was going so you wouldn't worry."

"You did fine," Jack said. "Drew's a good guy. A doctor, actually—in his residency now."

"But is he the kind of guy who will take advantage of a girl with a broken heart?" Nate asked. "Because my sister…"

"I don't know a thing about his love life," Jack said. "He said he'd had a breakup, so that might make them sympathetic to each other. I'll tell you what I know. Every time I've talked to him he's seemed like a stand-up guy. His brother-in-law was a disabled marine in a nursing home for a few years before he died, and Erin said that Drew, along with the rest of the family, helped take care of him. Erin thinks that had an impact on him, drew him to medicine. And…he has four-wheel drive. That should put your mind at ease."

"She *was* smiling," Nate admitted. "You should'a been there last year. Sitting in that church, waiting for the wedding to start. Just like in all things, the rumors that the groom didn't show started floating around the guests, maybe before Sunny had even heard it. It was awful. How do you not know something like that is coming? How could she not know?"

Jack gave the bar a wipe. "You can bet she's been asking herself that question for about a year."

"Tell me about the photography business," Drew said as they drove.

"You don't have to ask that," she said. "I can tell you're a gentleman and that's very polite, but you don't have to pretend to be interested in photography. It bores the heck out of most people."

He laughed at her. "When I was a kid, I took pictures sometimes," he said. "Awful pictures that were developed at the drugstore, but it was enough to get me on the yearbook staff, which I only wanted to be on because Bitsy Massey was on it. Bitsy was a cute little thing, a cheerleader of course, and she was on the yearbook committee—most likely to be sure the lion's share of the pictures were of her. I was in love with her for about six months, and she never knew I was alive. The only upside to the whole thing? I actually like taking pictures. I admit, I take a lot with my cell phone now and I don't have any aspirations to go professional, but I wasn't just being polite. In fact," he said, reaching into his pocket for his cell, "I happen to have some compound fractures, crushed ankles, ripped out shoulders and really horrible jaw fractures if you'd like to—"

"Ack!" she yelled, fanning him away with her hand. "Why in the world would you have those?"

"Snap 'em in E.R., take 'em to report and explain how we treated 'em and have the senior residents shoot us down and call us fools and idiots. So, Sunny—how'd it happen for you—picture taking? A big thug named Rock who liked to pose for you?"

"Nothing of the sort," she said indignantly. "I got a camera for Christmas when I was ten and started taking pictures. It only takes a few good ones before you realize you *can*. Take good pictures, that is. I figured out early what they would teach us about photography in college later—to get four or forty good pictures, just take four hundred. Of course, some subjects are close to impossible. Their color, angles, tones and shadows just don't work, while others just eat the camera, they're so photogenic. But..." She looked over at him. "Bored?"

"Not yet," he answered with a grin.

"It was my favorite thing," she said. "My folks kept saying there was no real future in it and I'd better have a backup plan, so I majored in business. But friends kept asking me to take pictures because I could. Pretty soon I had the moxie to ask them to at least pay the expenses—travel costs like gas for the car, film, developing, mounting, that sort of thing. Me and my dad put a darkroom in the basement when I was a junior in high school, but right after that we went digital and got a really good computer, upscale program and big screen. I built a website, using some of my stock for online advertising, and launched a price list that was real practical for people on a budget—but the product was *good*. My darkroom became a workroom. I could deliver finished portraits in glossy, matte, texture, whatever they wanted, and I could do it quickly. Friends told friends who told friends and by my sophomore year I was booked every weekend for family reunions, birthday parties, christenings, weddings, engagement parties, you name it. The only thing I didn't have when I dropped out of school to do this full-time was a studio. Since I did all my shooting on location at the site, all I needed in a studio was a desk, computer, big-screen monitor, DVD player and some civilized furnishings, plus a whole lot of albums and DVDs and brochures of photo packages. The money was good. I was set up before I was set up. I was lucky."

"I bet you were also smart," Drew said.

She laughed a bit. "Sort of, with my dad running herd on my little business all the time. He wasn't trying to make me successful, he was looking out for me, showing me the pitfalls, helping me not fail. When it became my means of income, I think he was a little ambivalent about me quitting college. And my mom? Scared her to death! She's old-fashioned—go get a practical job! Don't bet on your ingenuity or worse, your talent!"

"Your guy," Drew asked. "What did he do?"

"Highway Patrol. He liked life on the edge."

"Did he like your photographs?"

Without even thinking she answered, "Of him. He liked being in front of the camera. I like being behind it."

"Oh, he was one of the photogenic ones?"

"He was," she admitted. "He could be a model. Maybe he is by now."

"You don't keep in touch?"

"Oh, no," she said with a mean laugh.

"Not even through friends?"

"Definitely not through friends." She turned to look at him. "You? Do you keep in touch?"

He shrugged but his eyes were focused on the road. "Well, she's going to marry one of the residents at the hospital. We're not in the same service—he's general surgery. But she turns up sometimes. She's polite. I'm polite." He took a breath. "I hate that. I don't know how she feels, but I don't feel polite."

"So you are angry," she said, a note of surprise in her voice.

"Oh, hell yes," he replied. "It's just that sometimes the line is blurred, and I get confused about who I'm angriest with—her or me. She knew what she was signing up for, that residents don't have a lot of time or money or energy after work. Why couldn't we figure that out without all the drama? But then, I'm guilty of the same thing—I was asking way too much of her. See? Plenty of blame to go around."

There was quiet for a while. The road was curvy, banked by very tall trees heavy with snow. The snow was falling lightly, softly. The higher they went, the more snow there was on the ground. There were some sharp turns along the road, and a few drop-offs that, in the dark of night, looked like they were bottomless. He drove slowly, carefully, attentively. If he looked at her at all, which was rare, it was the briefest glance.

"Very pretty out here," she said quietly.

He responded with, "Can I ask you a personal question?"

She sucked in her breath. "I don't know...."

"Tell you what—don't answer if it makes you the least bit uncomfortable," he suggested.

"But wouldn't my not answering tell you that—"

"Did you fall in love with him the second you met him? Like right off the bat? Boom—you saw him, you were knocked off your feet, dead in love?"

No! she thought. "Yes," she said. She looked across the front seat at him. "You?"

He shook his head first. "No. I liked her right away, though. There were things about her that really worked for me, that work for a guy. Like, for example, no guessing games. She was very upfront, but never in a bitchy way. Not a lot of games with Penny, at least up until we got to the breaking-up part of our relationship. For example, if we went out to dinner, she ordered exactly what she liked. If I asked her what she'd like to do, she came up with an answer—never any of that 'I don't care' when she really did care. I liked that. We got along, seemed like we were paddling in the same direction. I wanted to be a surgeon, and she was a nurse who liked the idea of being with a doctor, even though she knew it was never easy on the spouse. When I asked her if she wanted to move in with me before the residency started she said, 'Not without a ring.'" He shrugged. "Seemed reasonable to me that we'd just get married. I'm still real surprised it didn't work out that way. I really couldn't tell you exactly when it stopped working. That's the only thing that scares me."

She stared at his profile. At that moment she decided that if she ever broke a bone, she'd want him to set it. "But by then you were madly in love with her, right? By the time you got to the ring?"

"Probably. Yeah, I think so. The thing is, Penny seemed exactly right for me, exactly. Logical. Problems that friends of mine had with wives or girlfriends, I didn't have with Penny. Guys envied me. I thought she was the perfect one for me."

She heard Glen's voice in her head. *I thought you were the best thing for me, the best woman I could ever hook up with for the long haul....*

"Until all this fighting started," he went on. "Things had been so easy with us, I didn't get it. I thought it was all about her missing her friends, me working such long hours, that kind of thing. I'm still not sure—maybe it was about another guy and being all torn up trying to decide. But really, I thought everything was fine."

"What is it with you guys?" she said hotly. "You just pick out a girl who looks like wife material and hope by the time you get to the altar you'll be ready?"

Drew gave her a quick glance, a frown, then looked back at the road. And that's when it happened—as if it fell from the sky, he hit a buck. He knew it was a buck when he saw the antlers. He also saw its big, brown eyes. It was suddenly in front of the SUV—his oldest sister's SUV that he had borrowed to go up to the cabin. Though they weren't traveling fast, the strike was close, sudden, the buck hit the front hard, was briefly airborne, came down on the hood, and rolled up against the windshield with enough force for the antlers to crack it, splinter it.

Drew fought the car, though he could only see clearly out of the driver's side window. He knew that to let the SUV go off the road could be disastrous—there were so many drop-offs on the way to the cabin. He finally brought the car to rest on the shoulder, the passenger side safely resting against a big tree.

Sunny screamed in surprise and was left staring into the eyes of a large buck through the webbed and cracked windshield. The deer was lying motionless across the hood.

Drew turned to Sunny first. "Sunny…"

"We hit a deer!" she screamed.

"Are you okay? Neck? Head? Back? Anything?" he asked her.

She was unhooking her belt and wiggling out of it. "Oh, my God, oh, my God, oh, my God! He's dead! Look at him! He's dead, isn't he?"

"Sunny," he said, stopping her, holding her still. "Wait a second. Sit still for just a second and tell me—does anything hurt?"

Wide-eyed, she shook her head.

He ran a hand down each of her legs, over her knees. "Did you hit the dash?" he asked. "Any part of you?"

She shook her head. "You have to help the deer!" she said in a panic.

"I don't know if there's much help for him. I wonder why the air bags didn't deploy—the SUV must've swept the buck's legs out from under him, causing him to directly hit the grille, and since the car kept moving forward, no air bags. Whew, he isn't real small, either."

"Check him, Drew. Okay?"

"I'll look at him, but you stay right here for now, all right?"

"You bet I will. I should tell you—me and blood? Not a good combination."

"You faint?"

She nodded, panic etched on her face. "Right after I get sick."

He rolled his eyes. That was all he needed. "Do not get out of the car!"

"Don't worry," she said as he was exiting.

Drew assessed the deer before he took a closer look at the car. The deer was dead, bleeding from legs and head, eyes wide and fixed, blood running onto the white snow. There was some hood and grille damage, but the car might be drivable if he didn't have a smashed wind-shield. It was laminated glass, so it had gone all veiny like a spiderweb. He'd have to find a way to get that big buck off and then, if he drove it, he'd have a hard time seeing through the cracked glass.

He pulled out his cell phone and began snapping pic-tures, but in the dark it was questionable what kind of shots he'd get.

He leaned back in the car. "Can I borrow your cam-era? It has a nice, big flash, right?"

"Borrow it for what?"

"To get some pictures of the accident. For insurance."

"Should I take them?" she asked.

"I don't know if you'll have time before you get sick and faint."

Blood. That meant there was blood. "Okay—but let me show you how." She pulled the camera bag from the backseat, took the camera out and gave him a quick lesson, then sat quietly, trying not to look at the dead deer staring at her as light flashed in her peripheral vision.

But then, curious about where Drew was, she looked out the cracked windshield and what she saw almost brought tears to her eyes. With the camera hanging at his side from his left hand, he looked down at the poor animal and, with his right hand, gave him a gentle stroke.

Then he was back, handing her the camera. "Did you pet that dead deer?" she asked softly.

He gave his head a little nod. "I feel bad. I wish I'd seen him in time. Poor guy. I hope he doesn't have a family somewhere."

"Aw, Drew, you're just a tender heart."

"Here's what we have to do," he said, moving on. "We're going to have to walk the rest of the way. Fortunately it's only a couple of miles."

"Shouldn't we stay with the car? I've always heard you should stay with the car. What if someone comes looking for us?"

"It will be too cold. I can't keep it running all night. And if anyone gets worried by how long we're gone, they're going to look in Fortuna or Eureka. Or at least the route to those towns, which is where you told them we were going." He lifted a brow. "Why do you suppose you did that?"

She shook her head. "I didn't want my uncle Nate to

think we were going somewhere to be alone. Dumb. Very dumb."

"I need a phone, a tow truck and a warm place to wait, so here's what's going to happen. Hand me the camera case." She zipped it closed and he hung it over his shoulder. "There's a big flashlight in the glove box. Grab it—I'll have to light our way when we clear the headlights. Now slide over here and when you get out, either shield or close your eyes until I lead you past the deer, because the way my night's going if you get sick, it'll be on me."

She wrinkled her nose. "I smell it," she said. "Ick, I can *smell* it!"

"Close your eyes *and* your nose," he said. "Let's get past this, all right?"

She slid over, put her feet on the ground and stood. And her spike heels on her boots sank into the frozen, snowy ground. "Uh-oh," she said.

"Oh, brother. So, what if I broke the heels off those boots? Would you be able to walk in them?"

She gasped! "They're six-hundred-dollar Stuart Weitzman boots!"

He looked at her levelly for a long moment. "I guess the photography business is going very, very well."

"I had to console myself a little after being left at the

church. Giving them up now would be like another…
Oh, never mind…"

"You're right," he said. "I must have lost my mind."
He eased her backward, lifted her onto the seat with her
legs dangling out. Then he positioned the heavy camera
bag around his neck so it hung toward the front. Next
he turned his back to her, braced his hands on his knees
and bent a little. "Piggyback," he said. "Let's move it."

"I'm too heavy."

"No, Sunny, you're not."

"I am. You have no idea how much I weigh."

"It's all right," he said. "It's not too much."

"I'll go in my socks. It's just a couple of miles…"

"And get frostbite and from then on you'll be putting your prosthetic feet into your Stuart Weitzmans."
He looked over his shoulder at her. "The sooner we do
this, the sooner we're warm and with help on the way."

Sunny only thought about it for a second—she was
getting cold and she liked her feet, didn't want to give
them up to frostbite. She grumbled as she climbed on.
"I was just willing to leave Jack's so we could talk without everyone watching. I haven't really talked to a single
guy in a year."

"Close your eyes," he said. "What does that mean,
'really talked to a single guy'?"

"Obviously I ran into them from time to time. Bag

boys, mechanics, cable repairmen, cousins to the bride or groom... But after Glen, I had sworn off dating or even getting to know single men. Just not interested in ever putting myself in that position again. You know?"

"I know," he said a bit breathlessly. He stopped trudging up the hill to catch his breath. Then he said, "You lucked out with me—there's no better way to see a person's true colors than when everything goes to hell. Wrecked car, dead deer, spiked heels—it qualifies." He hoisted her up a bit and walked on.

"I'd like to ask you something personal, if you're up for it," she said.

He stopped walking and slid her off his back. He turned toward her and he was smiling. "Sunny, I can't talk and carry you—this top-of-the-line camera is heavy. Here's what you can do—tell me stories. Any stories you want—chick stories about shopping and buying six-hundred-dollar boots, or photographer stories, or scary stories. And when we get to the cabin, you can ask me anything you want."

"I'm too heavy," she said for the umpteenth time.

"I'm doing fine, but I can't carry on much of a conversation. Why don't you entertain us by talking? I'll walk and listen." And he presented his back again so she could climb on.

She decided to tell him all about her family; how her

mother, two aunts and Uncle Nate had grown up in these mountains; and how later, when Grandpa had retired and left the veterinary practice to Uncle Nate, they all went back for visits. Grandma and Grandpa lived in Arizona as did Patricia and her two sons. Auntie Chris lived in Nevada with their two sons and one daughter and Sunny, an only child, lived in Southern California.

"Am I heavier when I talk?" she asked him.

"No," he said, stopping for a moment. "You make the walk shorter."

So she kept going. She talked about the family gatherings at the Jensen stables, about how she grew up on a horse like her mom and aunts had. But while her only female cousin and best friend since birth, Mary, had ridden competitively, Sunny was taking pictures. She spoke about fun times and pranks with her cousins.

She told him how Nate and Annie had met over an abandoned litter of puppies and would be married in the spring. "I'll be a bridesmaid. It will be my third time as a bridesmaid and a lot of my girlfriends are getting married. I've never before in my life known a single woman who was left at the altar. I keep wondering what I did wrong. I mean, Glen worked out like a madman and he wanted me to work out too, but you can't imagine the exercise involved in carrying a twenty pound camera bag, running, stooping, crouching, lifting that heavy camera for literally hours. I just couldn't get excited about lifting weights on top of that. He said I should think about implants. I hate surgical procedures of any kind. Oh, sure, I've always wanted boobs, but not that bad. And yes, I'm short and my butt's too big and my nose is pointy.... He used to say wide hips are good for sex and nothing else. That felt nice, hearing that," she said facetiously. "I tried to take comfort in the sex part—maybe that meant I was all right in the sack, huh? And I'm bossy, I know I'm bossy sometimes. I liked to think I'm efficient and capable, but Glen thought it was controlling and he said it pissed him off to be controlled by a woman. There you have it—the recipe for getting left at the altar."

Then she stopped talking for a while. When she spoke again, her voice was quiet and his tread actually slowed. "I'd like you to know something. When we first met and I was so snotty and rude, I never used to be like that. Really. I always concentrated on being nice. That's how I built my business—I was nice, on time, and worked hard—that's what I attribute most of my success to. Seriously. That whole thing with Glen.... Well, it changed me. I apologize."

"No apology necessary," he said breathlessly. "I understand."

Then she was embarrassed by all her talking, talking

about boobs and hips and sex to a total stranger. Blessedly, he didn't make any further comment. It wasn't long before she could see a structure and some lights up ahead. He trudged on, breathing hard, and finally put her down on the porch that spanned the front of a small cabin.

She looked up at him. "It's amazing that you would do that. I would have left me in the car."

He gave her a little smile. "Well, you wanted to see the cabin. And now you will. We'll call Jack's, let everyone know what happened, that we're all right, and I'll light the fire, so we can warm up. Then I have a few things to tell you."

"But it's almost Christmas and, before you go, I just want to enjoy the holiday spirit. I want us to help deliver the Christmas boxes, go to a couple of parties, sing around the tree, eat some great food and—" she smiled into his eyes "—and make love all night long. I don't know if you'll store up the memories, but dammit, I will."

ANGIE FROM *MY KIND OF CHRISTMAS*

6

Drew immediately started stacking wood in the fireplace on top of some very big pinecones he used as starters.

Sunny looked around—showplace, all right. She appreciated the plush leather furniture, beautiful patterned area rug, spacious stone hearth, stained shutters, large kitchen. There were two doors off the great room—bedrooms, she assumed. It wasn't messy, though books and papers were stacked on the ottoman and beside the long, leather sofa, and a laptop sat open on the same ottoman. There was a throw that looked like it might be cashmere that was tossed in a heap at the foot of the sofa.

"Should I go ahead and call Jack's?" she asked him.

He looked over his shoulder at her and smiled. "No

hurry. No way I'm getting a tow truck tonight, on New Year's Eve. In fact, I wouldn't count on New Year's Day either—I'm probably going to have to get my brother-in-law to drive up here in his truck to get me and tow Erin's car home. We're not late yet, so no one's worried." He lit a match to the starter cones and stood up as the fire took light. He brushed the dirt off his hands. "I hate to think about you being rescued too soon. I think we still have some things to talk about."

"Like?"

He stepped toward her. There was a softness in his eyes, a sweet smile on his lips. "You wanted to ask me something personal. And I have to tell you something." His hands were on her upper arms and he leaned down to put a light kiss on her forehead. "You're not too short. You're a good height." He touched her nose with a finger, then he had to brush a little soot off of it. "Your nose looks perfect to me—it's a very nice nose. And your chest is beautiful. Inviting, if you can handle hearing that from a man who is not your fiancé. I was never attracted to big boobs. I like to look at well-proportioned women. More than that, women in their real, natural bodies—implants might stay standing, but they're not pretty to me." His hands went to her hips. "And these?" he asked, squeezing. "Delicious. And your butt? One of the best on record. On top of all that I think you have the greatest laugh I've heard in a long time and your smile is infectious—I bet you can coax excellent smiles out of photo subjects with it. When you smile at me? I feel like I'm somebody, that's what. And the fact that you were a little ornery? I'm okay with that—you know why? Because when someone does something that bad to you, they shouldn't just get away with it. It hurts and turns you a little mean because it's just plain unfathomable that a guy, even a stupid guy, can be that cruel. I'm really sorry that happened, Sunny. And I hope you manage to get past it."

She was a little stunned for a moment. No one had ever talked to her like that, not that she'd given anyone a chance with the way she pushed people away. But he was so sexy and sweet it was *killing* her. "Just out of curiosity, what would you have done?"

"If I was left in my Vera Wang?" he asked, wide-eyed.

She laughed in spite of herself. "No, if you realized you didn't want to get married to the woman you were getting married to!"

"First of all, it would never have gotten that far if I wasn't sure. Invitations would never be mailed. Getting married isn't just some romantic thing—it's a lot of things, and one is a serious partnership. You have to be in the same canoe on at least most issues, but it's okay to be different, I think. Like my sisters and their guys?

I would never have coupled them up, they're so different from their guys. But they're perfect for each other because they have mutual respect and a willingness to negotiate. They keep each other in balance. Plus, they love each other. Jesus, you wouldn't believe it, how much they're in love. It's almost embarrassing. But when they talk about being married, it's more about how they want their lives to go, how they want their partnership to feel."

"And you were that way with... Penny?" she asked.

"I thought I was," he said. "Thought she was, too."

"What if you're wrong next time, too?" Sunny asked.

"Is that what you're afraid of, honey?" he asked her gently.

"Of course! Aren't you?"

He stared at her for a second, then walked into the kitchen without answering. "Let's hope good old Erin stocked something decent for a cold winter night, huh?" He began opening cupboards. He finally came out with a dark bottle of liquid. "Aha! Brandy! Bet you anything this isn't Erin's, but Aiden's. But it's not terrible brandy—at least it's Christian Brothers." He lifted the bottle toward her.

"Sure, what the hell," she said, going over to the sofa to sit. She raised the legs of her jeans, unzipped her boots and pulled them off. She lifted one and looked at it. Now why would she bring these to Uncle Nate's stable? These were L.A. boots—black suede with pointy toes and spike heels. The boots she normally brought to the stable were low-heeled or cowboy, hard leather, well-worn. The kind that would've made it up that hill so she wouldn't have to be carried.

She threw the boot on the floor. Okay, she had wanted to be seen, if possible, and judge the look on the face of the seer. Her confidence was pretty rocky; she needed to feel attractive. She wanted to see a light in a male eye like the one she had originally seen in Glen's—a light she would run like hell from, but still....

Drew brought her a brandy in a cocktail glass, not a snifter. He sat down beside her. "Here's to surviving a deer strike!" he said, raising his glass to her.

She clinked. "Hear, hear."

They each had a little sip and he said, "Now—that personal question? Since I can breathe and talk again."

"It's probably a dumb question. You'd never be able to answer it honestly and preserve your manhood."

"Try me. Maybe you're right about me, maybe you're not."

"Okay. Did you cry? When she left you?"

He rolled his eyes upward to find an answer. He shook his head just a bit, frowning. "I don't think so. Didn't cry, didn't beg." He leveled his gaze at her. "Didn't sleep either, and since I couldn't sleep I worked even more hours. I kept trying to figure out where I'd gone wrong. For two years we seemed to be fine and then once the ring was on the finger, everything went to hell."

"So what *did* you do?" she wanted to know.

"I did my chores," he said. "All the things she wanted me to do that when I didn't, drove her crazy. There were little rules. If you're the last one out of the bed, make it. If you eat off a plate, rinse it and put it in the dishwasher. If something you take off is dirty it doesn't go on the floor, but in the hamper. I thought if she came back, she'd see I was capable of doing the things that were important to her."

That almost broke her heart. "Drew…"

"In medicine we have a saying, if you hear hoofbeats, don't expect to see a zebra. I was thinking horses—it's pretty common for surgeons to have relationship problems because of the pressure, the stress, the time they have to spend away from home. Horses. I brought her with me to my residency program, took her away from her mom, away from her job and girlfriends, and then I had even less time for her than I'd had as a med student. And we fought about it—about my hours, her loneliness. But when she left me, she didn't go back home. It took me so long to figure that out. I thought it meant she was still considering us. She moved a few miles away. Not because I was still a consideration, but because there was a guy. I never suspected a guy. I didn't even know about him for six months after we broke up. It was a zebra all along."

"Ow. That must have hurt you bad."

He leaned toward her. "My pride, Sunny. At the end of the day, I missed her, hated giving up my idea of how we'd spend the rest of our lives, but it was mostly my pride that was hurt. I'm real grateful to Penny—she walked away while all we had at stake was some cheap, hand-me-down furniture to divide between us. If we weren't going to make it together, if she wasn't happy with me, I'm glad she left me before we invested a lot more in each other. See," he said, taking Sunny's hand in his, "I think I put Penny in charge and I went along, and that wasn't fair. When a man cares about a woman, he owes it to her to romance her, pursue her, *convince* her. I learned something there—you don't just move along toward something as serious as marriage unless just about every emotion you have has been engaged. Like I said, we grew on each other. Lots of times I asked myself why I thought that was enough."

"But what I want to know is, will you ever be willing to risk it again?" she asked.

"Yes, and I look forward to it," he answered.

"You're just plain crazy! A glutton for punishment!"

"No, I'm reformed. I always heard it was a good idea

to fall in love with your best friend and I bought that. I thought if you could meet someone you really liked and she also turned you on, all the mysteries of life were solved. I still think you'd better be good, trusted friends with the person you marry, but by God, there had better be some mind-blowing passion. Not like when you're sixteen and carry your brain in your... Well, you know. But next time, and there will be a next time, I want it all—someone I like a lot, trust, someone I respect and love and someone I want so bad I'm almost out of my mind."

"Do you think you'll ever find that?" Sunny asked.

"The important thing is that I won't settle for less. Now, you've had a year to think about it—what's your conclusion about what happened?"

She pursed her lips and frowned, looked down for a second, then up. "I was about to marry the wrong guy and he bolted before he could make the biggest mistake of his life. But don't look at me to thank him for it—the mess he left was unbelievable. Over a hundred gifts had to be returned, my parents had paid for invitations, a designer gown, flowers and several big dinners—including the reception dinner. Flowers were distributed to the wedding party so they wouldn't just be wasted... It was horrendous."

"Have you ever wondered," he asked her, "what one

thing would make that whole nightmare a blessing in disguise?"

"I can't imagine!" she said.

Funniest thing, he thought. *Before tonight, neither could I.*

He moved very slowly, scooting closer to her. He lifted the glass of brandy out of her hand and placed both hers and his on the coffee table. He put his hands on her waist and pulled her closer, leaning his lips toward hers. He hovered just over hers, waiting for a sign that she felt something, too; at least a stirring, a curiosity, that would be enough for now. Then slowly, perhaps reluctantly, her hands slid up his arms to his shoulders and that was just what he needed. He covered her mouth with his in a hot, searing kiss. He wanted to see her face when he kissed her, but he let his eyelids close and allowed his hands to wander around to her back, pulling her chest harder against his, just imagining what more could happen between them.

The kiss was warm and wet and caused his heart to thump. He'd had quite a few brief fantasies linked to desires. Earlier, out by the Christmas tree in town, he'd had a vision of kissing her and then licking his way down her belly to secret parts that would respond to him with powerful satisfaction. He wanted nothing as much as to lie in her arms, skin on skin, and explore every small corner of her beautiful body.

But that wasn't going to happen now. Not tonight. Not tomorrow.

He pulled away reluctantly.

"I haven't been kissed in a year," she whispered. "I had decided I wasn't ever going to be kissed again. It was too dangerous."

"No danger here, Sunny. And you'll be happy to know you haven't lost your touch. You're very good at it." He looked into those hypnotic blue eyes as he pushed a lock of her hair over her ear. "If I had married Penny, if Glen had shown up when he was supposed to, I wouldn't be kissing you now. And I have to tell you, Sunny, I can't remember ever feeling so good about a kiss…"

She could only sigh and let her eyes drift closed. "We are a bad combination," she whispered.

"I can't believe that…"

"Oh, believe it." She opened her eyes. "You were a guy who just went along with what a woman wanted and I was a woman who, without even thinking about it too much, pushed a man into a great big wedding he didn't want." She swallowed and her eyes glistened. "I hate to admit this to anyone, but Glen kept telling me things—like he just wasn't comfortable with the size of that wedding, and he wasn't sure our work schedules would be good for us, or this or that. I told him not to worry, but I never changed anything. I kept saying I couldn't—that photographers work weekends. But that's not really true, they don't have to work *every* weekend. Portraits for events like anniversaries and engagements can be done before the parties are held, belly shots and babies can be done on weekdays. But the important thing is that until five minutes ago, I wasn't willing to admit our breakup had anything to do with me. And I might be admitting it to you because I'll probably never see you again."

"Listen—I might have been a go-along kind of guy, but I was never that spineless. Glen let it go too far. He doesn't get off that easy."

She gave him a weak smile. "I'm glad I met you. I didn't want to meet a guy, get to know a guy, and I sure didn't want to like a guy, but… Well, I'm not sorry."

"You know what that means, don't you?"

She shook her head.

"After you go through something like a bad breakup and you meet someone new, you check it out and you either find someone better for you, or you recognize right off that you haven't found the right one yet. But at least you keep moving forward until the guy and the life that's right for you comes into focus. And until that happens, we get to kiss."

"You're an opportunist. I could smell it on you the second I met you."

"Now you call your uncle and tell him about the deer accident, tell him we're safe and warm and I'll be looking for a tow truck in the morning. If you want him to, you can ask him if he'll come and rescue you. He can come now or later. A little later or much, much later. You could even stay the night, if you felt like it."

"No I couldn't," she said with a laugh.

"Then will you ask him to wait till after midnight? It's not that far off."

"I think I'll just wait awhile to call," she said. "If I know my uncle, he'll be on the road as soon as he gets my call."

That made Drew smile. "I know I'm probably a poor substitute for the guy you wanted to be kissing at midnight, but—"

"Actually, Dr. Foley, I think maybe you're a big improvement. And I might've gone a long time without knowing that."

Sunny waited a little bit and then called her uncle, letting him know where she was, what had happened and that she was fine. While she was on the phone, Drew quickly downloaded the pictures of the bloody deer onto his laptop and deleted them from her camera. Then, while the fire roared, they sat on the leather sofa, very close together, with their feet propped up on the ottoman. At times their legs were on top of each other's. They kissed now and then. Other times they talked. Sunny didn't say too much more about Glen, and she didn't want to hear any more about Penny.

She didn't tell him that Glen wasn't always nice to her. Oh, it went a bit further than the comment about the wide hips. Glen was the kind of guy who stayed out too late "unwinding" after work, criticized her appearance as being not sexy enough for his tastes and when they did have time together, he was never happy with how they were going to spend it—almost as if he'd rather she be working. She had thought about snatching his phone and looking at old text messages, listening to voice mails, but she was a little afraid of what she might find so she convinced herself she was being paranoid. By the time she realized it wasn't such a positive match, she was wearing a ring and had made deposits on wedding stuff.

It was too late.

But what she did want to ask Drew was, "What makes you think you'll do any better the next time you have a relationship?"

He turned to her with a smile and said, "Good! I really wanted you to ask me that." He ran the knuckle of his index finger along her cheek. "Do you have any idea what attracts men and women to each other?"

She just shook her head. "I thought it was a learned behavior...."

"Maybe, but I bet it's more. I bet it's a real primal mating thing that has no logical explanation. Like you see someone and right away, *bam,* you gotta be with that person. And I bet sometimes all the other elements fall into place, and sometimes they don't. That kind of un-explainable thing—you see a woman on the other side of the room and your heart just about leaps out of your chest. You go brain-dead and you're on automatic. All of a sudden you're walking over to her and you don't know why, you just know you have to get closer. Everything about her pulls you like a magnet. You feel kind of stu-pid but you just walk up to her and say, 'Hi, my name is Drew' and hope for the best, even though she's looking at you like you're an idiot."

"Slick," she said. "Have you actually been able to use that technique very often?"

"I've never even tried it before, I swear. Listen, it's kind of embarrassing to admit this, but that never hap-pened with Penny. It was comfortable, nice, that's all. No fireworks, no mind-blowing passion..."

"But you said it was good with her! You said sex was good."

"I might be kind of easy to please in that department. The worst sex I ever had was actually pretty good. I want what *else* there is! How did what's-his-name reel you in?" he asked.

Yo. Me and you!

"He wasn't too slick, as a matter of fact. He thought he was. I never told him his great pickup line didn't impress me. Thing was, he was cute. And I worked all the time. I hadn't been out on a date in a long time and he was..." She shrugged. "Handsome and interested." She tilted her head and smiled at him. "I think I'm telling you all these things because you're safe."

His large hand closed over her shoulder. "I don't want to be safe," he said. "And I want to see you again."

"Want to go off, live our solitary lives and meet back here for New Year's Eve every year...kind of like a take-off on *Same Time, Next Year*?"

"Did you know what Jack had planned for midnight?" Drew asked. "Did you write your resolution?"

She shook her head, then nodded. "I wrote that I had to stay away from men. He put it in the fishbowl."

"At midnight everyone was going to pull out a resolution, ending up with someone else's. Really corny, don't you think?" he asked her, reaching into the pocket of his jeans. "It's going to be for laughs, not for real. Some skinny girl could get a resolution to lose twenty pounds. But I wrote this one before I knew much about you." He presented a slip of paper. "Look, Sunny—it's midnight."

"No, it's not," she said. "It's like three minutes till."

"We can stretch it out," he said, handing her the paper. "I have no idea why I stuck this in my pocket. I put a different one in the fishbowl."

She took it, opened it and read, "Start the new year by giving a new guy a chance."

Her cheeks got a little pink. She was flattered, she was feeling lusty and attracted, but… "But, Drew, I'm not going to see you again."

"If you want to, you will…"

"You're just looking for a replacement fiancée," she said. "And long-distance relationships are even harder to keep going than the close kind."

"We can start with football tomorrow. I have beer and wings. Unfortunately I have no car, but I bet you can wrangle one from the uncle."

"That's cute, but—"

"It's midnight," he said, closing in on her. His lips hovered right over hers. "Sunny, you just do something to me."

"Thanks," she said weakly. "Really, thanks. I needed to think I was actually attractive to someone."

"You're way more than that," he said, covering her mouth in a deep and powerful kiss. He put his arms around her waist and pulled her onto his lap, holding her against him. His head tilted to get a deeper fit over her mouth, their tongues played, her fingers threaded into his hair. At long last their lips parted. "Let's just give it a try, see where it goes."

"Can't work. I live in the south. L.A. area...."

"Me, too."

She jumped, startled. She slid off his lap. "You said Chico..."

"No, I didn't. My family is in Chico. I lived there while I went to med school, while I dated Penny, but I don't live there anymore. I'm in residency at UCLA Medical."

She slid away from him. "Uh-oh..."

He shook his head. "I'm just saying we keep getting to know each other, that's all. Neither one of us is likely to keep moving forward in a relationship that doesn't feel good. We're wiser—we know too much now. But for God's sake, Sunny, what if it's good? You gonna walk away from that?"

"I don't want to take any chances!"

"I don't blame you," he said. "It's midnight. Kiss in a new year. And just think about it."

She looked into his eyes for a long moment, then she groaned and put the palms of her hands on his bristly cheeks and planted a good, wide, hot one on his mouth.

Against her open mouth he said, *"Yeah!"* Then he

moved against her mouth, holding her tight, breathing her in, memorizing the taste of her.

A car horn penetrated the night. "Awww," he groaned. "Your uncle broke every speed limit in Humboldt and Trinity Counties."

"I told him to stay at Jack's till midnight, but I knew he wouldn't listen," she said. She pulled away from him, slid down the couch and reached to the floor for her boots. Without looking at him she said, "Listen, thanks. Really, thanks. I needed to drop the rage for a while, have a real conversation with a guy, test the waters a little bit. Kiss—I needed to kiss." She zipped the first boot. Then she looked at him. "I'm just not ready for more."

"But you will be," he said. "I can hang loose until you're more comfortable."

"I'll think about that," she said, reaching for the other boot.

The horn sounded again.

"He's going to be pounding on the door real soon," she said, zipping the boot.

"Will you come back tomorrow?" he asked.

She shook her head. "I need to think. Please understand."

"But how will I find you? How will you find me?"

"Doesn't Jack know your family? Don't they know where you are?"

He grabbed her just as the horn blasted another time. He held her upper arms firmly but not painfully, and looked deeply into her eyes. "The second I saw you I lost my mind and wanted to sit right down by you and talk to you. I wanted a lot more than that, but I'm no caveman. Sunny, all I want is to know more about you, to know if there's an upside to our mistakes—like maybe the right ones were meant to come along just a little later. I'd hate to stomp on a perfectly good spark if it's meant to be a big, strong, healthy flame. I—"

There was a pounding at the door.

Sunny sighed and pulled herself from his grip. "Well, here's a bright side for you," she said. "I'm going to kill my uncle."

The entire town was alive with Christmas. As the wagon rode down the main street, everyone came outside to wave and join in carol singing. They laughed at one another's off-key voices and a few friendly snowball fights broke out along the way.

MY KIND OF CHRISTMAS

7

Sunny threw open the door and glared at her uncle Na-thaniel. "Not real patient, are you?"

Nate had his hands plunged into his jacket pockets to keep warm. He glared back. "A—you didn't go where you said you were going to go. And B—you didn't come out when I honked. Something could have been *wrong!*"

"A—I'm twenty-five and can change my plans when it suits me. And B—something could have been *right!*" She turned toward Drew. "Thank you for everything. I'll get this lunatic out of here."

"Sunny," Drew said. "UCLA Medical. Orthopedics Residency. I stand out like a sore thumb. I'm the one the senior residents are whipping and screaming at."

She smiled at him. "I'll remember. I promise."

Sunny grabbed her jacket, her camera bag and pulled the door closed behind her as she left. Nathaniel let her pass him on the porch. She stomped a little toward the truck until her skinny heels stuck into the snow-covered drive and she had to stop to pull them out.

"Must've been tough, walking from that wrecked car to the cabin in those boots," Nate observed.

She glared over her shoulder at him. "He carried me."

"Are you kidding me?" Nate said. "It was two miles!"

"Piggyback," she said, trying to balance her weight on the balls of her feet until she got to the truck. She pulled herself up into the backseat of the extended cab with a grunt.

Annie, who sat in the front of the truck, had her arms crossed over her chest. When she looked into the backseat, there was a frown on her face. "Are you all right?" she asked grimly.

"Of course, I'm all right," Sunny said. "Are you angry with me, too?"

"Of course not! I'm angry with Nathaniel!"

"Because...?"

"Because you were laughing with Drew Foley and I didn't want to crash your party!"

Sunny laughed lightly. "Oh, you two," she said. "It wasn't a party," she said just as her uncle was getting behind the wheel. "It was supposed to be a tour of the cabin, but it turned into a deer accident and a two-mile trek. Poor Drew. He had to carry me because of my stupid boots."

"But were you ready to leave?" Annie asked, just as Nate put the truck in gear.

No, Sunny thought. Not nearly ready. She loved everything about Drew—his voice, his gentle touch, his empathy for kids and animals, his scent.... Oh, his scent, his lips, his *taste*. But she said, "Yeah, sure. Thanks for coming for me. Sorry if I was a bother."

"Sorry if I was a lunatic," Nate said, turning the truck around. "I have a feeling if I have daughters, Annie will have to be in charge."

"First smart thing you've said in an hour," Annie informed him.

"Well, I have a responsibility!" he argued.

Sunny leaned her head forward into the front of the cab, coming between them. "You two didn't have your New Year's kiss, did you? Because whew, are you ever pissy!"

"Some people," Annie said, her eyes narrowed at Nate, "just don't listen."

Winter in the mountains was so dark; the sun wasn't usually up before seven in the morning. But Sunny was.

In fact, she'd barely slept. She just couldn't get Drew out of her mind. She got up a couple of times to get something from the kitchen, but she only dozed. At five-thirty she gave up and put the coffee on.

By the time it was brewing, Annie was up. Before coming into the kitchen she started the fire in the great room fireplace. She shivered a bit even though she wore her big, furry slippers and quilted robe.

"Why are you up so early?" Sunny asked, passing a mug of coffee across the breakfast bar.

"Me? I'm always up early—we have a rigid feeding schedule for the horses."

"This early?"

"Well, I thought I heard a mouse in the kitchen," Annie said with a smile. "Let's go by the fire and you can tell me why *you're* up."

"Oh, Annie," she said a bit sadly, as she headed into the great room. "What's wrong with me?"

"Wrong?" Annie asked. She sat on the big leather sofa in front of the fire and patted the seat beside her. "I think you're close to perfect!"

Sunny shook her head. She sat on the sofa, turned toward Annie and pulled her feet under her. "I made up my mind I wasn't getting mixed up with another guy after what Glen did to me, then I go and meet this sweetheart. He's pretty unforgettable."

"Oh? The guy from the bar?"

Sunny sipped her coffee. "Sounds funny when you put it that way. Drew—a doctor of all things. Not a guy from a bar. He was up at his sister's cabin to study and only came into town to get a New Year's Eve beer. I never should have run into him. And even though he's totally nice and very sweet, I promised him I'd never get involved again, with him or anyone else. I told him I just wasn't ready."

"Smart if you ask me," Annie said, sipping from her own steaming cup.

"Really?" Sunny asked, surprised. Wasn't this the same woman who lectured her about letting go of the anger and getting on with her life?

Annie gave a short laugh. "After what happened to you? Why would you take that kind of chance again? Too risky. Besides, you have a good life! You have work you love and your parents are completely devoted to you."

"Annie, they're my parents," she said. "They're wonderful and I adore them, but they're my parents! They don't exactly meet all my needs, if you get my drift."

Annie patted Sunny's knee. "When more time has passed, when you feel stronger and more confident, you might run into a guy who can fill some of the blank spots—and do that without getting involved. Know what I mean?"

"I know what you mean," Sunny said, looking down. "Problem is, those kind of relationships never appealed to me much."

"Well, as time goes on..." Annie said. "I imagine you'll get the hang of it. You're young and you've been kicked in the teeth pretty good. I understand—you're not feeling that strong."

Sunny actually laughed. "I had no idea how strong I was," she said. "I got through the worst day of my life. I helped my mom return over a hundred wedding gifts..." She swallowed. "With notes of apology."

"You're right—that takes strength of a very unique variety. But you told me you don't feel too confident about your ability to know whether a guy is a good guy, a guy you can really trust," Annie said.

Sunny sighed. "Yeah, it's scary." Then she lifted her gaze and a small smile flitted across her mouth. "Some things are just obvious, though. You know what Drew said is the best and worst part of his job as an orthopedic surgery resident? Kids. He loves being able to help them, loves making them laugh, but it's really hard for him to see them broken. What a term, huh? Broken? But that's what he does—fixes broken parts."

"That doesn't mean you'd be able to count on him to come through for the wedding dance..." Annie pointed out.

But Sunny wasn't really listening. "When that deer was lying on the hood of the SUV I tried not to look, but he was taking pictures for the insurance and I had to take a peek out the windshield. He gave the deer a pet on the neck. He looked so sad. He said it made him feel bad and he hoped the deer didn't have a family somewhere. Annie, you grew up around here, grew up on a farm—do deer have families?"

"Sort of," she said softly. "Well, they breed. The bucks tend to breed with several does and they run herd on their families, keep 'em together. They—"

"He's got a soft spot," Sunny said. "If I ever gave a new guy a chance, it would be someone with a soft spot for kids, for animals...."

"But you won't," Annie said, shaking her head. "You made the right decision—no guys, no wedding, no marriage, no kids." Sunny looked at her in sudden shock. "Maybe later, when much more time has passed," Annie went on. "You know, like ten years. And no worries— you could meet a guy you could actually trust in ten years, date a year, be engaged a year, get married and think about a family... I mean, women are now having babies into their forties! You have lots of time!"

Sunny leaned toward her. "Did you hear me? He loves

helping kids. He carried me to the cabin—two miles. He petted the dead deer! And he should have broken the heels off my Stuart Weitzmans so I could walk in the snow, but he carried me instead because I just couldn't part with—" Sunny looked at Annie with suddenly wide eyes. "What if he's a wonderful, perfect, loving man and I refuse to get to know him because I'm mad at Glen?"

Annie gave Sunny's hand a pat. "Nah, you wouldn't do that. You're just taking care of yourself, that's all. You don't have a lot of confidence right now. You're a little afraid you wouldn't know the right guy if he snuck up on you and kissed you senseless."

Sunny touched her lips with her fingertips. "He kisses *great.*"

"Oh, Sunny! You let him *kiss* you?"

Sunny jumped up so fast she sloshed a little coffee on her pajamas. "I have plenty of confidence, I always have," she said. "I started my own business when I was twenty and it's going great. I know I get help from my dad, but I was never unsure. And I can't even think about being alone another ten years! Or sleeping with guys I don't care about just to scratch an itch—bleck!"

Annie shrugged and smiled, looking up at her. "All part of protecting yourself from possible hurt. I mean, what if you're wrong? Scary, huh?"

"Oh, crap, one hour with Drew and I knew what was

wrong with Glen! I just couldn't..." She stopped herself. She couldn't stop that wedding!

"You said it yourself—you shouldn't get mixed up with another guy," Annie reminded her softly. "You wouldn't want to risk getting hurt." Annie stood and looked Sunny in the eyes. "Give it eight or ten years. I'm sure the right guy will be hanging around just when you're ready."

Sunny stiffened so suddenly she almost grew an inch. She grabbed Annie's upper arm. "Can I borrow your truck? I have something important to do."

"In your pajamas?" Annie asked.

"I'll throw on some jeans and boots while you find your keys," she said.

Sunny dashed to the kitchen, put her coffee mug on the breakfast bar and as she was sailing through the great room Annie said, "Sunny?" Sunny stopped and turned. Annie took a set of keys out of the pocket of her quilted robe and tossed them.

Sunny caught them in surprise, then a smile slowly spread across her face. *Who carries their car keys in their robe?* "You sly dog," she said to Annie.

Annie just shrugged. "There are only two things you have to remember. Trust your gut and take it one day at a time." Annie raised a finger. "One day at a time, sweetheart. Nice and easy."

"Will you tell Uncle Nate I had an errand to run?"

"You leave Uncle Nate to me," Annie said.

By the time Sunny was standing in front of the cabin door, it still was not light out. It was only six-thirty, but there were lights on inside and the faintest glow from the east that suggested sunrise. Drew opened the door.

"We never open the door that fast in L.A.," she said.

"There weren't very many possibilities for this part of town," he said. And he smiled at her. "I'm pretty surprised to see you. Coming in?"

"In a minute, if you still want me. I have to tell you a couple of things."

He lifted a light brown brow. "About my nose? My hips?"

"About me. First of all, I never lie. To anyone else or to myself. But my whole relationship with Glen? I wouldn't admit it to anyone, but it was one lie after another. I knew it wasn't going well, I knew we should have put on the brakes and taken a good, honest, deep look at our relationship. But I couldn't." She glanced down, then up into his warm brown eyes. "I couldn't stop the wedding. It had taken on a life of its own."

"I understand," he said.

"No, you don't. It was the wedding that had become a monster—a year in the making. Oh, Glen should take some responsibility for going along with it in the beginning, but it was entirely my fault for turning off my eyes, ears and *brain* when it got closer! I'd invested in it—passion and energy and money! My parents had made deposits on everything from invitations and gowns to parties! And there was an emotional investment, too. My friends and family were involved, praising me for the great job I was doing, getting all excited about the big event! Not only did I feel like I was letting everyone down, I couldn't give it up."

"I understand," he said again.

"No, you don't! The wedding had become more important than the marriage! I knew I should snoop into his text messages and voice mails because lots of things were fishy, but I didn't because it would ruin the wedding! I should have confronted our issues in counseling, but I couldn't because I knew the only logical thing to do was to postpone the wedding! The wedding of the century!" A tear ran down her cheek and he caught it with a finger. "I knew it was all a mistake, but I really didn't see him not showing up at the last minute as a threat, so that made it easy for me to lie when everyone asked me if there were any clues that it would happen." She shook her head. "That he would leave me at the altar? I didn't see that coming. That we weren't right for each other? I managed to close my eyes to that because I was very busy, and very committed. That's the truth about me. There. I traded my integrity for the best wedding anyone had ever attended in their life! And I've never admitted that to anyone, ever!"

"I see," he said. "Now do you want to come in?"

"Why are you awake so early?" she asked with a sniff.

"I don't seem to need that much sleep. I'd guess that was a real problem when I was a kid. Sunny, I'm sorry everything went to hell with your perfect wedding, but I'm not threatened by that. I'm not Glen and I have my own mistakes to learn from—that wouldn't happen with me. And guess what? You're not going to let something like that happen again. So the way I see it, we have only one thing to worry about."

"What's that?" she asked.

"Breakfast. I was going to have to eat canned beans till you showed up. I don't have a car. Now you can take me to breakfast." He grinned. "I'm starving."

"I brought breakfast. I grazed through Uncle Nate's kitchen for groceries," she explained. "I wasn't going to find anything open on the way over here."

"You are brilliant as well as beautiful. Now we only have one other thing to worry about."

"What?"

"Whether we're going to make out like teenagers on the couch, the floor or the bed after we have breakfast."

She threw her arms around him. "You should send me away! I'm full of contradictions and flaws! I'm as much to blame for that nightmare of a wedding day as Glen is!"

He grinned only briefly before covering her mouth in a fabulous, hot, wet, long kiss. And after that he said, "Look. The sun's coming up on a new day. A new year. A new life. Let's eat something and get started on the making out."

"You're not afraid to take a chance on me?" Sunny asked him.

"You know what I'm looking forward to the most? I can't wait to see if we fall in love. And I like our chances. Scared?"

She shook her head. "Not at all."

"Then come in here and let's see if we can't turn the worst day of your life into the best one."

★ ★ ★ ★ ★

In a large saucepan of boiling salted water, cook parsnips, potatoes and garlic until tender, about 10 to 12 minutes. Drain.

In a food processor in 2 batches, puree together parsnip mixture, buttermilk, mustard and salt just until smooth.

Transfer to a serving dish; stir in chives.

PAIGE'S LEMON BLUEBERRY MUFFINS

STREUSEL
4 tbsp all-purpose flour
3 tbsp packed brown sugar
Pinch of salt
4 tsp unsalted butter, melted
and slightly cooled

MUFFIN
2 cups all-purpose flour
2 ½ tsp baking powder
½ tsp salt
1 cup granulated sugar
1 tbsp lemon zest
2 tbsp lemon juice
½ cup unsalted butter,
softened
2 eggs
⅔ cup milk
1 ½ cups blueberries,
divided

Preheat oven to 400 °F. Line 12-cup muffin pan with paper liners.

Streusel: in a small bowl, stir together flour, brown sugar and salt; using a fork, stir in butter until moistened. Set aside.

Muffin: in a bowl, whisk together flour, baking powder and salt. In large bowl, using your fingers, rub together sugar, lemon zest and lemon juice. Using an electric mixer, beat in butter until fluffy then beat in eggs 1 at a time. Scrape down sides and bottom of bowl. Stir in flour mixture, alternating with milk, making 3 additions of flour mixture and 2 additions of milk. Stir in 1 cup of the blueberries.

Divide batter among prepared muffin cups. Sprinkle remaining ½ cup of blueberries over the tops, pressing slightly. Sprinkle with streusel. Bake until cake tester inserted in centers comes out clean, about 10 minutes. Let cool in the pan on a rack for 10 minutes. Remove from the pan and let cool completely.

SLOW COOKER MULLED WINE

The perfect drink to enjoy with friends while decorating the town square!

2 bottles dry red wine
8 whole cloves
6 strips orange zest
2 star anise
1 cinnamon stick

1 1-inch piece ginger, thinly sliced
½ cup granulated sugar
½ cup vodka
Half of an orange, thinly sliced

In a slow cooker, combine wine, cloves, orange zest, star anise, cinnamon stick, ginger and sugar. Cover and cook on low for 3 hours.

Add vodka; stir to combine. Divide orange slices among glasses; pour wine mixture over top.

HOMEMADE REAL PUMPKIN SPICE LATTE

8 oz milk (any preferred kind)
2 tbsp canned pumpkin puree
1 tbsp plus 1 tsp maple syrup

⅛ tsp ground nutmeg, divided
Pinch of ground cloves, divided
4 oz espresso
¼ cup whipped topping

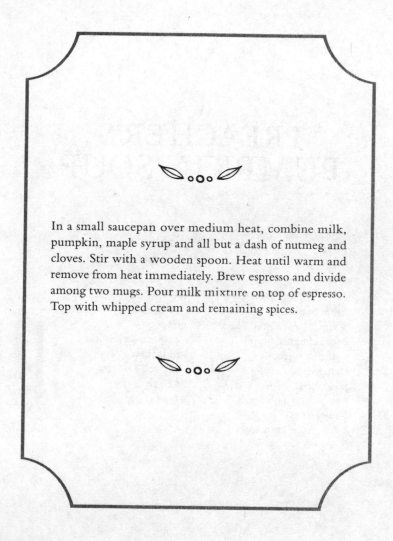

In a small saucepan over medium heat, combine milk, pumpkin, maple syrup and all but a dash of nutmeg and cloves. Stir with a wooden spoon. Heat until warm and remove from heat immediately. Brew espresso and divide among two mugs. Pour milk mixture on top of espresso. Top with whipped cream and remaining spices.

PREACHER'S PUMPKIN SOUP

2 tbsp butter
¼ cup chopped green pepper
2 tbsp chopped onion
1 large sprig parsley, chopped
⅛ tsp dried thyme
1 tbsp curry powder
1 bay leaf
1 cup canned tomatoes

1 14 oz can of pumpkin puree
2 cups chicken stock
1 tbsp flour
1 cup milk or cream
1 tsp salt
⅛ tsp pepper

Melt butter and add green pepper, onion, parsley, thyme, curry powder and bay leaf over medium heat. Cook 5 minutes. Add tomatoes, pumpkin and chicken stock. Cover and simmer 30 minutes, stirring occasionally. Remove bay leaf. Puree in a blender or food processor. Blend together flour and milk, and stir into soup. Add salt and pepper and cook once more over medium heat, stirring frequently, until mixture boils and thickens. Can be served hot or cold.

CLASSIC GINGERBREAD DOUGH

6 tbsp unsalted butter, softened
¼ cup granulated sugar
2 tbsp fancy molasses
1 cup all-purpose flour

3 tbsp cocoa powder
1 tsp ground ginger
¼ tsp cinnamon
¼ tsp baking soda
Pinch of salt

In a bowl using an electric mixer, beat butter with sugar until fluffy, about 1 minute. Beat in molasses. In a separate bowl, whisk together flour, cocoa powder, ground ginger, cinnamon, baking soda and salt; stir into butter mixture in 2 parts to make soft dough, mixing with hands or kneading to bring together. Refrigerate until chilled, about 1 hour.

Preheat oven to 350 °F. Line 2 baking sheets with parchment paper.

Between parchment paper, roll dough to ⅛-inch thickness. Using cookie cutters, cut into desired shapes. Reroll scraps as needed. Arrange cuttings 1 inch apart on prepared pans. Refrigerate until firm, about 15 minutes.

Bake, 1 sheet at a time, until fragrant and firm, 9 to 11 minutes. Let cool on the pan on a rack for 5 minutes; transfer to rack to cool completely.

ROYAL ICING

1 tbsp meringue powder
2 tbsp water (plus more as
needed)

1 cup icing sugar

In a bowl using an electric mixer, beat meringue powder with water on medium speed until foamy, about 2 minutes. Beat in icing sugar until stiff and glossy, about 4 minutes. Beat in additional water, ½ tsp at a time, until desired consistency is reached. Cover with plastic wrap until cookies are completely cool.

Spoon icing into piping bag fitted with desired tip and decorate cookies as you choose. Let stand until dry, about 30 minutes.

This recipe can also be used to create a gingerbread house.

JACK'S BAR'S BEEF AND MUSHROOM PIE

The filling for this pie is as comforting as comfort food can get. Baking it between layers of flaky pastry is how they serve it at Jack's Bar, but you can also eat this as a stew with some crusty bread on the side or serve it over creamy mashed potatoes (using Preacher's recipe). However you choose to enjoy this savory dish, you'll understand why it's the most popular menu item at Jack's!

FILLING
675 g stewing beef cubes
¼ tsp each of salt and pepper
5 tsp vegetable oil
3 slices bacon, chopped
225 g cremini mushrooms, quartered
1 onion, chopped
3 cloves garlic, minced
2 tsp chopped fresh thyme

1 cup beef broth
1 cup brown ale
¼ cup tomato paste
2 bay leaves
1 tbsp all-purpose flour
1 tbsp water
1 Pastry—double crust (recipe to follow)
1 egg yolk
2 tsp water

Sprinkle beef with half each of the salt and pepper. In a Dutch oven, heat 2 tsp of oil over medium-high heat; brown beef, in batches and adding another 2 tsp of oil as needed. Transfer to a plate; drain any fat from pan.

Add bacon to pan; cook for 2 minutes. Add mushrooms; cook until no liquid remains, about 5 minutes. Transfer to plate; cover and refrigerate until needed.

Add remaining 1 tsp oil to pan; cook onion, garlic, thyme and remaining salt and pepper until onion is softened and light golden, about 5 minutes.

Add broth, ale, tomato paste and bay leaves; bring to a boil, stirring and scraping up browned bits. Return beef and any accumulated juices to the pan. Reduce heat, cover and simmer until beef is tender, about 2 hours. Discard bay leaves.

Whisk flour with 1 tbsp water; whisk into stew and cook until slightly thickened, about 5 minutes. Stir in reserved bacon mixture. Set aside to cool slightly while preparing pastry.

On a lightly floured surface, roll out half of the pastry to a ⅛-inch thickness; fit into 9-inch pie plate. Trim to leave ¾-inch overhang. Pour filling into pie shell.

Roll out remaining pastry to ⅛-inch thickness. Whisk egg yolk with 2 tsp water; brush some over pastry rim in pie plate. Fit pastry over filling; trim to leave ¾-inch overhang. Fold overhang under bottom pastry rim and flute edge. Brush top with remaining egg mixture; cut steam vents in top.

Bake on a rimmed baking sheet on bottom rack in 425°F oven for 20 minutes. Reduce heat to 350°F; bake until the bottom is golden and the filling is bubbly, 60 to 65 minutes. Let cool in pan on rack for 10 minutes before serving.

DOUBLE CRUST PASTRY

This recipe is perfect for Jack's Bar's Beef and Mushroom Pie but can be used for any pie you choose.

2 ½ cups all-purpose flour
¾ tsp salt
½ cup cold unsalted butter, cubed

½ cup cold lard or vegetable shortening, cubed
¼ cup cold water
3 tbsp sour cream
1 egg

In a bowl, whisk flour with salt. Using a pastry blender or two knives, cut in butter and lard until mixture resembles coarse crumbs.

Whisk together cold water, sour cream and egg; drizzle over flour mixture, tossing with a fork and adding up to 1 tsp more cold water if necessary until rough dough forms.

Divide in half; shape into discs. Wrap each and refrigerate until chilled, about 30 minutes.

Just living is not enough… One must have sunshine, freedom, and a little flower.

—HANS CHRISTIAN ANDERSEN

1

Maggie Sullivan sought refuge in the stairwell between the sixth and seventh floors at the far west end of the hospital, the steps least traveled by interns and residents racing from floor to floor, from emergency to emergency. She sat on the landing between two flights, feet on the stairs, arms crossed on her knees, her face buried in her arms. She didn't understand how her heart could feel as if it was breaking every day. She thought of herself as much stronger.

"Well now, some things never change," a familiar voice said.

She looked up at her closest friend, Jaycee Kent. They had gone to med school together, though residency had

separated them. Jaycee was an OB and Maggie, a neurosurgeon. And…they had hidden in stairwells to cry all
those years ago when med-school life was kicking their
asses. Most of their fellow students and instructors were
men. They refused to let the men see them cry.

Maggie gave a wet, burbly huff of laughter. "How'd
you find me?" Maggie asked.

"How do you know you're not in my spot?"

"Because you're happily married and have a beautiful daughter?"

"And my hours suck, I'm sleep-deprived, have as many
bad days as good and…" Jaycee sat down beside Maggie. "And at least my hormones are cooperating at the
moment. Maggie, you're just taking call for someone,
right? Just to stay ahead of the bills?"

"Since the practice shut down," Maggie said. "And
since the lawsuit was filed."

"You need a break. You're recovering from a miscarriage and your hormones are wonky. You need to get
away, especially away from the emergency room. Take
some time off. Lick your wounds. Heal."

"He dumped me," Maggie said.

Jaycee was clearly shocked. "*What*?"

"He broke up with me. He said he couldn't take it

anymore. My emotional behavior, my many troubles. He suggested professional help."

Jaycee was quiet. "I'm speechless," she finally said. "What a huge ass."

"Well, I was crying all the time," she said, sniffing some more. "If I wasn't with him, I cried when I talked to him on the phone. I thought I was okay with the idea of no children. I'm almost thirty-seven, I work long hours, I was with a good man who was just off a bad marriage and already had a child..."

"I'll give you everything but the good man," Jaycee said. "He's a doctor, for God's sake. Doesn't he know that all you've been through can take a toll? Remove all the stress and you still had the miscarriage! People tend to treat a miscarriage like a heavy period but it's a death. You lost your baby. You have to take time to grieve."

"Gospel," Maggie said, rummaging for a tissue and giving her nose a hearty blow. "I really felt it on that level. When I found out I was pregnant, it took me about fifteen minutes to start seeing the baby, loving her. Or him."

"Not to beat a dead horse, but you have some hormone issues playing havoc on your emotions. Listen, shoot out some emails tonight. Tell the ones on the need-to-know list you're taking a week or two off."

"No one knows about the pregnancy but you and Andrew."

"You don't have to explain—everyone knows about your practice, your ex-partners, the lawsuit. Frankly, your colleagues are amazed you're still standing. Get out of town or something. Get some rest."

"You might be right," Maggie said. "These cement stairwells are killing me."

Jaycee put an arm around her. "Just like old times, huh?"

The last seven or eight miles to Sullivan's Crossing was nothing but mud and Maggie's cream-colored Toyota SUV was coated up to the windows. This was not exactly a surprise. It had rained all week in Denver, now that she thought about it. March was typically the most unpredictable and sloppiest month of the year, especially in the mountains. If it wasn't rain it could be snow. But Maggie had had such a lousy year the weather barely crossed her mind.

Last year had produced so many medical, legal and personal complications that her practice had shut down a few months ago. She'd been picking up work from other practices, covering for doctors on call here and there and working ER Level 1 Trauma while she tried to figure out how to untangle the mess her life had become. This, on her best friend and doctor's advice, was a much needed break. After sending a few emails and making a few phone calls she was driving to her dad's house.

She knew she was probably suffering from depression. Exhaustion and general misery. It would stand to reason. Her schedule could be horrific and the tension had been terrible lately. It was about a year ago that two doctors in her practice had been accused of fraud and malpractice and suspended from seeing patients pending an investigation that would very likely lead to a trial. Even though she had no knowledge of the incidents, there was a scandal and it stank on her. There'd been wild media attention and she was left alone trying to hold a wilting practice together. Then the parents of a boy who died from injuries sustained in a terrible car accident while on her watch filed a wrongful death suit. Against her.

It seemed impossible fate could find one more thing to stack on her already teetering pile of troubles. *Hah. Never challenge fate.* She found out she was pregnant.

It was an accident, of course. She'd been seeing Andrew for a couple of years. She lived in Denver and he in Aurora, since they both had demanding careers, and they saw each other when they could—a night here, a night there. When they could manage a long weekend, it was heaven. She wanted more but Andrew was an ER doctor and also the divorced father of an eight-year-old daughter. But they had constant phone contact. Multiple texts and emails every day. She counted on him; he was her main support.

Maggie wasn't sure she'd ever marry and have a family but she was happy with her surprise. It was the one good thing in a bad year. Andrew, however, was *not* happy. He was still in divorce recovery, though it had been three years. He and his ex still fought about support and custody and visits. Maggie didn't understand why. Andrew didn't seem to know what to do with his daughter when he had her. He immediately suggested terminating the pregnancy. He said they could revisit the issue in a couple of years if it turned out to be that important to her and if their relationship was thriving.

She couldn't imagine terminating. Just because Andrew was hesitant? She was thirty-six! How much time did she have to *revisit the issue*?

Although she hadn't told Andrew, she decided she was going to keep the baby no matter what that meant for their relationship. Then she had a miscarriage.

Grief-stricken and brokenhearted, she sank lower. Exactly two people knew about the pregnancy and miscarriage—Andrew and Jaycee. Maggie cried gut-wrenching tears every night. Sometimes she couldn't even wait to get home from work and started crying the second she pulled the car door closed. And there were those stairwell visits. She cried on the phone to Andrew; cried in his arms as he tried to comfort her, all the while knowing he was *relieved*.

And then he said, "You know what, Maggie? I just can't do it anymore. We need a time-out. I can't prop you up, can't bolster you. You have to get some help, get your emotional life back on track or something. You're sucking the life out of me and I'm not equipped to help you."

"Are you kidding me?" she had demanded. "You're dropping me when I'm down? When I'm only three weeks beyond a miscarriage?"

And in typical Andrew fashion he had said, "That's all I got, baby."

It was really and truly the first moment she had realized it was all about him. And that was pretty much the last straw.

She packed a bunch of suitcases. Once she got packing, she couldn't seem to stop. She drove southwest from Denver to her father's house, south of Leadville and Fairplay, and she hadn't called ahead. She did call her mother, Phoebe, just to say she was going to Sully's and she wasn't sure how long she'd stay. At the moment she had no plan except to escape from that life of persistent strain, anxiety and heartache.

It was early afternoon when she drove up to the country store that had been her great-grandfather's, then her grandfather's, now her father's. Her father, Harry Sullivan, known by one and all as Sully, was a fit and hardy seventy and showed no sign of slowing down and no interest in retiring. She just sat in her car for a while, trying to figure out what she was going to say to him. How could she phrase it so it didn't sound like she'd just lost a baby and had her heart broken?

Beau, her father's four-year-old yellow Lab, came trotting around the store, saw her car, started running in circles barking, then put his front paws up on her door, looking at her imploringly. Frank Masterson, a local who'd been a fixture at the store for as long as Maggie could remember, was sitting on the porch, nursing a cup of coffee with a newspaper on his lap. One glance told her the campground was barely occupied—only a couple of pop-up trailers and tents on campsites down the road toward the lake. She saw a man sitting outside his tent in a canvas camp chair, reading. She had expected the sparse population—it was the middle of the week, middle of the day and the beginning of March, the least busy month of the year.

Frank glanced at her twice but didn't even wave. Beau trotted off, disappointed, when Maggie didn't get out of the car. She still hadn't come up with a good entry line. Five minutes passed before her father walked out of the store, across the porch and down the steps, Beau following. She lowered the window.

"Hi, Maggie," he said, leaning on the car's roof. "Wasn't expecting you."

"It was spur of the moment."

He glanced into her backseat at all the luggage. "How long you planning to stay?"

She shrugged. "Didn't you say I was always welcome? Anytime?"

He smiled at her. "Sometimes I run off at the mouth."

"I need a break from work. From all that crap. From everything."

"Understandable. What can I get you?"

"Is it too much trouble to get two beers and a bed?" she asked, maybe a little sarcastically.

"Coors okay by you?"

"Sure."

"Go on and park by the house. There's beer in the fridge and I haven't sold your bed yet."

"That's gracious of you," she said.

"You want some help to unload your entire wardrobe?" he asked.

"Nope. I don't need much for now. I'll take care of it."

"Then I'll get back to work and we'll meet up later."

"Sounds like a plan," she said.

Maggie dragged only one bag into the house, the one with her toothbrush, pajamas and clean jeans. When she was a little girl and both her parents and her grandfather lived on this property, she had been happy most of the time. The general store, the locals and campers, the mountains, lake and valley, wildlife and sunshine kept her constantly cheerful. But the part of her that had a miserable mother, a father who tended to drink a little too much and bickering parents had been forlorn. Then, when she was six, her mother had had enough of hardship, rural living, driving Maggie a long distance to a school that Phoebe found inadequate. Throw in an unsatisfactory husband and that was all she could take. Phoebe took Maggie away to Chicago. Maggie didn't see Sully for several years and her mother married Walter Lancaster, a prominent neurosurgeon with lots of money.

Maggie had hated it all. Chicago, Walter, the big house, the private school, the blistering cold and concrete landscape. She hated the sound of traffic and emergency vehicles. One thing she could recall in retrospect, it brought her mother to life. Phoebe was almost entirely happy, the only smudge on her brightness being her ornery daughter. They had switched roles.

By the time Maggie was eleven she was visiting her dad regularly—first a few weekends, then whole months and some holidays. She lived for it and Phoebe constantly held it over her. *Behave yourself and get good grades and you'll get to spend the summer at that god-awful camp, eating worms, getting filthy and risking your life among bears.*

"Why didn't you fight for me?" she had continually asked her father.

"Aw, honey, Phoebe was right, I wasn't worth a damn as a father and I just wanted what was best for you. It wasn't always easy, neither," he'd explained.

Sometime in junior high Maggie had made her peace with Walter, but she chose to go to college in Denver, near Sully. Phoebe's desire was that she go to a fancy Ivy League college. Med school and residency were a different story—it's tough getting accepted at all and you go to the best career school and residency program that will have you. She ended up in Los Angeles. Then she did a fellowship with Walter, even though she hated going back to Chicago. But Walter was simply one of the best. After that she joined a practice in Denver, close to her dad and the environment she loved. A year later, with Walter finally retired from his practice and enjoying more golf, Phoebe and Walter moved to Golden, Colorado, closer to Maggie. Walter was also seventy, like Sully. Phoebe was a vibrant, social fifty-nine.

Maggie thought she was possibly closer to Walter than to Phoebe, especially as they were both neurosurgeons. She was grateful. After all, he'd sent her to good private schools even when she did every terrible thing she could to show him how unappreciated his efforts were. She had been a completely ungrateful brat about it. But Walter turned out to be a kind, classy guy. He had helped a great many people who proved to be eternally grateful and Maggie had been impressed by his achievements. Plus, he mentored her in medicine. Loving medicine surprised her as much as anyone. Sully had said, "I think it's a great idea. If I was as smart as you and some old coot like Walter was willing to pick up the tab, I'd do it in a New York minute."

Maggie found she loved science but med school was the hardest thing she'd ever taken on, and most days she wasn't sure she could make it through another week. She could've just quit, done a course correction or flunked out, but no—she got perfect grades along with anxiety attacks. But the second they put a scalpel in her hand, she'd found her calling.

She sat on Sully's couch, drank two beers, then lay down and pulled the throw over her. Beau pushed in through his doggie door and lay down beside the couch. The window was open, letting in the crisp, clean March air, and she dropped off to sleep immediately to the rhythmic sound of Sully raking out a trench behind the house. She started fantasizing about summer at the lake but before she woke she was dreaming of trying to operate in a crowded emergency room where everyone was yelling, bloody rags littered the floor, people hated each other, threw instruments at one another, and patients were dying one after another. She woke up panting, her heart hammering. The sun had set and a kitchen light had been turned on which meant Sully had been to the house to check on her.

There was a sandwich covered in plastic wrap on a plate. A note sat beside it. It was written by Enid, Frank's wife. Enid worked mornings in the store, baking and preparing packaged meals from salads to sandwiches for campers and tourists. *Welcome Home*, the note said.

Maggie ate the sandwich, drank a third beer and went to bed in the room that was hers at her father's house.

She woke to the sound of Sully moving around and

saw that it was not quite 5:00 a.m. so she decided to go back to sleep until she didn't have anxiety dreams anymore. She got up at noon, grazed through the refrigerator's bleak contents and went back to sleep. At about two in the afternoon the door to her room opened noisily and Sully said, "All right. Enough is enough."

Sully's store had been built in 1906 by Maggie's great-grandfather, Nathaniel Greely Sullivan. Nathaniel had a son and a daughter, married off the daughter and gave the son, Horace, the store. Horace had one son, Harry, who really had better things to do than run a country store. He wanted to see the world and have adventures so he joined the Army and went to Vietnam, among other places, but by the age of thirty-three, he finally married and brought his pretty young wife, Phoebe, home to Sullivan's Crossing. They immediately had one child, Maggie, and settled in for the long haul. All of the store owners had been called Sully but Maggie was always called Maggie.

The store had once been the only place to get bread, milk, thread or nails within twenty miles, but things had changed mightily by the time Maggie's father had taken it on. It had become a recreational facility—four one-room cabins, dry campsites, a few RV hookups, a dock on the lake, a boat launch, public bathrooms with showers, coin-operated laundry facilities, picnic tables and grills. Sully had installed a few extra electrical outlets on the porch so people in tents could charge their electronics and now Sully himself had satellite TV and Wi-Fi. Sullivan's Crossing sat in a valley south of Leadville at the base of some stunning mountains and just off the Continental Divide Trail. The camping was cheap and well managed, the grounds were clean, the store large and well stocked. They had a post office; Sully was the postmaster. And now it was the closest place to get supplies, beer and ice for locals and tourists alike.

The people who ventured there ranged from hikers to bikers to cross-country skiers, boating enthusiasts, rock climbers, fishermen, nature lovers and weekend campers. Plenty of hikers went out on the trails for a day, a few days, a week or even longer. Hikers who were taking on the CDT or the Colorado Trail often planned on Sully's as a stopping point to resupply, rest and get cleaned up. Those hearties were called the thru-hikers, as the Continental Divide Trail was 3100 miles long while the Colorado Trail was almost five hundred, but the two trails converged for about 200 miles just west of Sully's. Thus Sully's was often referred to as *the crossing*.

People who knew the place referred to it as Sully's.

Some of their campers were one-timers, never seen again, many were regulars within an easy drive looking for a weekend or holiday escape. They were all interesting to Maggie—men, women, young, old, athletes, wannabe athletes, scout troops, nature clubs, weirdos, the occasional creep—but the ones who intrigued her the most were the long-distance hikers, the thru-hikers. She couldn't imagine the kind of commitment needed to take on the CDT, not to mention the courage and strength. She loved to hear their stories about everything from wildlife on the trail to how many toenails they'd lost on their journey.

There were tables and chairs on the store's wide front porch and people tended to hang out there whether the store was open or closed. When the weather was warm and fair there were spontaneous gatherings and campfires at the edge of the lake. Long-distance hikers often mailed themselves packages that held dry socks, extra food supplies, a little cash, maybe even a book, first aid items, a new lighter for their campfires, a fresh shirt or two. Maggie loved to watch them retrieve and open boxes they'd packed themselves—it was like Christmas.

Sully had a great big map of the CDT, Colorado Trail and other trails on the bulletin board in the front of the store; it was surrounded by pictures either left or sent back to him. He'd put out a journal book where hikers could leave news or messages. The journals, when filled, were kept by Sully, and had become very well known. People could spend hours reading through them.

Sully's was an escape, a refuge, a gathering place or recreational outpost. Maggie and Andrew liked to come for the occasional weekend to ski—the cross-country trails were safe and well marked. Occupancy was lower during the winter months so they'd take a cabin, and Sully would never comment on the fact that they were sharing not just a room but a bed.

Before the pregnancy and miscarriage, their routine had been rejuvenating—they'd knock themselves out for a week or even a few weeks in their separate cities, then get together for a weekend or few days, eat wonderful food, screw their brains out, get a little exercise in the outdoors, have long and deep conversations, meet up with friends, then go back to their separate worlds. Andrew was shy of marriage, having failed at one and being left a single father. Maggie, too, had had a brief unsuccessful marriage, but she wasn't afraid of trying again and had always thought Andrew would eventually get over it. She accepted the fact that she might not have children, coupled with a man who, right up front, declared he didn't want more.

"But then there was one on the way and does he step up?" she muttered to herself as she walked into the store through the back door. "He complains that I'm too sad for him to deal with. The *bastard*."

"Who's the bastard, darling?" Enid asked from the kitchen. She stuck her head out just as Maggie was climbing onto a stool at the counter, and smiled. "It's so good to see you. It's been a while."

"I know, I'm sorry about that. It's been harrowing in Denver. I'm sure Dad told you about all that mess with my practice."

"He did. Those awful doctors, tricking people into thinking they needed surgery on their backs and everything! Is one of them the bastard?"

"Without a doubt," she answered, though they hadn't been on her mind at all.

"And that lawsuit against you," Enid reminded her, *tsking.*

"That'll probably go away," Maggie said hopefully, though there was absolutely no indication it would. At least it was civil. The DA had found no cause to indict her. *But really, how much is one girl supposed to take?* The event leading to the lawsuit was one of the most horrific nights she'd ever been through in the ER—five teenage boys in a catastrophic car wreck, all critical. She'd spent a lot of time in the stairwell after that one. "I'm not worried," she lied. Then she had to concentrate to keep from shuddering.

"Good for you. I have soup. I made some for your dad and Frank. Mushroom. With cheese toast. There's plenty if you're interested."

"Yes, please," she said.

"I'll get it." Enid went around the corner to dish it up.

The store didn't have a big kitchen, just a little turning around room. It was in the southwest corner of the store; there was a bar and four stools right beside the cash register. On the northwest corner there was a small bar where they served adult beverages, and again, a bar and four stools. No one had ever wanted to attempt a restaurant but it was a good idea to provide food and drink—campers and hikers tended to run out of supplies. Sully sold beer, wine, soft drinks and bottled water in the cooler section of the store, but he didn't sell bottled liquor. For that matter, he wasn't a grocery store but a general store. Along with foodstuffs there were T-shirts, socks and a few other recreational supplies—rope, clamps, batteries, hats, sunscreen, first aid supplies. For the mother lode you had to go to Timberlake, Leadville or maybe Colorado Springs.

In addition to tables and chairs on the porch there

were a few comfortable chairs just inside the front door where the potbellied stove sat. Maggie remembered when she was a little girl, men sat on beer barrels around the stove. There was a giant ice machine on the back porch. The ice was free.

Enid stuck her head out of the little kitchen. She bleached her hair blond but had always, for as long as Maggie could remember, had black roots. She was plump and nurturing while her husband, Frank, was one of those grizzled, skinny old ranchers. "Is that nice Dr. Mathews coming down on the weekend?" Enid asked.

"I broke up with him. Don't ever call him nice again," Maggie said. "He's a turd."

"Oh, honey! You broke up?"

"He said I was depressing," she said with a pout. "He can kiss my ass."

"Well, I should say so! I never liked him very much, did I mention that?"

"No, you didn't. You said you loved him and thought we'd make handsome children together." She winced as she said it.

"Obviously I wasn't thinking," Enid said, withdrawing back into the kitchen. In a moment she brought out a bowl of soup and a thick slice of cheese toast. Her

soup was cream of mushroom and it was made with
real cream.

Maggie dipped her spoon into the soup, blew on it,
tasted. It was heaven. "Why aren't you my mother?"
she asked.

"I just didn't have the chance, that's all. But we'll
pretend."

Maggie and Enid had that little exchange all the time,
exactly like that. Maggie had always wanted one of those
soft, nurturing, homespun types for a mother instead of
Phoebe who was thin, chic, active in society, snobby and
prissy. Phoebe was cool while Enid was warm and cud-
dly. Phoebe could read the hell out of a menu while Enid
could cure anything with her chicken soup, her grand-
mother's recipe. Phoebe rarely cooked and when she did
it didn't go well. But lest Maggie completely throw her
mother under the bus, she reminded herself that Phoebe
had a quick wit, and though she was sarcastic and ironic,
she could make Maggie laugh. She was devoted to Maggie and craved her loyalty, especially that Maggie like
her more than she liked Sully. She gave Maggie everything she had to give. It wasn't Phoebe's fault they were
not the things Maggie wanted. For example, Phoebe
sent Maggie to an extremely good college prep boarding school that had worked out on many levels, except

that Maggie would have traded it all to live with her father. Foolishly, perhaps, but still... And while Phoebe
would not visit Sully's campground under pain of death,
she had thrown Maggie a fifty-thousand-dollar wedding
that Maggie hadn't wanted. And Walter had given her
and Sergei a trip to Europe for their honeymoon.

Maggie had appreciated the trip to Europe quite a lot.
But she should never have married Sergei. She'd been
very busy and distracted and he was handsome, sexy—
especially that accent! They'd looked so good together.
She took him at face value and failed to look deeper
into the man. He was superficial and not trustworthy.
Fortunately, or would that be unfortunately, it had been
blessedly short. Nine months.

"This is so good," Maggie said. "Your soup always
puts me right."

"How long are you staying, honey?"

"I'm not sure. Till I get a better idea. Couple of weeks,
maybe?"

Enid shook her head. "You shouldn't come in March.
You should know better than to come in March."

"He's going to work me like a pack of mules, isn't he?"

"No question about it. Only person who isn't afraid to
come around in March is Frank. Sully won't put Frank
to work."

Frank Masterson was one of Sully's cronies. He was about the same age while Enid was just fifty-five. Frank said he had had the foresight to marry a younger woman, thereby assuring himself a good caretaker for his old age. Frank owned a nearby cattle ranch that these days was just about taken over by his two sons, which freed up Frank to hang out around Sully's. Sometimes Sully would ask, "Why don't you just come to work with Enid in the morning and save the gas since all you do is drink my coffee for free and butt into everyone's business?"

When the weather was cold he'd sit inside, near the stove. When the weather was decent he favored the porch. He wandered around, chatted it up with campers or folks who stopped by, occasionally lifted a heavy box for Enid, read the paper a lot. He was a fixture.

Enid had a sweet, heart-shaped face to go with her plump body. It attested to her love of baking. Besides making and wrapping sandwiches to keep in the cooler along with a few other lunchable items, she baked every morning—sweet rolls, buns, cookies, brownies, that sort of thing. Frank ate a lot of that and apparently never gained an ounce.

Maggie could hear Sully scraping out the gutters around the store. Seventy and up on a ladder, still working like a farm hand, cleaning the winter detritus away.

That was the problem with March—a lot to clean up for the spring and summer. She escaped out to the porch to visit with Frank before Sully saw her sitting around and put her to work.

"What are you doing here?" Frank asked.

"I'm on vacation," she said.

"Hm. Damn fool time of year to take a vacation. Ain't nothing to do now. Dr. Mathews comin'?"

"No. We're not seeing each other anymore."

"Hm. That why you're here during mud season? Lickin' your wounds?"

"Not at all. I'm happy about it."

"Yup. You look happy, all right."

I might be better off cleaning gutters, she thought. So she turned the conversation to politics because she knew Frank had some very strong opinions and she could listen rather than answer questions. She spotted that guy again, the camper, sitting in his canvas camp chair outside his pop-up tent/trailer under a pull-out awning. His legs were stretched out and he was reading again. She noticed he had long legs.

She was just about to ask Frank how long that guy had been camping there when she noticed someone heading up the trail toward the camp. He had a big backpack and walking stick and something strange on his head. Maggie squinted. A bombardier's leather helmet with earflaps? "Frank, look at that," she said, leaning forward to stare.

The man was old, but old wasn't exactly rare. There were a lot of senior citizens out on the trails, hiking, biking, skiing. In fact, if they were fit at retirement, they had the time and means. As the man got closer, age was only part of the issue.

"I best find Sully," Frank said, getting up and going into the store.

As the man drew near it was apparent he wore rolled-up dress slacks, black socks and black shoes that looked like they'd be shiny church or office wear once the mud was cleaned off. And on his head a weird WWII aviator's hat. He wore a ski jacket that looked to be drenched and he was flushed and limping.

Sully appeared on the porch, Beau wagging at his side, Frank following. "What the hell?"

"Yeah, that's just wrong," Maggie said.

"Ya think?" Sully asked. He went down the steps to approach the man, Maggie close on his heels, Frank bringing up the rear and Enid on the porch waiting to see what was up.

"Well there, buddy," Sully said, his hands in his pockets. "Where you headed?"

"Is this Camp Lejeune?"

Everyone exchanged glances. "Uh, that would be in North Carolina, son," Sully said, though the man was clearly older than Sully. "You're a little off track. Come up on the porch and have a cup of coffee, take off that pack and wet jacket. And that silly hat, for God's sake. We need to make a phone call for you. What are you doing out here, soaking wet in your Sunday shoes?"

"Maybe I should wait a while, see if they come," the man said, though he let himself be escorted to the porch.

"Who?" Maggie asked.

"My parents and older brother," he said. "I'm to meet them here."

"Bet they have 'em some real funny hats, too," Frank muttered.

"Seems like you got a little confused," Sully said. "What's your name, young man?"

"That's a problem, isn't it? I'll have to think on that for a while."

Maggie noticed the camper had wandered over, curious. Up close he was distracting. He was tall and handsome, though there was a small bump on the bridge of his nose. But his hips were narrow, his shoulders wide and his jeans were torn and frayed exactly right. They met glances. She tore her eyes away.

"Do you know how you got all wet? Did you walk through last night's rain? Sleep in the rain?" Sully asked.

"I fell in a creek," he said. He smiled though he also shivered.

"On account a those shoes," Frank pointed out. "He slipped cause he ain't got no tread."

"Well, there you go," Maggie said. "Professor Frank has it all figured out. Let's get that wet jacket off and get a blanket. Sully, you better call Stan the Man."

"Will do."

"Anyone need a hand here?" Maggie heard the camper ask.

"Can you grab the phone, Cal?" Sully asked. Sully put the man in what had been Maggie's chair and started peeling off his jacket and outer clothes. He leaned the backpack against the porch rail and within just seconds Enid was there with a blanket, cup of coffee and one of her bran muffins. Cal brought the cordless phone to the porch. The gentleman immediately began to devour that muffin as Maggie looked him over.

"Least he'll be reg'lar," Frank said, reclaiming his chair.

Maggie crouched in front of the man and while speaking very softly, she asked if she could remove the hat. Before quite getting permission she pulled it gently off his head to reveal wispy white hair surrounding a bald dome. She gently ran her fingers around his scalp in search of a bump or contusion. Then she pulled him to his feet and ran her hands around his torso and waist. "You must've rolled around in the dirt, sir," she said. "I bet you're ready for a shower." He didn't respond. "Sir? Anything hurt?" she asked him. He just shook his head. "Can you smile for me? Big, wide, smile?" she asked, checking for the kind of paralysis caused by a stroke.

"Where'd you escape from, young man?" Sully asked him. "Where's your home?"

"Wakefield, Illinois," he said. "You know it?"

"Can't say I do," Sully said. "But I bet it's beautiful. More beautiful than Lejeune, for sure."

"Can I have cream?" he asked, holding out his cup.

Enid took it. "Of course you can, sweetheart," she said. "I'll bring it right back."

In a moment the gentleman sat with his coffee with cream, shivering under a blanket while Sully called Stan Bronoski. There were a number of people Sully could have reached out to—a local ranger, state police aka highway patrol, even fire and rescue. But Stan was the son of a local rancher and was the police chief in Timber-lake, just twenty miles south and near the interchange. It was a small department with a clever deputy who worked the internet like a pro, Officer Paul Castor.

Beau gave the old man a good sniffing, then moved down the stairs to Cal who automatically began petting him.

Sully handed the phone to Maggie. "Stan wants to talk to you."

"He sounds like someone who wandered off," Stan said to Maggie. "But I don't have any missing persons from nearby. I'll get Castor looking into it. I'm on my way. Does he have any ID on him?"

"We haven't really checked yet," Maggie said into the phone. "Why don't I do that while you drive. Here's Sully."

Maggie handed the phone back to her dad and said, "Pass the time with Stan while I chat with this gentleman."

Maggie asked the man to stand again and deftly slid a thin wallet out of his back pocket. She urged him to sit, and opened it up. "Well now," she said. "Mr. Gunderson? Roy Gunderson?"

"Hm?" he said, his eyes lighting up a bit.

Sully repeated the name into the phone to Stan.

"And so, Roy, did you hurt anything when you fell?" Maggie asked.

He shook his head and sipped his coffee. "I fell?" he finally asked.

Maggie looked at Sully, lifting a questioning brow. "A Mr. Gunderson from Park City, Utah," Sully said. "Wandered off from his home a few days ago. On foot."

"He must've gotten a ride or something," Cal said.

"His driver's license, which was supposed to be renewed ten years ago, says his address is in Illinois."

"Stan says he'll probably have more information by the time he gets here, but this must be him. Dementia, he says."

"You can say that again," Maggie observed. "I can't imagine what the last few days have been like for him. He must have been terrified."

"He look terrified to you?" Frank asked. "He might as well be on a cruise ship."

"Tell Stan we'll take care of him till he gets here."

Maggie went about the business of caring for Mr. Gunderson, getting water and a little soup into him while the camper, Cal, chatted with Sully and Frank, apparently well known to them. When this situation was resolved she meant to find out more about him, like how long he'd been here.

She took off Roy's shoes and socks and looked at his feet—no injuries or frostbite but some serious swelling and bruised toenails. She wondered where he had been and how he'd gotten the backpack. He certainly hadn't brought it from home or packed it himself. That would be too complicated for a man in his condition. It was a miracle he could carry it!

Two hours later, the sun lowering in the sky, an ambulance had arrived for Roy Gunderson. He didn't appear to be seriously injured or ill but he was definitely unstable and Stan wasn't inclined to transport him alone. He could bolt, try to get out of a moving car or interfere with the driver, although Stan had a divider cage in his police car.

What Maggie and Sully had learned, no thanks to Roy himself, was that he'd been cared for at home by his wife, wandered off without his GPS bracelet, walked around a while before coming upon a rather old Chevy sedan with the keys in the ignition, so he must have helped himself. The car was reported stolen from near his house, but had no tracking device installed. And since Mr. Gunderson hadn't driven in years, no one put him with the borrowed motor vehicle for a couple of days. The car was found abandoned near Salt Lake City with Roy's jacket in it. From there the old man had probably hitched a ride. His condition was too good to have walked for days. Roy was likely left near a rest stop or campgrounds where he helped himself to a backpack. Where he'd been, what he'd done, how he'd survived was unknown.

The EMTs were just about to load Mr. Gunderson into the back of the ambulance when Sully sat down on the porch steps with a loud huff.

"Dad?" Maggie asked.

Sully was grabbing the front of his chest. Over his heart. He was pale as snow, sweaty, his eyes glassy, his breathing shallow and ragged.

"Dad!" Maggie shouted.